Zauberkraft: Red

By Juliet Waldron

Amazon Print 978-1-77362-685-7

BWL Publishing Inc.

Books we love to write ...
Authors around the world.

http://bwlpublishing.ca

Chapter One

"Ha! See her coming out of the pines over there?" Christoph von Hagen, his hazel eyes narrowing, lifted a muscular arm to point. "Just as I thought. She went through the rocky thicket south of von Beiler's woods. Now she's angling this way, the crafty vixen."

The red Arabian mare with the taffy colored tail had begun a wild gallop across the pasture. The breakneck daring left no doubt that a superbly confident rider was astride.

It was a game, a game played by young aristocrats, a wild and dangerous game of Fox and Hounds. Several 'foxes', given a head start, must reach the safety of a goal, riding across rough country, while the 'hounds', rode after them in hot pursuit.

The well-to-do players wagered among themselves on every possible outcome, but the prize for any fox who escaped was the largest, particularly because it so rarely happened. Today escape was to be rewarded with a spirited yearling colt.

"But," the speaker went on, a wry smile on his handsome face, "no one will ever catch that whirlwind of hers on the flats."

Christoph von Hagen and his cousin Max had ridden fast, intent upon getting ahead of the hunt and setting an ambush for the last uncaught 'fox' at a steep hill just before the goal. Sitting easily on a powerful bay, Christoph was an Austrian nobleman in his middle twenties. He was tall, erect, and, under the fine tailoring of his elegant clothes, muscular. His dark, curly hair was captured in a black queue ribbon, and his large eyes flashed with intelligence and humor.

Along with an exceptional body, men and women alike agreed that von Hagen was good looking. Men described his face as "open" or "forthright." The praise of the women was a good deal warmer, tending towards the classical. "Like some pagan god" was the phrase most frequently whispered behind fluttering fans at the valley's parties.

Von Hagen's companion shaded his eyes with his hand, trying to get a better look at the horse blazing across the flower dotted green below. His more ordinary blonde good looks were diminished by proximity to the dark handsome giant.

"Hers? A female? Riding like that?" Fox and Hounds was considered too dangerous for the gentler sex. And wasn't this fox astride? Astride and wearing trousers?

"The Devil," the smaller man abruptly exclaimed. He'd answered his own question. "It's Caterina von Velsen and her red Moroccan."

"And you know how well that rascal rides." Christoph said with a broad grin. "Besides, there's not a horse around that can catch that mare of hers over the flat, not even my Brandy." One strong hand gave his mount's glossy, sweating neck a pat.

"We've got to get her, Max. Right now."

As if he understood the urgency, the bay stallion reared. In the next instant horse and rider were plunging down the hill, showering earth and green grass behind.

"Christoph," called his companion, hurriedly spurring after. "The dike! You can't go that way!"

If von Hagen heard, he paid no attention. The big bay, black mane and tail flying, continued on course straight towards a lethal looking heap of broken stone. It would have to be taken in one leap, for landing atop it, would certainly break the horse's legs. No one had risked his mount across von Beiler's dike in a generation. Max could hardly believe Christoph would. Cousin von Hagen's horse

3

was a rare Prussian, bred in the stables of the warrior Elector Frederick, and worth a small fortune.

As he came parallel to the dike, Max reined in to watch the impossible. First came the gathering of the powerful burnished hindquarters of the Prussian, then the breathtaking leap as the bay tucked up his high black stockings and rose skyward.

Max gave a whoop as giant horse and rider flew over the murderous pile with all the elan of a bird of prey. The clean landing on the other side led at once to a resumption of the same regular hoof beat thunder, a relentless charge. Giving another sportsman's cheer, Max kicked and used his whip, beginning a hasty circumnavigation of the dike.

As he rode forward, he could see the hurtling fox— Caterina von Velsen—speeding on a parallel course. Her mare was fully extended, never more than one foot on the ground. The girl's hat, which she'd worn to hide her hair, had blown off and now her thick braid writhed like a red snake behind her.

More riders, a troop, boomed over the hill. Throwing a glance over her shoulder, Caterina knew that of two foxes, she must be the only one left.

There was a momentary flash of triumph. The yearling would be hers, and how proud Papa would be!

On the other side of the willow banked river she could see the beginnings of the manicured grounds attached to the von Beiler's Schloss. Anticipating the bridge—the goal, the ground on the other side—Caterina's gaze swung ahead. That was when she saw a rider coming towards her from an impossible direction, the other side of the insurmountable stone dike.

"Gottesblut!" Cursing was unladylike, but it was precisely what she felt. She had at once recognized the big Prussian bay and his equally imposing rider.

Christoph! The only one with the horse, the skill and the guts to try it…

Both horses thundered towards the bridge. For a moment it looked as if they would meet head on. Caterina reined her red mare hard. An impossibly sharp turn later, horse and rider plunged off the high bank, landing with a huge splash in the river.

It was deep here, perhaps deeper than Caterina expected, for it had been awhile since she'd been hunting around von Beiler's. Her mount came up swimming. Swollen by a recent rain, the water was rushing, carrying them swiftly downstream beneath the bridge.

"Come on, Star," she urged, grasping the mare's flowing mane. The bank was lower on the goal side; the water was shallower. It would be easy to get up. She could still win.

As horse and rider swept beneath the bridge, there was a drum roll of hooves above and then an overwhelming deluge. Caterina was still blind and gasping when a man's big hand came out of the water and seized her braid.

"Got you! Got you, Fraulein Fox."

"Ow! Let me go! You cheat!"

Furious, struggling with him in the water, she let go of the horse and began to lash at him with her riding crop.

"Hey! Foxes don't carry those," he cried, wrenching it out of her hand. "And I didn't cheat. Brandy jumped the dike fair and square." Firmly putting one big hand on the top of Caterina's red head, he dunked her.

In the meantime, the mare had continued her push to the bank. When Cat came up again, choking and sputtering, the first thing she saw was Star scrambling out, her flaxen tail a darkened, dripping tatter.

Christoph, so tall, soon found the bottom as well. With an arm around his coughing quarry, he breasted the water. In another few minutes, he dumped Cat unceremoniously onto the bank.

"Bully! You didn't have to drown me."

Grinning, von Hagen threw his considerable length onto the grass beside her. He was equally sodden, but his expression was one of complacent satisfaction.

"You hit me with your crop, so I defended myself. Don't be a poor sport, Caterina. You were a clever fox, absolutely the best I've ever chased."

"Why did you have to come back from Vienna? And what are you going to do now that you're here, tell Wili more lies and then let her down again?"

"Scratch, scratch, fierce cousin Cat." Christoph pinched her nose. "You know your sweet sister always forgives me. Some day you'll fall in love yourself and then you'll be some fellow's pretty toy too, Stork Legs."

"Smug. Selfish!" She launched a swing at him. "I'll never be anyone's toy!"

Taking advantage of aspects of the situation which Caterina's innocence overlooked, von Hagen rolled onto his back and allowed her to get astride. Then he lay there, laughing as he warded off her slaps, whooping whenever she landed one.

As he teased, riders were pounding over the bridge, a whole crowd piling in, out of breath from the wild pursuit.

"Did the fox cross the water?" The question—for gulden and hunting dogs and dueling pistols were at stake—was asked repeatedly and anxiously as each new arrival clattered across the bridge. "No, the fox was caught by her red hair as she swam," said Max von Beiler, who'd come around the dike just in time to see the watery drama of Caterina's capture.

"A female fox?"

"Well, 'female' is debatable. It's cousin Cat."

"Damn. I should have known. Valkyrie and that red Moroccan."

"And so the red fox's papa owes me five gulden!"

"Me too!"

Caterina, overhearing, stopped hitting the laughing Christoph, jumped to her feet and shook a dripping fist.

"I'm a better rider than all of you chicken hearts. If this lunatic hadn't jumped the dike, I would have won."

This set off a renewed flurry of excitement. The late arrivals hadn't seen Christoph's feat.

"He jumped the dike? Jesus, Mary and Joseph!"

"What a risk to take with the Prussian!"

"Cousin Chris doesn't take risks." Max gave his opinion. "He knew he could do it."

6

Debate was immediate. Had it been insanity or luck? Had it been horse power, the expertise of the rider, or both? Ignored now, Caterina stood, water streaming off her. She was red headed and tall. Her eyes, green as bottle glass, blazed with fury. What would have been fair skin if she'd been a more conventionally house-bound female was lightly tanned and dusted with tiny golden freckles. Her budding womanliness was shown off to advantage by a man's riding habit, jacket, shirt and knee breeches, all of it plastered to her willowy frame.

Christoph, who had been admiring her, decided to remind her of his presence. Seizing one of her long legs, he tumbled her down again.

"By God," he cried, strong arms locking around her, "Come here, Coz. I'd like to teach you to kiss as well as you ride."

Howls of laughter erupted from the onlookers as Christoph wrestled Caterina close. The whole time he kept whispering that one little kiss wouldn't hurt, that "Your sister won't mind." Arms locked against his formidable chest, resisting with all her might, Caterina thought that Christoph was just doing what he always did–seeing how far he could get.

As they tussled, witty encouragement was shouted from the bridge.

"Give the skinny tomboy a lesson."

"Just what our hell Caterina needs."

"Yes!" Max was laughing. "Kisses, a wedding and babies. Then I won't have to worry that she's going to show up on that winged steed of hers and lose me my wagers."

"Swine!" Somehow she was managing to keep him away. "Especially you, Christoph von Hagen. Let me go!"

"As you wish, Fraulein von Velsen." Just as suddenly as he'd started, he released her. Still, there was that unbearable smile, those bright eyes flashing amusement.

"Hey, little cuz, don't you know that a woman who sits down on top of a fellow runs a risk he might get the wrong idea about what she's after?"

"By the Blessed Mother!" Cat protested, reddening and angrily beginning to pummel Christoph again. "Your mouth! I'm a lady!"

"Then ACT like one!" The roar came from her half brother, Theo, who'd just ridden up. His square face red, he leapt off his horse and caught Cat by the back of the jacket, yanked her onto her feet and then gave her a tremendous shove in the direction of Star, who had calmly settled down to cropping the grass a few feet away from the arms and legs turmoil on the ground. "GET HOME!"

Theo was short and burly, nothing like his elegantly proportioned half sister. Seizing her again, he dragged her to her horse and gave her such an angry boost to the saddle that he practically tossed her over. To Theo, Cat's riding astride and all the rest of her tom boy stuff was a never ending source of embarrassment.

Muddy chin held high, Caterina reined Star briskly around and headed towards the gray stone manor. In a moment she'd risen to a perfectly seated canter, wet red braid bouncing on her back.

* * *

As she approached the gray stone Schloss on the hill, her heart was heavy, sinking with every rocking stride of the sorrel beneath her. Not only had she been ignominiously caught by that wretched Christoph, losing the wagers she knew Papa had made, but Mama would have a fit when she saw her. Lady von Velsen thoroughly disapproved of her daughter playing fox and had spent all yesterday afternoon quarreling with Papa about it. What would happen when Mama inevitably found out the rest?

"There she was, Mama, rolling on the ground like a wild Indian. An absolute disgrace to her sex, not to mention the entire family."

That would certainly be Theo's version. Cat had a strong premonition that this was the last game of Fox and Hounds she'd ever play.

In her heart was not only disappointment, not only fear of parental displeasure, but something else just as disturbing. Something to do with her half sister's fiancé, that fellow who thought he was God's gift to women, cousin Christoph.

It had started in the close up moment when he'd been trying to kiss her. Those brilliant eyes, the brown flecked so beautifully with green, those elegant features, the mouth tempting her, the whispers…

She knew what her sister, what everybody knew, about Christoph's adventures with women. Up till this instant Cat had always considered herself immune to the young rake's charm. After all, hadn't he been around, in and out of the house, courting her big sister, flirting with the maids, most of her young life? Hadn't they raced their horses, hunted together?

Hadn't he rudely nicknamed her "Stork Legs" and "Red"? Hadn't he tugged her braids, buried her in hay in the barn, battled with her as if she were a little brother and told her a thousand times to "get lost" when he wanted to kiss and cuddle Wili?

Now, since this afternoon's wrestling against his hard body, Caterina felt something new, a strange, uncomfortable excitement. She'd tested her strength against his, against a might with which he could have easily overwhelmed her. For some reason, he had pushed her to the limit and then, wearing that wicked, knowing grin, he had let go, had chosen not to take the kiss he'd won.

The thing that had resulted, the unimaginable thing, was that now she wished he had kissed her. What would it have been like to have that beautiful mouth meet hers? "Damn you, Christoph von Hagen." She began to chant the words aloud, desperately trying to drive the thoughts from her head. "I'm not like all the others. I don't want you to kiss me. I don't. I don't. I don't."

* * *

9

Down by the bridge the young men were passing around a flask of fiery brandy. Theo had ridden off after Caterina, ready to make his complaint to "Madame Mama" about his "wild savage" of a half sister.

"I couldn't let on while Theo was here but, by God, I could hardly get up." Christoph confessed with a grin. He sipped from the flask Max had handed him and then passed it to the next man.

"You unprincipled fellow," said one of the cousins, laughing. "You can't mean that skinny child aroused your interest?"

"Well, she seems to have aroused something I usually think of as signifying interest," Christoph murmured.

"Good God! But why?"

There was a general chuckle of disbelief, but von Hagen, with a mixture of amusement and seriousness replied, "You fellows have no imagination. Here and now I predict that in one year our leggy gosling cousin Red will become a swan."

"And there, may I remind you, gentlemen," Max chimed in, "speaks a renowned judge of woman flesh."

"Well, I think it's just the experience of a wet woman in his arms talking," one of the cousins replied. "Five gulden says that at sixteen Caterina von Velsen will be as skinny and as unremarkable as she is today."

You're on." Christoph laughed, clasped the challenger's hand. "Next year, mark my words, Caterina von Velsen will take your breath away."

"Whatever happens, by next year her papa will probably start looking for a husband for her," Max added meditatively. "She's got a nice little dowry, but it's hard to imagine our wild Caterina wedded and with a full belly on. Beauty or not, who among us noble bachelors would be so brave as to marry her?"

There was a general negative shaking of heads.

"It seems the Landrat will have to set his lures up north where no one knows her. Munich might just be far enough away," someone jokingly suggested.

"Well, after the tussle I just had," said von Hagen with a chuckle, "I think that the fellow who takes Red Caterina to wife had better know how to ride like a champion or he'll never have a prayer of staying in the saddle."

"Ah, but Chris," Max shouted through the following laughter. "I'm afraid that pronouncement disqualifies all of us and leaves you, conqueror of the killer dike, the only possible contender."

"God defend! Did you see the way she used that crop?"

"Well, good sir," Max teased, "then you better hurry up and wed gentle Wili. Mark my words, Christoph von Hagen, it's the only way to save yourself."

Continuing to joke and relive the various adventures of the hunt, the cousins mounted their horses once more. Making excuses for their poor showing and making new wagers, they began a lively trot towards the ivy covered Schloss on the hill.

Christoph was a preoccupied, half hearted participant. In order to stay out of trouble with his elders, he knew he'd have to spend the next few days keeping his fiancé close company. Wili von Velsen was a sweet creature, not exciting or clever, but pretty enough and reassuringly in love with him. He was fond of Wili, so it was no hardship to spend a few weeks going through the motions of courting her. Of course, at first she'd be sulky about how long he'd stayed in Vienna, but he was confident he could soon charm her out of that.

Ordinarily, Christoph enjoyed the rural pleasures of his Donau valley home, but as he rode up the hill with the others he felt something interfering with his usual relaxed anticipation of a few weeks of ease and more or less chaste amusement. Before him floated a vision, one that glowed with what he, with his experience of life and love, uncomfortably recognized as the compulsion of a new divinity.

Those astonishing emerald eyes, that thin girlish face, the lines as straight and pure as a sculpted angel's! The thick red braid, which he suddenly imagined loosened, cascading across a pillow; the tiny freckles, a golden dust scattered across even the most intimate, satin places. Most provocative was the remembered sensation of a strong, lithe body wrestling angrily and competently against his, a body which belonged—alarmingly—to skinny Red Caterina.

* * *

Wilhelm von Velsen, a man with an aspect of forbidding dignity, was Chief Magistrate of the valley, the Landrat. He was by birth an aristocrat, a man unaccustomed to submitting humbly to lectures. His continued silence now was ample acknowledgement that he'd earned what his wife was dishing out.

"This is your fault, sir. Ever since you saw how well she could ride, you have indulged her, spoiled her. This is where it leads! Rolling on the ground with Christoph von Hagen as if they were school boys! Theo says Christoph wasn't about to discourage her, either. Engaged to Wili, and now the scoundrel's putting his hands all over our Caterina."

"Gottesblut! That young dog!" The square face of the Landrat was quite red. A huge ham fist landed on the table, making the delicate blue and white china jump.

Caterina's father had been in a temper from the moment he'd heard that the wagers he'd made on his fox had been lost, but now an eruption was pending. Lady Albertine pressed her advantage, although she knew it had to be done with care. She wanted her husband to pull the reins in on Caterina, pull them in hard, but she didn't want the house party spoiled by a rampage. It would be, she knew, a near thing.

"I told you how Caterina treats good Frau Pluncke. The brat just throws down her sewing and climbs out the school room window, right down the ivy, saddles that mare of hers and rides away. It's a regular thing now, whenever she's set a task she doesn't fancy."

Lady von Velsen was determined, for once, to get it all said. She herself was an able horsewoman, but she also

12

boasted a fine hand with a needle. More than that, she was an active and able overseer of her husband's large household, from kitchen to laundry.

"She's fifteen, Wilhelm. Fifteen! Quite old enough to marry. Didn't I tell you she shouldn't be allowed to play fox? Theo said that if it had been anyone but von Hagen who'd put his hands on Caterina like that, he'd have called him out."

"Your Theo's a damned trouble maker," the Landrat grumbled. He knew what Theo, his wife's son by her first marriage, thought about his little sister. "But the lawless young dog—Christoph! Where is he?" The Landrat gripped the table, preparatory to heaving his barrel body from the chair.

"Very dutifully and lovingly sitting in an upstairs window seat," said Lady von Velsen, beginning to rub her husband's massive shoulders, "being most attentive to your Wili. I don't think we want to interrupt that."

"No," growled the Landrat, subsiding beneath her hands. "Damn him. He has a hell of an eye for strategy."

"Indeed. All the more reason to press for a wedding."

"He has to go back to his regiment in three weeks. He's only got a short leave and then it's off to the Turkish wars."

"Isn't it always the same story?"

Lady Albertine took a seat beside her husband. The conversation was getting away from her, moving in the direction of the other looming family problem, the long promised and long delayed marriage of Christoph von Hagen to the Landrat's daughter by his first marriage, Wilhelmina.

"At his winter leave then," muttered her husband. "I'll insist upon it."

"Make him promise, Wilhelm, have a talk with his father. Cousin Rupert is just as sick of it as we are. You know, Wili will be twenty-three in October."

"Yes, her best breeding years already gone by. Gottesblut! You'd think that land down by the river would be incentive enough for him to take her. He could marry,

13

get us a grandson and still run off to play soldier to his heart's content. These young people nowadays—"

"And Caterina?" Lady von Velsen interrupted. "You'll speak to Caterina? It has to stop, Wilhelm. She's just too old to go parading around in trousers." Lady von Velsen leaned forward anxiously, one arm still around her husband. She didn't want to lose this opportunity to make him see how serious the problem was. "The child can barely thread a needle, but that's nothing compared to the rest. She hasn't a ghost of a notion about anything a woman should, about cookery or about managing a house. Why, when she marries, her servants will waste, steal, commit riot."

"Mmmmraaah," growled the Landrat.

"Of course," his wife said soothingly, "I know how disappointing it's been, my giving you only that girl."

She was patting her husband's back firmly and rhythmically as if she were burping an enormous baby. Perhaps the entire message could be delivered without causing an explosion. "She's really a good child, but she knows you wish she had been a boy and so she plays the son's part, following you and Herr Longenecker around, messing endlessly with that horse of hers, but it's plain cruelty to let her go on this way. And, oh, Wilhelm, just think. What if she refuses to marry and gets, gets—" Lady von Velsen's voice dropped to a whisper, as if just saying the words aloud might make them come true. "What if she gets like Aunt Teresina? You know how she fascinated Caterina. And Grandpapa Tanucci always blamed himself, said that her—oddities, were the result of his indulgence."

Just audibly, the Landrat groaned. A case horribly in point. For lack of a son he'd raised a tomboy instead of a proper daughter. The awful consequences were just now coming home.

Chapter Two

Almost a year later, when Christoph returned to the valley, he arrived not dashingly on horseback, but reclining in a chaise. Wili wept to see him, for her handsome darling was worn, gaunt and pale. When he walked, it was frowning with effort and leaning heavily upon a cane. Pain from the terrible wound he had taken fighting the Turks had aged him, scoured deep lines around his eyes and mouth.

With tears in his eyes, Christoph took Wili into his big arms. When he called her "my darling wife," hearts in both families soared. Now, at last, after this near tragedy, the knot was to be tied! The pair were allowed a long time alone together in the study.

"He says he's sorry," Wili said tearfully to Lady von Velsen. "He says that all these years he's been fond of me, but that he just couldn't imagine being married. Now he says that he's come to understand that a caring, tender friend is the best kind of wife there is. He says he's ashamed and sorry. He swears to make it all up to me."

"Oh, my darling," Lady von Velsen exclaimed, embracing her step daughter, "I'm so glad! Your papa and I want you to be happy so much."

Cat nodded, smiled, but said nothing. Of course she was happy that Wili was to get her wish and be married to Christoph at last. Nevertheless, there was a queer aching sadness whose source was a mystery, a mystery which was hidden behind a dark forbidding door, one she neither cared nor dared to open. A wedding date was set. Cat's sixteenth birthday, just after the spring equinox, passed almost unnoticed in the whirl of activity and planning.

The bridegroom to be came to stay at the von Velsen Schloss while completing his recovery. Wili spent her days with him. She tirelessly prepared delicacies to nurture him. Soon, with so much care and comfort, the beloved invalid began to regain color and strength. His limp lessened. The cane was discarded.

No one could quite believe how changed Christoph was. He was always unceremoniously gathering Wili up to hug and kiss her. Suddenly all Wili's tears were ones of joy.

As the wedding day drew closer, Christoph took his bride-to-be for long, lonely drives from which Wili returned looking rosy and tousled. This alarmed Lady von Velsen, but when the Landrat only smiled.

"Never mind, lady wife. All it means is that we may have a head start on a grandson. If I understand that boy, and I think I do by this time, this means he's in earnest at last."

With his elders Christoph was solemn and respectful. He spent his evenings having long serious talks with the Landrat about land, law, tenants and farming. In every way he seemed much older. With Caterina he was formal and proper, suddenly more a distant older relative than playful cousin.

As weeks passed Wili floated deliriously around the Schloss, babbling endlessly about her sweetheart, about her wedding. While Cat was truly happy to see her so elated, at the same time she felt increasingly sad, as if she'd lost something precious, although she didn't know quite what. In the hustle and bustle of preparations, strict discipline relaxed and Cat spent a lot of time out of the house, riding Star aimlessly around and trying not to think too much.

* * *

One afternoon about a month before the wedding, everyone went out for a ride. The physician had just given Christoph permission to do so and he couldn't wait.

16

In the party was Oncle Rupert, Christoph and Wili, Landrat Wilhelm and Caterina. Wili wasn't as bold a rider as Cat, but like most country gentry, she knew what she was about on horseback.

As they cantered through a lush riverside meadow, the bride-to-be laughed gaily, urged her little gelding on. Christoph, delighted at being up on his Prussian again, kept daring everyone to ride faster. The pace rose to a gallop.

Wili's mount stumbled. Letting out a sound like a human scream, the horse pitched forward.

Wili's astonished cry mingled with that of her mount. Swiveling out of the saddle in a classic side saddle fall, she crashed straight onto her back among the flowers.

When Cat reached the spot, she leapt down beside her sister. Wili's body was quivering all over in an ugly, spasmodic shudder and her neck was oddly twisted. Heavy golden hair spilled from beneath her loosened cap onto the green.

Nearby her poor horse staggered and moaned, holding up a front leg from which bone protruded and blood bubbled. Cat crouched in the grass beside Wili, too stunned to make a sound. Her sister's gray eyes, usually benignly alight, were empty. There was not even a spark left to which Caterina could bid farewell.

* * *

One by one, the other riders joined her. Christoph, far ahead, was the last to arrive. He threw the reins over his horse's head and dismounted in a single bound. Only too well did the soldier know the face of death!

"No!" He went to his knees beside Cat and seized her limp body in his arms. "No! Wili! No! This can't be!"

An explosion split the air. Cat looked up to see Wili's little horse tumble to the ground. Oncle Rupert had discharged a hunting piece point blank into his head, ending the poor creature's agony. At this crowning desolation, Cat began to sob.

17

* * *

A few days later, in the first hot days of June, they laid Wili beside her mother, the Landrat's gentle first wife. Kinfolk and neighbors, as well as a crowd of servants, all stood together, faces pinched and eyes red. When it was over, the terrible last words said, the coffin delivered into the crypt, Lady von Velsen and Caterina, breathless with crying, walked wordlessly out into the bright sunlight.

It was the Landrat who had something to say. He went straight up to Oncle Rupert on the church steps and loudly declared, "In the name of God, Rupert von Hagen, promise me here and now that your son will marry Caterina."

Everyone froze. Rupert's mouth opened and closed like a fish out of water. When not even a croak came out, Wilhem von Velsen declared, "By God, we'll still have a wedding. On the sixth Monday hence."

Rupert stammered, his round cheeks pale, "'Pon my honor, Wilhelm von Velsen—it shall be as you say."

Like everyone in hearing, Rupert was shocked, but he understood his kinsman's now desperate need to arrange the matter. Upon the Landrat's death, the bulk of the von Velsen lands would revert to Christoph as the nearest male heir. The grafting of the two family branches by marriage was the only way Wilhem von Velsen had to pass his beloved land on to his grandchildren.

"Marry him?" Caterina turned to stare at Christoph, who, white faced, was just emerging from the dark passage that led to the crypt. "No! I won't!" She caught her heavy black skirts, prepared to run somewhere, anywhere, but her portly father anticipated. One great hand, moving with astonishing alacrity, took immediate, rough possession of her arm.

"If you disgrace me now, I shall beat you black and blue right here in the street."

He never let go, not during the carriage ride home, not until he had dragged Cat all the way up the long, curving staircase toward her bedroom.

"There will be no nonsense. You will do as I say, Caterina. In six weeks you'll be married. While we wait, you will remain in your room. It will give you time to prepare."

"But Papa," Cat cried, "I don't want to be married. Not to him. Not now. Please don't make me. Please!"

"Husband," Lady von Velsen seemed equally alarmed by turn things had taken, "This may be right in a few months, but do you really think—"

"Not another word from either of you! A wedding is planned and a wedding there shall be. The idea came to me in church, and as nothing much ever comes to me there except sleep, I believe it is a sign from God."

"You act as if Wili and I are of no more importance to you than one of your mares," Cat shouted. "One is dead, so another takes her place in the breeding barn."

"This defiance is the punishment I deserve for indulging you, for not teaching you a woman's place and duty. Heaven knows, your mother has warned me a thousand times."

Instead of the expected fury, the Landrat's face was grave. Cat thought she'd never seen her father look so cold.

"The law, Caterina, says that you are mine and just exactly like those mares. You know that our lands will revert to my cousin's family when I die, as it seems I am fated to do, without sons. By God, girl, my name may vanish, but that good black earth down by the river shall not pass away from my blood!"

The Landrat was like a mountain peak in a storm, scowling, intractable. It took all Cat's strength to speak again.

"But Papa—Christoph is a rake, and—oh, I despise him."

"Enough, Caterina. Our cousin was unkind to Wili, unkind and thoughtless. I know you grieve for your sister. We all do, but see what ruin delay has brought us! If I'd forced them to it last summer, why, my heart near cracks when I remember..."

19

"But, but—I'm not ready to be married. Mama will tell you." In the face of his stony resolve, Caterina was prepared to humble herself

"I know, Caterina, but it can't be helped. Now just remember that I am your father. Yes, if you like, your master, and I say you shall marry him."

"I won't! I can't!"

"Too late I see," her father roared, "you are nothing but an ungrateful brat! By Christ and all his Saints, you shall do as I say!" The Landrat's head spun. The death of one beloved child, the defiance of the other! One huge hand came flying, but Cat was so furious that the head rattling slap didn't stop her.

"Hit me! Go on!" Cornered, she feared nothing, not even her father's towering rage. "I shan't marry that lying rake. I shan't!"

Her father, who had hold of her arm, slapped again. Cat's head rang.

"Wilhelm! Have you lost your mind? You wouldn't treat a serving girl—or even a dog this way." Lady von Hagen flung herself upon her husband's thick arm.

"A serving girl wouldn't act the way this hussy does! Not a creature on two legs or four acts—she thinks she's master here!" The Landrat panted, his square face was purple.

"I won't marry him! I won't!" Cat repeated, still struggling with all her might and main to escape.

"Shame! Shame on you both!" Her mother cried. "Caterina! How dare you defy your father?"

"Damn her! She has driven me mad!"

"Leave this room at once, sir," Lady von Hagen exclaimed, "and let me speak to my daughter alone."

"Your daughter? Entirely yours, I think! The red-headed she-devil!"

"Wilhelm! How dare you?" Lady von Velsen gave her own red head an imperious, wild horse toss.

Faced by two outraged and exceedingly tall women, the Landrat prudently retreated. The bedroom door crashed shut behind him and then the key ground with awful finality in the large, square lock.

* * *

"Oh, Mama! Please don't let him make me marry Christoph." Caterina threw herself into her mother's arms. It wasn't unusual for girls of sixteen to be married, but up till this moment Cat had considered marriage only the remotest possibility. Now it was rushing in with all the finality of a death sentence.

Lady von Velsen soothed her daughter, stroked the flaming hair and reflected with melancholy upon how long it had been since she'd had the pleasure of holding this fiercely independent child in her arms. Finally, she took Cat's chin in her hand, tipped it up to gaze into her eyes, so exactly like her own.

"If you're ready now, Caterina Maria Brigitte, we'll talk. And I will talk first, because I'm your mama."

She drew her daughter towards the window seat, the place where Cat had endured so many maternal lectures. When Caterina's red head nestled against her shoulder, Lady von Velsen began.

"You're going to have to grow up now, grow up faster and harder than I'd choose, but there's nothing else to be done. This is a terrible thing for us all, for your papa, too, you must believe it, to think of a wedding when we should all be grieving. Duty will carry us through. Duty, Caterina! Everyone's duty—yours, mine, Papa's, and young von Hagen's too, for at last he seems understand his."

Caterina began a protest, but the cool, stern voice of her mother rose, continued.

"Your Papa needs a grandchild, he needs to know that his land, the land which he loves so much, which you love so much, will be passed on through you."

This speech held more power than slaps. How often had Caterina and her Papa ridden that land together, those lush green pastures where the cattle grazed and grew so fat, the shaded, leafy bowers where the ancient willows stooped

21

to finger the water! Now that Wili was gone, it was all in Caterina's hands, the sweetest water and the richest meadows in the valley. In a vision, all senses engaged, Caterina experienced it, the smell of dark earth after plowing, the summer grain, the sedate, ruffling rows of turnip. Above were the hillside vineyards, clustered with grapes.

"By this marriage, Caterina," Lady von Velsen said, "This beautiful place will pass to your children and grandchildren."

"But, oh! Mother of God! Wili's dead!"

"Yes. Our dear sweet Wili's dead and there's nothing to be done except to go on with living."

For a time nothing more was said. They wept and embraced. "I know you aren't prepared for marriage, but here it is, and we shall just have to make the best of it. I know you're brave. I've seen you take those fences on a hunt just as cool as any of the men, but now it's time for a different kind of bravery. It's well known that you're as brave as a man, Caterina. Now let's see if you're as brave as a woman."

Cat's green eyes widened.

"Yes, my dear," Lady von Velsen went on softly, stroking her daughter's pale cheek, "you've never thought like that, have you? You've always imagined that courage is only for men, but that's because women's bravery is taken for granted. I think you are going to discover that every day we have to be both braver and stronger than any man. You're still so young and I knew someday you'd learn, but this is forcing the lesson, like bitter medicine. I wish there were more time, Caterina, but there isn't."

Cat had never seen her mother like this. Mesmerized, she listened.

"You must stop acting like a child and start acting like a woman, a noblewoman, born not only to wealth and privilege, but to responsibility and duty. Life is hard for women, whether they are noble or common. We are seldom allowed to make our own choices and I blame your papa for making it harder for you. No matter how well you ride,

22

or what you know about hunting or about horses or the business of the manor, you're still a woman with a woman's destiny and not the son he wanted so much."

7"But it's not fair," Cat exclaimed. "Wili loved Christoph. She wanted him and I don't. Oh, I don't!" She hadn't cried while trading blows with her father's heavy hands, but now Cat leaned against her mother's warm bosom and began to sob.

"There, there, baby," Lady von Velsen soothed, caressing her child's scarlet head. "It will be difficult at first. To say anything else would be a lie. Christoph has been irresponsible and cruel, but I believe the terrible thing that has happened will temper his resolve to do the right thing. He's your kinsman, Caterina, and once he was your playmate. He will be good to you. I'm sure of it."

Caterina clung to her mother and trembled. The secret desire she had felt for Christoph ever since last year was now doubly shameful. Into her mind came images of things witnessed in the barn and pasture, of the swift collision of brute pairing, all mingled with memories of that day at the riverbank, memories that had haunted her continuously since it had happened. She remembered the feel of his muscle. She remembered the amused speculation in his brilliant eyes as he'd tumbled her on top of him, as he'd caressed her, aroused her, and then, so casually—set her free.

In six weeks the scene would play differently. A ring would be on her finger. Duty to family would provide the voluptuary with both impulse and excuse. In the sanctity of the fresh linen bridal chamber, in the very house she'd grown up in, she imagined his beautiful, self satisfied smile as he exercised his rake's expertise upon her.

Safe in her mother's arms, Cat shuddered, swore an oath to herself. Married or not, Christoph would not find possession easy. Even if he consummated the marriage by force or by seduction, the mere act would not make her weak like all the others. She would never pine for him, never be reduced to a lovesick toy, a toy he could abandon or pick up as the mood took him.

Chapter Three

7

"Soon it will be time to put on your dress."

"No." Cat spat the word, didn't break her pacing. "I can't!"

Lady von Velsen had spent much of the last few weeks sharing her daughter's bedroom prison. For the first time since she'd been a very little girl, Cat had been glad to have her company. All her life it had seemed as if Mama had been the one pulling on her reins, yet now, in close quarters and under duress, Cat suddenly understood how much she was loved.

"Now, Caterina," Mama said, "you know I wouldn't agree with Papa if I thought you were going to a truly bad man, to a harsh or cruel one. I think that when Christoph was so close to death he was forced to reflect for the first time in his life. When he returned to us this spring, he had changed. He'd not only made up his mind to do his duty, but to cherish Wili as a gentleman should."

"He's sorry now, but how long will it last?"

"I think he finally understood your sister, how truly, truly good she was. I think he'd begun to truly care for her. What has happened has hurt him just badly as it has the rest of us."

Cat wearily rested her head against her mother's shoulder. She had heard the same thing every day for the last six weeks.

"The problem has always been that Christoph von Hagen was made for women to fall in love with. He's handsome; he's intelligent and strong and brave. But I'm

24

beginning to believe that he is good at heart too, that he is, at last, the kind of man Oncle Rupert wanted to raise. It may take awhile, but I think that in awhile you are going to have that rarest of things for people like us—love in your marriage."

"Oh, I will never..."

"I hear guests," her mother interrupted, "It's time for you to dress."

"All right," Cat whispered, a lump in her throat, "but I only want you. Don't call the maids."

Nodding, Mama got up and crossed the room. "I'll just put my head out and tell them," she said.

There were some words at the door, for there were not only maids waiting, but the Landrat himself tramping bull footed up and down in the corridor.

With only one person to help, getting ready took a while, but Lady von Velsen didn't rush. First she brought out a new white shift and chemise. Once Cat had slipped out of her morning gown, she donned those and then sat to pull on silk stockings and tie on the bright ribboned knee garters. Next, her mother set to work helping her tall, slender daughter into the back laced stays just arrived from Vienna.

When all the crisscross lacing was done, a ring of pillow was tied and settled at her waist. Next a heavy white on white patterned silk dress, intended to be worn again at some future introduction at Court, was slipped on.

After Lady van Velsen tied up the polonaise tapes that would puff up the back of the dress, Caterina held her arms out to accept the sleeves. Then, with a button hook from the dressing table, her mother set about fastening the close fitted bodice.

Finally, seating her daughter in front of the mirror, she declared, "I'm no hairdresser. Won't you let Ute come in?"

Caterina fiercely shook her head "no."

"If I braid your hair, our cousin Wagensperg will think you are terribly provincial."

"Who cares what that awful snob thinks? I don't want my hair all ratted up like a hay stack."

25

Lady von Velsen sighed, but proceeded to make two thick plaits, to coil and pin. In a few minutes a shining crown of red braid graced Caterina's elegant head.

"Just like a Donau farmer's bride." Her mother said smiling into the mirror. "Still, why should a girl with hair like yours smother it under a wig or use powder? Now," she coaxed, "why don't we put on a little rouge?"

Caterina lifted her hand, tried to brush the lamb's wool puff away, but Mama insisted, making a couple of passes along the line of her daughter's high boned cheeks.

When this was done, a plain gauze veil was brought, but before Lady von Velsen put this on, she wanted Caterina to cross over to the long mirror.

"I don't want to. This is the most horrible day of my life."

"In two years, my contrary child, I'll wager you won't think so. I absolutely insist that you look into that mirror."

Taking Caterina's hand, she drew her reluctant daughter after her.

"Caterina Maria Brigitte, see! There's someone very beautiful."

When she looked at her reflection, there was an astonishing stranger, a tall beauty whose slender waist was accentuated by the swelling of panniers, whose small breasts were raised in perfect alabaster rounds by the tightly laced stays. Above the long oval of her face, above her straight angel's nose, above the level green eyes, Caterina's thick hair flamed, a glorious scarlet crown.

"Oh, my angel!" Lady von Velsen's eyes welled with tears.

While mother and daughter shared a long embrace, chatter bubbled up from below. Dogs barked, hurried footsteps tapped along the corridor.

"The veil now, love."

As it came floating down, Caterina's world became enveloped in the sort of mist encountered in dreams. Holding her mother's hand, she went out through that door she hadn't passed for six weeks, along the hall and down the stairs, towards the cheerful clamor of servants and family.

At the bottom of the long staircase, the Landrat appeared, dressed in his best black brocade. The retreat of his own sandy hair was hidden beneath an enormous brown curly wig, the one he wore when he sat judgment. His eyes, usually an icy shade of blue, warmed at the sight of his daughter.

"Gottesblut! A princess!" A huge smile expanded across his broad face. "Where did you find her, my Lady?"

"She's been here all the time, it seems," her mother replied, meeting his light tone.

"Now, Caterina Maria," the Landrat appropriated his daughter's hand, "I trust that we are finished with your nonsense?"

"I am not aware of any behavior that could be termed nonsense, Father. I am here to do my duty."

"Gottesblut! Still that martyred tone, as if I were asking my beautiful red filly to stand for some toothless, potbellied donkey instead of the finest purebred stud in the valley." The pressure of anticipation had apparently sent the Landrat early to his brandy bottle.

"Wilhelm. Please." Lady von Velsen glanced around, hoping that no one had heard.

"It's the plain truth and she knows it," the Landrat rumbled, continuing to gaze at Cat with boundless approval. "Please be a good girl. And please, in the name of all that's holy, stop looking as if I'm taking you to be hanged."

* * *

Coming through the door of the house chapel, the place where she'd heard Mass ever since she could remember, today so crowded with expectant relatives, Caterina caught sight of her destiny. Christoph, tall and broad shouldered, had turned to watch her approach. The expression on his handsome face was appropriately solemn, but Cat thought she detected a distinct gleam of surprise in his brilliant eyes. The bridegroom's curly, dark hair was unpowdered and simply caught with a black queue ribbon. For the ceremony, he had chosen to wear his military blue and buff.

Some men were improved by a uniform, but Christoph needed no embellishment. Standing there, square jawed, he was a living, breathing ideal of chivalry. Medals of valor and rank, bestowed by the Emperor after the last campaign, twinkled on his chest.

A renegade thought whispered that it was just as her father had said. There was a deep physical surge, a moment of abandoned elation at the sight of him, but at once the twin specters of guilt and resentment arose to squash it.

The long bridal Mass began. Cat, peering through her veil, saw Christoph attentive. With eyes that seemed unnaturally bright, he listened to the priest, and pronounced the responses of the ritual.

At last the words of the vow were spoken. Gently but firmly the heavy gold band slipped into place upon her finger. The cousin she'd shared so many wild rides with, the one who'd chased her, tickled her, buried her in hay and teased her, calling her "Red" and "Stork Legs", who had so many times led on and let down her poor sister, had, with dizzying finality, become Caterina's husband.

When he lifted her veil, she was surprised to see tears shining in his dark lashes. The unexpected sight moved her so that she, in a sudden impulse of charity, lifted her head and demurely accepted the tender brush his lips gave hers.

Once more, unbidden, came the earlier, unseemly excitement. The clean manly smell of him was good, as was the up close view of his regular features. Although brief and cousinly, the kiss, for some reason Cat couldn't fathom, moved her powerfully.

* * *

As they'd walked out of the chapel, the wedding ring burning her finger to the bone, Cat had taken her hand out

28

of his. For an instant he'd looked at her quizzically, but he had not tried to recapture it.

She was furious with herself for blushing—as if she were in happy anticipation of what was to come. How humiliating it was to feel the burning in her cheeks, how impossible to meet the guest's speculative eyes...

* * *

The wedding supper soured her mood. Some of the rowdy cousins, led on by Max, weren't above acting as if this were a regular wedding, as if they neither knew nor cared that Wili was barely cold in her grave.

"Remember what he said last year when she was fox? About keeping his seat?" The whole group seated at the far end of the table burst out laughing.

"By God!" Theodor shouted, leaping to his feet and thumping the table.

"You weren't present," was the provocative reply.

Christoph glowered at these rude cousins, but they were undismayed. Grins and elbowing continued.

On the other side, Aunt Wagensperg's round fish eyes, aglitter with interest, surveyed her. Caterina began to wonder if this lady, who spent time in Baden and Vienna, would be taking stories of this wedding back to one of Christoph's mistresses.

Meanwhile course after delicious course came in. Many gushing toasts were offered to the "most handsome couple ever" and many ardent wishes for "the blessing of children" from Oncle Rupert and the Landrat, who had both pledged their only children in this all important rite.

No more than the formalities of the table passed between the new husband and wife. Cat picked at a breast of pheasant and ate some of the ripe, luscious berries that had been scattered along the cloth. She sipped a little of the dizzying Moselle her father had broken out for the occasion. Every other dish, the one of turkey stuffed with pigeons and song birds, of delicate poached bream in egg

29

sauce, of roast piglet surrounded with heaps of savory glazed vegetables, she waved away.

Christoph made no attempt to converse. He wasn't eating much either, although he was filling his glass regularly.

Cat had expected him to attempt to proprietarily touch her, but he didn't. When he did speak, he kept saying things that sounded like echoes of the speeches with which Mama had daily plied her. He was nothing like his usual gay, cavalier self.

Cat understood that he was sorry. Oh, yes, so sorry! And what good did it do poor Wili who had lived whole years in anticipation of this day? Watching him sitting there, drinking too much, ill at ease, sending an occasional caution in the direction of those others who were exactly the way he used to be, Cat grew angry.

"Don't think I'm fooled," she finally hissed, "because I'm not. Even though you act so solemn, all I can think of is that Wili loved you and that at every turn you broke her heart."

She had expected anger, but all she saw in Christoph's eyes was pain, so much, in fact, that no retort came.

Caterina's father, seated on her left, was not so affected. "Caterina," he growled. "None of that. Remember what I told you."

"Yes, I remember. You said that in this world a woman has less choice than a mare."

His fist hit the table so hard that all the china and most of the guests jumped. Caterina leapt to her feet. To her great surprise her father was right beside her, moving his bulk with all the terrifying speed of a wounded bear.

"All right, my girl." His hand closed on her arm like a trap. "If you want to leave the table, it's fine with me. You aren't eating anything anyway and your husband—" the Landrat shot a furious look at Christoph, "—will soon slide under the table."

He turned to face the speechless guests. "Well, you young dogs," he shouted, making the guilty cousins quiver, "You've done enough joking! If you aren't too drunk to stand, let's get to it. Let's put these two into bed. They can sort out their quarrels there."

With a whoop the young men jumped to their feet, rushed to the head of the table, and, with a united effort, lifted the muscular six feet of the bridegroom.

"Here, you, Wagensperg!" one of them shouted. "We need all the help we can get. He's as heavy as a bull calf." Skinny Count Wagensperg let out a whinnying giggle and rushed to add whatever strength was in his spindly arms to the task.

The Landrat maintained a ferocious grip on Cat's arm as he dragged her down the hall. Lady von Velsen ran alongside, clucking and scolding Papa for his crudeness and Caterina for creating such a disgraceful scene.

The women trailed after, eyes full of anticipation. Wili's special girl friends and most of the von Velsen household servants were crying, but it seemed to Caterina that everyone not an intimate of the family wore the usual wedding night smirk.

When they arrived in the bridal chamber, Christoph was set upon his feet. Max von Beiler played valet and untied his cousin's stock, pulled off his jacket and unbuttoned his waistcoat. Christoph's servant, a one legged veteran of those fierce Turkish wars, hobbled in and began to neatly lay his clothes aside.

Mama began to say that Cat should be undressed behind the lacquered screen and put into a nightgown, but Papa didn't agree.

"She'll only start her nonsense again. Just get the dress and stays and all that underneath baggage off. She can go to bed in her shift." In spite of his wife's scolding, the Landrat refused to relinquish his hold on Cat's arm for an instant. He called to his butler, who stood in the crowd of servants that had followed the gentry up the stairs.

"Bring me the key to this room at once," he ordered.

As the butler made his way through the crowd, the Landrat turned his attention back to Caterina.

"Now, vixen, will you continue to make a fool of yourself and disgrace your family?"

31

For a moment they glared at each other. Cat had been entertaining some second thoughts, thoughts that had nothing to do with shame or fear. Once she had the dress and panniers off, she'd be more agile, far more able to defend herself.

The room was on the second floor but there was neither any of the useful ivy nor a tree close to the window. Papa had already thought of those earlier and, to Cat's utter chagrin, had not only the ivy, but the pretty little plum tree cut down.

Still, she'd gauged the height. Perhaps, if worse came to worse, she'd jump anyway and hope she didn't break a leg—or her neck.

"No, Father," she said, demurely lowering her eyes. She extended her free hand, the one on which Papa didn't have a death grip, and spoke to her mother. "Help me undress," she said, giving the gesture all the dignity that was possible while surrounded by her male relatives.

So, behind the lacquered screen, encompassed her kinswomen, all of whom were soothing and clucking encouragement, Cat was relieved of her beautiful dress, of the clumsy impediment of panniers, of the pinching stays. Her thick hair was uncoiled and brushed until it fell down her back in a scarlet mantle. The chamber pot was set out, the windows opened to the cool, pleasant June night.

Mama insisted that Caterina get into bed, and there she sat, kneeling in the plump new featherbed, ready to leap as soon as that awful man made a move towards her.

Her husband was, she knew, far from sober. All the time his valet and the others had been helping him undress, he'd seemed unsteady. Cat had seen him boisterous during the hard drinking times of Carnival and Christmas, but never before as drunk as this.

Papa had noticed too. Before going out, he'd taken Christoph by the arm and advised in an undertone, "Listen, my boy, I'll be locking you in. There is nothing outside she can climb down and I think it's high enough that even our bold Cat won't try to jump. Just sleep a little and tend to her when you're able."

From Max and his friends there had been some disbelieving chuckles when Christoph, with an expression of relief, had nodded, apparently ready to take his father in law's advice.

The door locked behind the revelers with a smart snap, leaving the bride and groom alone. In the light of a few discreetly placed lamps, the new husband and his young wife regarded each other. From the other side of the closed door came the sounds of people jostling and joking.

"Well..." von Hagen began, moving towards the bed with the same apologetic expression he'd had on all evening.

"Don't you dare!" Cat cried, heart in her throat.

At once she wished she hadn't been so loud. From outside came the echo of the cousins repeating her words and laughing.

"Gottesblut!" This was her father, his shout obliterating every other sound. "Don't you fellows know a thing about breeding a nervous filly? Get downstairs and stay there—the lot of you!"

"Your papa is a pithy speaker." Christoph winked at her. Once again he began an unsteady approach.

"You better leave me alone." Bounding out of bed, Cat began to back towards the window. "I promise you, no matter what Papa says, I'll jump."

"That won't be necessary," von Hagen replied. He had reached the bedpost now and was leaning on it, regarding her with a bemused expression. "You don't have to break your neck to avoid me. It's clear I'm not wanted. I don't know what stories you've heard about me, but rest assured I've always believed finesse to be infinitely more challenging than rape."

Unsteadily he let himself down onto the thick featherbed. "Now, if you'll excuse me, cousin, I'm going to go to sleep."

From where she stood in the dimly lit room, Cat watched the upheaval under the covers.

"And if you're sensible," he continued calmly, "you'll join me and do the same. I imagine you're pretty worn out

33

after this hell we've just been through. I promise you, little cousin, no matter what your papa and mine may want, there is no immediate prospect of any—breeding." And with that, the new bridegroom pulled the covers around his ears. Not five minutes later his steady, even breathing told Cat that, somehow or other, the cool villain had gone straight to sleep.

Caterina went to sit on the sofa in front of the fire place. Because the house was officially in mourning, there could be no dancing, but the sounds of cheerful, drunken conversation continued to float up from below.

Time passed, and a night chill flowed into the room. After awhile Caterina grew cold. As quietly as possible, she stood, crept across the room and found a blanket that had fallen from the foot of the bridal bed in which to wrap herself.

"Caterina?"

Thoroughly startled, she jumped back, blanket clutched against her bosom.

"You don't have to stay out there. I'm sorry I fell asleep on you, but sleeping when you can is a soldier's trick. Come on, Cat, get in with me. Then you can tell me all about why you're so upset."

"My sister is dead. Isn't that enough?"

"Oh, Caterina."

He sat up. Prudently she stepped back again.

"Do you really think I'm not grieving for Wili?" he asked.

"You can't feel like I do." Cat felt tears prick. "You were horrible to her."

"Yes, I was horrible and unkind and stupid to boot. She'd forgiven me, though, and I—"

"Where you were concerned, Christoph, Wili was soft-headed. What were you going to do, anyway? Get her belly full and then run back to your mistress? Or is it mistresses?"

"Absolutely not, Caterina. I'm done with that. The promise I made before the priest will be kept. As it's turned out, you are the one I made the promise to."

34

There followed the rustle of bedclothes being invitingly lifted.

"Come on, Red, get in," he coaxed. "It seems we both could use some comforting."

When she didn't reply, simply retreated to the sofa with her blanket, he observed, "You're going to have to get used to sleeping with me sometime. And all I want is to hold you. I give you my word nothing else will happen."

"The worth of your word is well known, Herr Graf," Caterina snapped, using the baronial title the Emperor had just conferred. "Especially if it is given to a woman."

"Suit yourself, Lady von Hagen," came his reply. His voice was always compelling, but now, coming out of the darkness, it seemed particularly gentle, full of compassion. "We shall talk it all out in the morning. Both our heads will be clearer then."

"I have nothing to say to you," she retorted, trying to ward off the confusion she felt. Why was he being like this?

"Well, Caterina, you may have nothing to say to me, but I have some important things to say to you. Right now though, I think we are both too upset. Tomorrow will be soon enough. So," he concluded in that same gentle tone of voice, "good night, little cousin."

Chapter Four

In the woods on the ridge, an owl hooted. The night dragged on as Cat sat on the sofa, wide awake. She drew up her knees and let her thoughts wander, considered and rejected a host of desperate plans. The whole time she fingered the locket she always wore, the one with the picture of Saint Brigitte.

Aunt Teresina Tanucci, the one the rest of the family spoke of with such aversion, had given it to her. This lady, a great aunt on her mother's side, was a strange old creature who had lived without a husband on what should have been her dower portion for some fifty years. In spite of the disapproval the Landrat felt for her spinister's life, he always said Teresina Tanucci was "an expert farmer, and a damned lucky one, too."

Still, she lived close to the bone, with little more refinement than her peasants. Too much was spent in taking care of strays of all kind, human and four legged. She took in, without preference, foundlings, cats, dogs, monkeys, hawks, and horses. Some of the babies who appeared at her doorstep in baskets, if they survived the precarious time of infancy, were taken in by the Sisters of Saint Hildegard, but many, those obviously from overflowing peasant families, were raised to work upon the land. Teresina took an abiding interest in all of them.

The Landrat sometimes referred to Aunt Teresina as "that smelly old badger." In fact, Auntie T was rather like that, fat and shuffling. Leaves or straw, somehow or other, was always stuck on her voluminous, out of fashion skirts, or in her gray and yellow hair.

"Dirt isn't healthy," she'd say fastidiously. The pronouncement had become a kind of family joke at von Velsen's. Although her rugs were regularly beaten and the servants always seemed to be scrubbing the walls and floors, the place still smelled strongly of the many animals she kept.

Her barn was filled by dairy cattle and oxen as well as old and lamed horses. From the latter, she had, over time, managed to breed some fleet, beautiful ones. In fact, she drove everyone who liked to bet crazy, because every few years she'd appear with one of her young studs at the St. Anne's Day races down in Passau and sweep all before her.

Occasionally she'd sell one of these champions, but she would never sell to anyone she suspected of treating animals badly. Many a young hell for leather, pockets full of gold, rode all the way out to her farm only to have to ride away again without making the expected purchase.

In fact, many years ago, someone had stolen a stallion he'd been refused. The following day, the horse had returned by himself, badly marked by spurs, mouth bloody from the use of a cruel bit. The thief, however, was worse off. His body was discovered in a ditch beside the Passau road, trampled and broken.

The peasants whispered that Auntie T had simply called the horse back. A lot of queer stories about Fraulein Tanucci's power over animals had always floated around the valley.

As soon as Caterina got her first pony, she'd wheedle Papa for a servant to ride with her to see Auntie and her menagerie. Sometimes both Wili and Caterina were allowed to ride by themselves to visit the squat little house whose acres cut a corner out of the hectare of their mother's dower land. Auntie was always glad to see them, although the girls sensed that neither of their parents was entirely pleased by these visits.

Still, it was always fun. There were always interesting things to see and do. Sometimes there were hawks with broken wings that needed mending. There were generations of cats, sitting in every window, scampering under the house or into the barn. Sometimes they'd find Auntie doctoring the cats for worms, forcing a mixture down their throats with a squirt. Sometimes she'd be with her peasants in the stables, running gnarled hands over the sleek sides of her cattle or her favorite mares.

Aunt Teresina was respected by the peasants as a healer. Doctors never went to her farm, for she knew all about herbs and surgery, too. If an arm or leg was broken, Aunt Teresina could set it. If a child or a newly birthed mother had a fever, she treated them with decoctions of plants and roots she found in the fields and forests of her own land. Peasants from all over made pilgrimages to her for cures.

The von Velsen girls learned much by following Auntie as she went through her day in the barn or as she slowly, leaning on her cane, traversed the woods or meadows. She showed the girls where to find special plants, told them what illnesses they cured. Later, in her kitchen she'd teach how each was prepared.

One spring, while Wili was visiting her von Hagen cousins, Cat was given permission to spend a week with Auntie T. She'd been excited to go, not to have to study regular schoolroom things, just be all day with her interesting and fond old aunt and all the animals.

It had been fun, just as much as she'd imagined, until the third night when she'd suffered from a horrible nightmare. She'd dreamed that a group of creatures with animal heads were all around her. It had been particularly terrifying because, unlike most bad dreams, she had been unable to make herself wake up. The monsters had held her next to a roaring pine fire in the woods and pricked her underarm with a needle while she'd screamed.

The next day she'd awoken feeling quite sick. Her underarm, the part to which the creatures had been so attentive, was sore and swollen. There was a queer nausea, almost the same as if she'd stolen too much wine, a thing she'd done with her sister at a Carnival party in Passau. The headache and nausea she felt seemed very much the same.

Aunt Teresina was the first thing Cat saw when she woke up, for she'd been sitting by her bedside. She had a basin in hand, had seemed to know that Cat would wake up and vomit. Then, utterly nonplussed, she'd taken the basin and gone out, leaving orders with her maids that Caterina was to be confined to her bed. One of her foundlings, an oversized lumpy adolescent called Trudchen, was set to nursing Caterina.

Trudchen, although only a few years older than her charge, was an excellent nurse. She carried broth and teas from the kitchen and coaxed Cat to swallow them, she brushed her long, red hair, helped her to wash and even, to Cat's utter astonishment, read aloud to her. Caterina's father would have been amazed, as he held the opinion that a peasant could never, under any circumstances, be taught to read.

"That sore place under your arm, Lady Cat, is from a brown spider. My mistress says that's why you had those all those awful bad dreams and why you're sick."

Bandages dipped in a herbal tincture were applied by Trudchen every hour. These proved to have a wonderfully numbing effect. On the third day, the perpetual stinging had subsided to an itch and the swelling had gone.

"Here, love," Auntie T said, when Cat's arm had healed, "tomorrow your mama wants you home, so here's a going away present. Promise me you'll always wear it." The square, mannish hands deposited a carved wooden locket on a chain around Cat's neck. The locket was large, the kind that usually contained a portrait of a husband or lover.

"Open it," her Aunt urged.

Cat did as she was told. There was a painting inside, but it proved to be of a lovely young woman whose tumbling brown curls were crowned with flowers. A dappled fawn was curled at her feet.

"Her friend is just like the little darling we saw when we went looking for mushrooms among the birches," Aunt Teresina reminded.

"Yes," said Cat, thinking of the beautiful rock still baby they'd spied on their first morning's foray into the woods. The fawn had been almost invisible in its hiding place beneath a flowering spray of wild apple.

"Who is the pretty lady, Auntie?"

"Who? Why, imagine a Tanucci woman not knowing! Especially you, Caterina Maria Brigitte!" An arm slipped around the girl's shoulders. Drawing her close, Auntie whispered, "She is our special guardian, Saint Brigitte."

"Why, I've never seen her pictured like that."

"Well, this is how she is known to the mountain folk."

"It was her Saint's Day the morning I woke up sick."

"Indeed it was," her aunt replied with a curious smile. "'Tis a late name day present for you. Now," she added, "I'm going to show you a secret. Pay close attention, Caterina Brigitte!"

Those old, rough fingers pressed one of the wooden rosettes that ornamented the case. Cat was surprised when the locket popped open again, this time in back.

"See how it opens? See the secret?"

Cat examined the newly revealed compartment. Inside was something that gleamed.

"It's a Protector for you now that you are growing to be a woman. Take it out, but be very careful."

It took Cat a moment to extract the object. It turned out to be an extremely thin blade, almost a needle, set on a small section of horn.

"If anyone ever tries to harm you, just fetch it out. Keep it in your hand like this," Auntie T demonstrated, palming the blade so that it disappeared. "Then take it like so," she said, her fingers moving deftly, "and do this!"

In a flash the gleaming point was against Cat's neck. Her eyes widened and she sat very still, hoping that Auntie T would be very, very careful!

"There, where the big vein swells! Don't hesitate, just push it in. If you cut that vein, whoever it is won't trouble you for long."

Cat's eyes remained wide as the old woman returned the blade to her.

"Now," Teresina Tanucci said crisply, "you show me that you know what to do."

40

Feeling very queer, Caterina did as she was told. She was surprised at how easy it seemed, almost as if she'd practiced already.

"Very good," said her aunt after a few minutes. "Now put it back and keep it a secret. No one should know! Not ever! Not your mama, not your papa, not dear Wili, not your favorite servant! Not any one! Show them the pretty saint, but not the secret! And practice taking the little protector out every night, so that you can do it easily. Practice holding it, imagine sticking it in."

"But, ah—why, Auntie?"

"So you won't be afraid to use it if you have to. You are pretty, Caterina, and men are evil! Now promise me that you'll always wear it, even when you sleep, and that you'll practice, exactly as I showed you, every night!"

It seemed awfully strange, but with Aunt Teresina's watery green eyes fixed upon her, Cat made the promise solemnly.

* * *

Even after she was at home again, Cat felt a queer compulsion to do as her Aunt had instructed. After the light had been blown out and she was hidden inside the bed curtains, she'd click open the locket, take out the needle like blade and then thrust it into the neck of an imaginary attacker.

She soon learned that there was punishment for neglecting the exercise. It came in the form of nightmares, nightmares filled with the same terrifying creatures she'd seen in the horrible dream.

Even stranger, when once she tried to tell Wili about the secret in the locket, her tongue had gone so thick she couldn't move it. Next, her throat closed and she began to choke. As she fought to get her breath, she felt utterly terrified. It was, all in all, such an alarming experience that Caterina never even considered telling anyone again.

* * *

After she received the protector, Auntie Teresina died. One of the peasants came to give the news to Landrat von Velsen.

"She had a lung sickness, sir, and a fever."

"And she did not send to us?"

"No, sir. She didn't want any doctors. She used her own remedies."

"And much good it's done her!"

"Well, time gets us all in the end, sir. Ah—that's what Lady Tanucci said, sir," the peasant added hastily, hoping not to annoy the Landrat.

"True enough." The Landrat's mind was beginning to work upon the family matters this death would precipitate. "Well, I'll send a wagon over to bring her to her family's burying place."

"Ah, sir, if it please you, your honor, we've already buried her, as she wished, up on the hill."

"Without a priest?" Cat's mother exclaimed.

"She didn't want a priest, Lady," the peasant mumbled, staring at his ragged foot wrappings. "Begging your pardon."

The Landrat sat silently, his broad forehead crumpled in thought. He was still pondering the property. As the magistrate of the district and the husband of a Tanucci heiress, it was occurring to him that he really didn't know how the land was to be disposed.

"Lady Tanucci said I was to bring you these papers, honored sir, and that you'd know what to do. That you'd be merciful and not put us off the land."

Out of his pocket, the man produced an ancient package of papers. It turned out to be several wills, the earliest dating from the days Aunt Teresina had first taken up residence at the farm.

The nearest living relative was Caterina's mother. The newer papers, witnessed by an attorney from Passau, expressed the wish that land would not go to the von Ployer half-brothers, but would pass to Caterina. Of course, it would end up being a matter for men of the two families to decide.

* * *

Here Caterina's musings ended, returning her to the present, to that darkened bedroom into which she was locked with a man she despised. Absently, she clicked open the locket, removed the blade and performed the exercise just as she had for years now.

Get a good grasp! Then thrust!

She tried, while doing the exercise, to make the attacker into Christoph, but her heart wasn't in it. After all, he hadn't yet offered to do her any harm. He was her playmate of old, dear Wili's beloved, and now, Blessed Saint Brigitte, her very own husband!

Returning the blade to its hiding place, Cat heaved a sigh of relief. Maybe she could sleep now; there hadn't been a private moment in which to accomplish the task all day and she knew for a fact that punishment for the sin of omission would have certainly come as soon as she'd fallen asleep.

Dragging the blanket over her head, Cat tried to relax, but memories of Aunt Teresina continued to pursue her. She began to think of how it had been, the day she'd ridden with Wili, Herr Longenecker, and a few servants to the farm after her Aunt's death.

The girls had been intending to put a knot of dried flowers on her grave and to bring some of her pet's home. The Landrat had wanted Herr Longenecker to count the livestock and put a stick into the grain bins to measure what was there.

At the farm, people were going about their tasks as usual, but the scene seemed different, somehow diminished.

"Where are all the animals?" Both Wili and Cat had burst out with the same question at once.

While there were still a few cats and dogs roaming the yard, the favorites were nowhere to be seen. Their Aunt's personal servant looked somewhat abashed. "The mistress said that they were to go with her," he finally admitted.

Then he said that they'd dug a very large grave and killed cats and dogs, all the crippled birds, even one of the horses, and had laid them down with her.

"Disgusting! Crazy! Like some pagan!" Lady von Velsen made no bones about what she thought. "And to think I let Caterina stay with her last spring!"

"Exactly what I thought at the time," her father replied.

This last eccentric act left a bad taste in everyone's mouth. It was a long time before the girls would talk about her again. Wili turned quite against her, especially after talking to the priest. Father Partsch, always jealous of Auntie T's influence with the peasants, had said that, gentlewoman or not, she must have been in league with "dark powers". The way she had wanted to be buried was certain proof!

A nasty stir in the ecclesiastical courts followed and some priestly witch hunters arrived. In order to forestall the burgeoning trouble, Papa ordered all the peasants on Auntie T's land to undergo baptism. Most did, but some disappeared and were not seen in those parts again. Two old women who flatly refused and who were found to have "witch marks" were taken to Passau and hanged. It might have been worse, except for the fact that the nobility and the local bishop (whose mother was a Tanucci) closed ranks. In the end, the outsiders were silenced and the matter was quashed.

"Was Auntie really a witch?" Cat whispered the question to her father one evening while the family was sitting solemnly after supper. "Father Partsch told Wili she was."

Lady Albertine shot an alarmed look at her husband. Her anxiety during the last few months had been palpable.

"Father Partsch better mind his own business," said the Landrat, gazing severely at his daughters. "Your aunt was mad, not bewitched. Imagine bringing all this trouble upon her family through the public exercise of that kind of eccentricity! She must have known what would happen, that the news would get around. We of noble blood, Caterina, have more than just our own skins to look after. We not only have our families, we have lands, servants and peasants in our care. Be sure that you always remember that!"

Trying to block out this last, ugly memory, Caterina rolled over for the thousandth time and threw her arm across her eyes, hoping to somehow quiet her mind.

Outside, June was rampant. Cool breezes swayed the moonlit trees. A nightingale filled the darkness with his poignant, silver-throated note spinning. It occurred to her that the last bird Wili had mended and freed, not two months ago, had been a nightingale.

In the darkness the man who should have belonged to her sister sighed and rolled over. Maybe, Cat thought, focusing upon the moonlit patch on the floor, maybe in the morning this whole thing would turn out to be nothing more than a terrible dream, a dream with the same awful reality as the dream she'd had all those years ago at Auntie T's.

Chapter Five

Caterina, stretching her long self out in the sunlight on the sofa, realized first that she had overslept enormously and second that morning had not exorcised the man in the bed. She could hear his regular breathing.

The soft squeal of a key in lock announced an opening door. Cat sat up to see Mama, accompanied by a servant who was carrying a tray of breakfast. She saw rolls, butter, cheese and slices of cold meat, eggs sitting staunchly erect in cups and a large red and white china pot steaming with tea. It looked most inviting after no dinner.

Then she saw a little frown begin to pucker her mother's forehead. Lady van Velsen had noticed they were sleeping apart.

"Madame Mama, you shouldn't be here," said Christoph. While she'd been thinking of breakfast, he'd suddenly sat up. The shirt in which he'd gone to bed was open, revealing a broad expanse of chest. "We're not really ready for congratulations yet."

Cat sprang off the sofa and dashed toward her mother. "Mama!" she cried. "Mama!"

Wine might have incapacitated her husband the night before, but not this morning.

"No running to Mama yet." Leaping from the bed, strong bare legs flashing, he caught Caterina by the arm.

"Let go!" Cat began at once to pummel his chest, but she might as well have been hitting the wall.

"Please go out and lock the door again," Christoph directed, over Cat's head. "We don't want to be disturbed.

46

Tell Herr Goran to get a chair and sit where he can hear if I shout." For a man who was holding a strong and frightened young woman by the wrists, his tone was remarkably relaxed.

"Don't go!" Cat pleaded, but Mama and the servant were already beating an embarrassed retreat.

As the key clicked once again, Caterina exclaimed, "Why can't she stay?"

"Because, cousin Kitty Cat, we have unfinished business."

Thinking she understood, she began to struggle wildly, but he gave her a hard shake and said sharply, "No! It's not what you think. I have a confession to make."

When she, surprised at his tone, quieted and met his eyes, he went on, "I'd rather not say this, but something tells me that if I am ever to gain your respect, I'm going to have to completely lose it."

In the aching silence that followed, he gazed deep into her eyes. Cat didn't think that she'd ever seen those usually laughing hazel eyes so troubled.

"If you remember, I said last night that there was no immediate prospect of any breeding."

Cat blushed, nodded. For the life of her, she couldn't imagine what he was going to say.

"Your sister and I—made love."

Cat gasped. Her heart began to pound wildly.

"Even if she and I were not married, well—we both wanted it. I think you can see now why it wouldn't really be right for you and me. Not for a time."

Caterina remained speechless. Her face had gone as red as her hair.

"We both need time to grieve."

When he tried to stroke her cheek, Cat jerked away.

"Don't touch me!"

The tears that had been welling spilled. She was to be spared his unwanted and for the last six weeks so fearfully anticipated attentions, but, the reason for her escape! Words burst from her lips, words she had no sense of choosing.

"You didn't love her. What are you anyway? A dog that jumps every bitch he gets near?"

"If that's true, then why not you?" Christoph retorted. "Of course I loved Wili. We were promised to each other for half our lives. It was the most natural thing in the world, and Wili had been kept waiting far too long."

"You aren't talking about a mare. You are talking about my dear, good sister!" Caterina didn't understand why, but the idea that he'd made love to Wili was repellent, almost as much as if he'd confessed that he'd been in bed with her mother. She stamped and then blurted, "You're even more wicked than I thought."

His reaction was surprising. Instead of raging, he sat down on the sofa, strong bare knees sticking out beneath the shirt. Resting his chin in his hand, Christoph stared at her steadily, as if trying to fathom a deep mystery.

"The fact of the matter is, Caterina, that making love to Wili was one of the few decent things I ever did for her. Now, especially now, I'm glad we didn't wait." In the pause that followed, Caterina felt a growing discomfort as she endured his gaze. Last night she had been angry and frightened. Now her emotions were a runaway, plunging here and there. It seemed impossible to identify exactly what she felt.

"Is it, perhaps—a touch of jealousy?"

"How dare you assume that I'm like all your others?" Cat felt as if she'd been struck by lightning. "I have never—I have never been—I never could—" Stumbling wildly, she finally exclaimed, "How could I be so wicked as to be in love with my sister's betrothed?" Then, of course, thinking of things she'd sometimes imagined, she flushed scarlet.

Christoph continued to look solemnly at her. If anything, he looked miserable. His words had come out wearily, as if arousing desire in yet another woman was more of a burden than he could, at the moment, bear.

"Could you please stop pretending I'm the enemy? I promised your mama and papa, and here I promise you. I'm going to be a good husband. I knew telling you about Wili would hurt, but I didn't want to start our marriage out with

48

a lie. Don't look so sad, little cousin," he continued, his eyes suddenly brightening. "I'm sure that the duties we owe each other will, some day, be performed with pleasure." One elegant hand stretched out to her. "Now, pax, Caterina. Nothing will happen until we are ready. Come and give me a kiss to seal the treaty."

Cat moved in his direction, but instead of joining him on the sofa, she leaned over, grabbed the handle of the breakfast tray and then dumped it, in a cascade of eggs and ham, bread, tea and fragile china, in his direction.

"Conceited monster!"

Christoph was astonishingly quick. He jumped, vaulting over the sofa back. The teapot missed him. Instead, it broke and emptied upon the floor.

"Damn!" he exclaimed breathlessly from the other side.

"I'm not jealous," Cat shouted. "I don't want you now and I will never want you!"

She turned and ran toward the window, fully intending to hurl herself out, but he came in three great strides and caught her around the waist.

A moment later she was tumbled onto the bed, his strong body holding her down. Once he'd established control of her whirlwind arms, he forced them up over her head.

"Let me go!"

"Not until you promise to calm down. You little fool, you could have killed yourself." Caterina turned her head away.

"Caterina," he said, staring down at her in dismay, "what on earth is going on? I knew you were grieving for Wili and angry with me, but I thought that down at the bottom you and I were friends."

"I never was your friend!" Then she added, "Christoph, please move. I can't breathe." "Good," he replied. Nevertheless, he did shift his weight a little. "I thought I was your favorite person in the world, at least for a gallop." His eyes were full of puzzlement and hurt. "Did I frighten you when I said I wanted a kiss?"

"No! I'm not frightened of anyone."

"I am your husband, you know. Mother Church says I'm entitled to not only a kiss this morning, but quite a bit more..." He lowered his handsome curly head and began to tentatively nuzzle against her cheek. The sensation was perversely exciting—and maddening.

"Don't. I hate you, Christoph von Hagen!"

"Because of how I treated Wili? Or because I made love to her? Or because I said that someday I hoped we might enjoy being married to each other?"

When she remained silent, his face grew sad. "Well, maybe you have cause to hate me, but she had better. Somehow, though, dear Wili never could hate. All those times she took me back, all those injured birds and rejected lambs and lost kittens she was always rescuing. Your sweet sister didn't have an unkind bone in her body."

His beautiful hazel eyes spilled over. "And I freely admit that I've been the biggest fool that ever was, that I've a lot to make up for. You know, Cat, I almost died this past winter. There's nothing like that to get a fellow thinking. And then a thing happened on my way here, something with a lady in Vienna, that made me decide to change myself, made me realize, once and for all, what a cold hearted bastard I've—"

"I don't want to hear about your mistresses!"

The anger Cat saw in his eyes wasn't surprising, but the pain was.

"She was and is a lady, Caterina," he said, "in spite of what she did with me. And you had better learn to think before you speak. We're married now, damn it, roped together till death do us part."

She had begun to struggle again, but, strong as she was, he had no trouble holding her.

"Do you know how easy it would be to just do what your papa wants, to get between your pretty legs and start making that baby they all want, with or without your assistance?"

"Go ahead." She was shaking, but still defiant. "Stop talking and be the brute you really are."

"Oh, Caterina!" Christoph shook his dark curly head and sighed despondently. Without another word, he sat up and let her go. "You really are a trial. Especially for a man with a broken heart, a hangover and a cut foot."

Cat rubbed her wrists and quickly rolled away from him, but he no longer seemed interested in what she was doing.

"Would you help me bandage this?" Sitting up, he pulled a foot into his lap.

At once Cat saw a trail of blood. The foot he was inspecting steadily dripped red. "I stepped on china," he explained, indicating the shards which lay about the floor.

"Um—let's just use this." Suddenly ashamed, she began to tug at the bottom of her petticoat.

"You don't mind ruining it?"

She was doubly annoyed when she couldn't tear it, so she offered him the hem. In his hands it came away as easily as if the cloth were rotten. Then, in a practiced manner, he bound his foot.

Food and bits of porcelain were scattered everywhere. Feeling ill at ease and not knowing exactly what to do, Cat got out of bed, knelt and began to pile china and food on the tray. The smashed eggs, the butter and hot tea made the floor quite slippery.

Christoph sat watching her pensively.

"I think what it needs is stitching." The makeshift bandage was already turning red. "Can you do it?"

"Mama will have to. Wili could have, but I'm afraid I'd just tear bigger holes in you."

"Wili wouldn't have tossed the breakfast on the floor either and I'd be eating your Mama's excellent food and kissing and cuddling instead of brawling with you, crazy brat."

Overwhelmed, Cat slammed the tray down on the table and burst into tears. It was true. Her sister would have been as happy this morning as she was miserable. As she leaned against the table and wept, he stood and then shuffled close. Big arms firmly enclosed her and Cat was drawn against him, against that beautiful, muscular body that every other girl in the valley dreamed of.

"Please. Don't."

"Oh, Caterina," he said softly, irresistibly turning her to face him. "Why are you like this? It's me, Christoph. I've never, ever forced a woman and I don't intend to start with my own little cousin. Believe me, I'm so damnably sorry about what has happened. I thought that if I married Wili it would make amends for everything. I thought I would come back here and make a clean start, make our papas happy, and make Wili happy at last. Listen to me, Cat. That's the same speech I made to Wili. She understood. She forgave me, she loved me, but, God, how wrong it's gone."

He drew her close. Even though her cheek was pressed against his bare, broad chest, even though she was experiencing for the first time all the sensations of intimacy, catching the scent of his man's body, feeling his muscle taut skin, this was indisputably not love making. Caterina turned her face towards him like a baby and let go of a brief, intense shower of tears against that formidable chest. Maybe he shed some too, for a series of tremors ran through him. The whole time his strong hands were comforting her, stroking the heavy, loose hair that fell in a fiery cascade down her long back.

"There, there," he murmured after awhile, "Just a little touch of you, my pretty Kitty Cat, to comfort us both."

He tilted her chin, used his thumbs to gently wipe away her tears. Somehow, in spite of the fact that she was so close to this nearly naked, splendid body, there was now nothing fearful about it. "We'll have to go out there eventually," he said, putting her hair back from her face, big brother fashion, "and then, pretty Red, your papa will want to see proofs that his grandson has been started."

Naturally, Cat went rigid when he said that, but he just smiled sadly.

"Don't worry, Cat. We've got a way to fool him. Take a look at the back of your petticoat." When Cat took the soft folds of muslin in hand and pulled it around, she was surprised to discover a long streak of red on the back.

"It's probably from my foot. Your nightgown fell in it while you were down on the floor picking up. I caution you though, don't tell anyone our secret, not your favorite maid, not even your mama. Your papa, not to mention mine, will have an apoplexy if he learns how this really went."

Cat nodded meekly. Inside she felt a wild surge of relief.

"We'll have to put up with some teasing and I'm sure your mama will question you."

In a courtly gesture, he caught her long hands and kissed them, one after the other. "So do we understand each other at last, Lady von Hagen? You have not only a new husband, but a whole new man to get to know. Shall we have a treaty? Keep the secret so that our fathers may continue to live, so that Theo and Max and all the others don't die laughing?"

"Of course," she said, fighting off the perverse tremor which his touch, his ever so careful touch, set off.

"Good. And I promise that if any of our cousins start, I'll break their heads or their arms, whichever is handiest." The chuckle that followed was harsh, as if this morning he'd enjoy doing that. "As for you, you're going to have to be on guard with your mama and that nosy Wagenspurg woman. She could worm a confession out of the Pope."

Caterina smiled because this was true.

"You have my word, Caterina. I'm going to take good care of you."

During this speech he'd tipped her chin and with a thumb executed a caressing tracery of her mouth. If he had done it only a half an hour ago she would have raged at him, but now, although it was an encroachment, she let it happen, let the chill course through her.

How hard it was going to be to deny him, how dangerous to allow those hands, those experienced, knowing hands, to touch. The gentle kiss in the chapel, the just performed tracery of her lips, why did it compel her so?

Was it because of the magnetism of his health, his strength, his purebred conformation? Suddenly, in spite of all that had happened, all that she'd said and sworn, it was just like that long ago day by the river. Her veins ran fire.

"Now, the kiss I asked for earlier," he said. "To seal our peace." Caterina's arms, moving by themselves, went around his neck. To be held so easily in his strong arms, to experience all these interesting sensations was so beguiling...

His mouth was firm on hers, the touch of his scratchy one day beard grazed her chin. She could feel his curls against the arm she had around his neck. Christoph was gentle, not even pursuing the tempting response of her parted lips.

"There," he said, releasing her. "Peace is declared. There will be no force. There has been more than enough of that employed by our fathers in bringing us together."

"I shall rely upon your word, Herr Graf." Caterina, still within his arms, desperately hoped that the spoken formality would master her racing heart.

"The time isn't now, not for either of us. Someday though, I think it will certainly be the greatest honor to cover every satin, gold dusted inch of you with kisses."

At the same moment, he released her. Cat stepped back, feeling rather foolish. All she could think of to say was: "Will you call for my mama now, Herr Graf?"

Chapter Six

Christoph called to his Hauptmann, Goran, who promptly came thumping on his wooden leg down the hall to unlock the door. Then her husband went out to dress in an adjoining chamber. Lady von Velsen entered with servants and began exclaiming at once over the wrecked china.

Caterina was sternly set to washing and dressing. At first her mother was immovable, but eventually the rumbles that came from the stomach of her daughter persuaded her to relent and have another pot of tea and some bread and butter sent from the kitchen.

"It's more than you deserve, though. Creating another scene this morning! I didn't think I'd live to see the day, but your husband has got all my admiration. He's showing the restraint of a man twice his age. Frankly, you deserve to starve until dinner."

There were questions, too, after the servants had gone. To these Cat made no answer, although her fair skin reddened furiously.

Of course, Lady von Velsen believed she knew what that meant. When the maid tried to gather up the stained shift, Mama took charge of it.

"The Landrat will want to see." She gave Cat a motherly look, but her daughter steadfastly refused to meet her eyes.

Caterina remained in the room until Christoph came to take her down to dinner. When she saw him again, dressed in a suit of dark green with plentiful lace at collar and cuffs, his dark curls brushed to a shine and falling over broad shoulders, Cat was beset by another of those traitorous moments of exultation. There wasn't another man anywhere to match him.

Arm in arm they walked into the crowded great room. It seemed that little had changed from last night. The place was still crowded with neighbors and cousins and all those extra servants. When a chorus of cheers and giggles greeted them, Christoph patted Cat's arm and sent a solemn, cautioning look around the room. Cat held up her chin, but felt the damnable blush coming on. She knew that there wasn't an imagination in the room that wasn't running wild.

* * *

Christoph's nature was demonstrative and affectionate. In public, he touched her. His hands glided down her long back, lingered tenderly. Cat accepted it, understanding that this was a necessary part of the deception. Meanwhile that renegade desire which had taken up residence gloried. There were times when she couldn't repress the flush of pleasure that came when his arm slipped around her.

In private, however, he was formal. All the time they stayed at her parent's house, Cat slept on the sofa, her man in the bed.

"You are so tall, you should really be the one to have it." She attempted to sound off-hand.

"I really shouldn't accept your offer, Red. It doesn't seem gentlemanly, but my choices are either the bed or the floor. The damned sofa would leave me nowhere to put my legs from the knee down. I'm surprised you fit."

"Well, I do if I curl up. So it's decided."

"Of course, we could share the bed. There is plenty of room and I am not bent upon ravishing you."

"I don't think it would be wise."

"Perhaps not, but I hope that it will be the same with you as with all the other kitty cats I know. After we are at Heldenberg and the really cold weather sets in, you'll find it more to your liking to cuddle."

Then without any more ceremony than if he'd been alone, he proceeded to toss off his dressing gown. The body revealed was harmonious as a pagan statue. There was only one defect, but the fault wasn't Nature's. One thigh was scarred and dimpled with three purple and white ragged crescents, the remnants of last year's wound.

The first time she saw him undress it almost took Cat's breath away, even though it was not the first time she'd seen a naked man. Once after a hunt she'd come upon her male cousins swimming in the river. Although her papa had hurried her away, yelling at the boys to "mind their damned manners", they'd made sure that she'd got an eyeful.

Now here was Christoph, exactly as naked and only a few feet away. Cat knew she'd never seen this much man. Like any male, whether a tail flaunting, big shouldered tom or a head tossing stallion, it was obvious that he enjoyed his body.

That first night when he'd so carelessly disrobed, she'd turned away, gone to the sofa and rolled herself up tightly in a blanket. She told herself that what everyone else wanted, she did not!

To assist her resolve, she conjured a memory of dear, lost Wili. Of Wili sobbing on her bed, of Wili crying in Mama's arms at a long ago Carnival in Passau, tears falling in room after room, in spring and summer and winter, over and over again. So many promises made, every one broken!

Cat asked herself how she could sensibly have much faith in this most recent of Christoph's so often sworn to conversions.

* * *

For several weeks the odd honeymoon went on, as did the hunting and gaming. A wedding was always a fine excuse for neighbors and relatives to do some extended visiting, and this time, right before the summer haying, was one of the few times of year in which gentlemen did not feel it necessary to be in daily attendance upon their lands.

Every morning the men breakfasted and then went riding, racing their horses across the pastures and wagering on the outcome. A field was dedicated to saber practice and the men made passes at a target from horseback, a game at which her husband excelled.

One day though, Caterina came upon her husband at the humblest sort of work. A section of stone wall had tumbled down and it seemed that the huge peasant who usually did this had strained his back. Christoph had come upon Jakab stretched out on the ground trying to relax a spasm and had good naturedly offered to finish the job for him. Now he, with jacket, shirt and stock discarded and the workman's leather gloves on, the lean hard muscles of his back and arms pumped, was lifting stones and fitting them into the wall.

"Peasant's labor, sir," scolded the Landrat who'd just come upon the scene. Then he chuckled and shot a joking smile at his daughter. "We never work a breeding bull."

Inwardly Caterina groaned. Her father's steady stream of earthy witticisms were driving her mad.

Christoph heaved a rock into place, wiped the sweat from his eyes with his arm and grinned.

"I don't mind, Oncle. It's exercise that a man who has been feasting for three weeks badly needs."

Indicating the servant prone on the ground, he added, "I didn't want to stand by and see your Jakab pop a gut. Besides, sometimes I do this on my own place. Heldenberg is so stony that we raise all our fences this way. It's interesting, like putting a puzzle together. Isn't that so, Jakab?" he called out.

A deferential answering grunt arose from the prone giant. "Ja, mein Herr Graf..."

Heaving up another sizeable rock and shifting it around in his hands close to his broad chest, Christoph paused for a moment to study its placement in the wall. Sweat was just beginning to trickle down his back.

"Well," said the Landrat, who had been admiring his son in law's physique, "don't wear yourself out, dear boy."

He squeezed Caterina's hand and smiled at her fondly. "You've other important business to attend to, haven't you?"

"Indeed, I have." Christoph neatly fitted the rock and then turned to send the Landrat a broad wink. "But I think there's little danger I'll ever be too tired for that kind of work."

"Now didn't I say so, Kitty Cat?" Her father beamed. "The finest stallion in the valley?"

"Papa!"

"Oh, come now. The time for maidenly modesty is past, isn't it?"

There was no answer. Caterina, embarrassed, had slipped her arm out of her father's, picked up her skirt and run. The Landrat, well used to her flights, simply watched her go.

"Tail high and head up, skittish as a two year old filly. I hope for your sake Son that breeding settles her down..."

* * *

During the weeks the visiting lasted, Christoph studiously left Caterina alone during the day, spending his time with the men. More often than not, he was the winner, although Max von Beiler, who hunted with Cat's father regularly and knew the land like the back of his hand, twice carried away the honors of the hunt. Lady von Velsen and the more accomplished female riders joined in the horseback sports, and, of course, Cat would have dearly loved to have been among them.

Her father, however, absolutely forbade it. "It's closing the door after the horse has been stolen, but I won't tempt fate again."

Cat fretted, but von Hagen acquiesced in her father's decision.

"Obey your papa, little wife. It's a small thing to humor him."

So she was imprisoned (for that was the way she thought of it) with the more sedentary ladies and old men.

59

They, of course, were on fire to tease tales of married intimacy from her, but after one morning gathering at which Cat burst into tears, called them "a bunch of evil minded gossips" and ran out of the room, they reverted to great formality in her presence. She contrived to be with them as little as possible, saying that she was going to her room, and then slipping away to visit Star.

If the mare was in the pasture, all Cat had to do was whistle and she would come, bobbing her head in greeting. With a gentle whicker, she'd lower a velvet nose to Caterina's hand searching for the green apple or whatever treat Caterina had thought to bring.

There was only one other person who had Star's confidence besides Cat, and Herr Longnecker was kept so busy with the extra animals of the guests that she often found her mare dusty and ungroomed. One day, Caterina called Star from among the other mares in pasture and got her haltered. Then she led her inside to do some grooming herself.

Here it was that Christoph, who had come in early from his ride, found her, wearing a dirty brown dress and an apron. When the bay stallion saw the mare, he gave a clarion call and pulled so hard that he nearly pulled his master off his feet. The mare stamped and kicked, tried to get her head around to face him.

At the ominous sound of a stallion trumpeting, a groom came running to assist in getting Christoph's big bay into one of the double walled stallion boxes.

"She shouldn't be inside, Lady," the groom said. "With all the stallions we've got at the moment, it'll cause a riot. She's coming on again. While the company's here and the barn is full, Herr Longnecker said she was to stay out in the little high pen or in the mare's box."

Embarrassed, Caterina patted her horse's neck. The mare was quivering all over, nostrils flaring, slamming one slender forefoot into the floor. The groom was right, of course. Cat had been so preoccupied by all her own troubles that she hadn't been thinking about Star.

"I'm sorry, Karl. She just looked so dirty and you know how she loves to be scratched."

"Well, my Lady," said the groom. "No harm done." Peering over the box door, he whistled softly. "Look at her shine! You've got a fine hand, Fraulein—ah, I beg your Ladyship's pardon."

He paused, staring at this girl he'd watched grow up. Married now to a handsome, rich nobleman and yet there she still was, grubbing with her horse, red hair in a long braid down her back, dirty hands, a smudge on her face. She might, he thought, and not for the first time, have made a better farmer's wife. Were there any other great ladies who understood so well all the earthy mysteries of horse craft?

"My Brandy fancies your Star," Christoph remarked. "Perhaps before we leave here on Thursday we should arrange—a marriage."

"She doesn't like him. I can tell."

She hadn't been told when she was to leave her father's house, but now, suddenly, here it was, only a few days away. It brought home the fact that she was Christoph's, just like the hilly eastern parcel, the twenty heifers, the two plow broke oxen, the Wurttemberg mares and several thousand gulden that comprised her dowry. She and Star belonged to Christoph von Hagen now, to do with exactly as he pleased.

"We are talking about horses, aren't we, my Lady?" Christoph raised an eyebrow, but the groom, humbly tugging a forelock, came to Caterina's rescue.

"Indeed, Herr Graf, so far your Lady's Star has only seen one stallion she's been willing to stand for, the von Melk's Barb."

"It is just as Karl says, Herr Graf." Cat was careful not to breach etiquette. She really felt a desperate need to protect Star. "The Barb died last winter ago and Papa and I and Herr Longenecker have been at our wit's end to find a stud ever since. She won't have any here," she added, firmly meeting her husband's eyes.

"Well, let's put them near each other for a while and see if his good looks change her mind." Her husband's reply was relaxed and cheerful. "Of course, like his master, he's not a particularly subtle fellow, but perhaps," he added, his hand coming to engulf hers, "the lady will take pity on him."

"I don't know."

"But isn't she a Barb? I've always understood they're hot blooded, that they go in and out of season until they're bred."

"Only half," Cat replied. "Fortunately she's cold blooded like her mother. Once we get through July, it usually stops."

"To begin again in January," said the groom with a shake of his head aimed at the mare.

After Star was safely inside the companionable safety of the mare's loose box, husband and wife began to walk back arm in arm. For awhile Christoph was silent, clearly pondering something. Then he said, "I didn't know you were so sentimental."

"What do you mean?"

"Well, I thought Wili was the one who nursed the runts, the one who felt that all creation had feelings just like people, that the only difference between the beasts and us was tails. You know, in breeding harness Star wouldn't run any risk of being injured. She's fast and brave, but crossed with my Prussian or one of your papa's Hanoverians, you might get more size and that speed of hers as well. Isn't that beauty of a sorrel filly in the back pasture hers?"

"Yes," Cat replied. "She's something, isn't she? But—I don't want her tied for breeding."

The kind of expression a parent puts on when he's indulging a child was taking possession of her husband's face, so Cat quickly added, "Besides, if she's carrying, I can't have the fun of riding her." The real reason, the thing Cat couldn't say, had to do with something that had happened with one of the horses during the spring of her thirteenth year.

Black Lady had been a favorite, a big, rangy horse, with the longest neck and the deepest chest anyone had ever seen on a mare. In fact, for two years she'd made a fine showing against the stallions at the races in Passau.

Usually the animals were put to pasture together and breeding got accomplished in the course of things, but this mare, fleet as a storm cloud, was possessed of a fury. She ran, she bit and fought and finally she'd kicked her stallion in the head and blinded him in one eye. To complete the disaster it soon became clear that she hadn't been successfully bred.

"I knew what a devil she was." The Landrat reproached himself endlessly. "You warned me, Longnecker. A man's a fool who doesn't listen to his Horse Master." He damned himself. He cursed the mare.

The stallion Black Lady had blinded was too good to destroy, but even for breeding the poor fellow was at a disadvantage now, so any mares he was to service were tied in a box stall

The next time Black Lady looked ready to breed, the Landrat had her harnessed, her feet tied to rings in the floor in a big box stall. Then he'd had Longnecker bring a stallion to serve her. It was done several days in a row.

"That she devil will throw a foal this time."

Cat had happened upon it, the grooms joking as the stallion leapt. Face burning, she'd slunk away, out of the barn. How terrible to see this brave female creature bound and forced.

Now, sooner or later, one way or another, just like Black Lady, Caterina herself would be bred. The thought produced a violent shudder.

Her husband, his arm around her, noticed. "What's the matter, sweetie?"

He made as if to draw her close, to give one of those warm, cousinly squeezes he'd been giving her, but the endearment was too much. Caterina yanked her arm out of his and then pelted away towards the house as fast as she could go.

Chapter Seven

Christoph's estate had the same name as the looming mountain upon whose shoulders it sat: Heldenberg. The surroundings were wild and the nearest town, the tiny village of Heldenruhe, was about seven miles away.

As the time of Cat's departure grew closer, Lady van Velsen seemed increasingly apprehensive. She fussed and fussed over her daughter, insisting that she spend her days overlooking housekeeping in every detail, from kitchen to the linen closet.

"A quick course?" Christoph teased when he discovered them at it. He leaned across a gleaming table and lifted a fat, ripe greengage from a basket in the center. After biting into it, he sent a nod of approval towards his mother in law. Inside the thin green and purple skin was a juicy golden center.

"Herr Graf," said Lady von Velsen, drawing herself up very straight, "I have always done my best to instruct Caterina in the duties she would be expected to perform as a gentleman's wife. I have tried persuasion and I have tried whippings. Both, as you probably know, to little avail." She looked so distressed that Cat felt she should say something.

"It's not Mama's fault, Graf von Hagen. It's just as she says."

For the first time she could see her mother's point of view. In a few days she would be mistress of a large household and she knew next to nothing about how to manage it.

"Housekeeping just wasn't as interesting to me as horses."

A ferocious look from her mother interrupted.

"No apologies, please, from either of you ladies." von Hagen said smiled. "Especially from Lady Albertine who has been trying to sow grain on stony ground. I have a capable staff in residence. They shall, I'm sure, continue to manage as they have in the past. When my wife becomes interested, as I'm sure she will, she can assert her own notions about housekeeping."

He finished the small fruit and dropped the pit upon a plate set beside the basket. It was awful to Cat to see her proud and capable mother standing there, apparently so embarrassed on account of her.

"Until she has notions, though," Christoph said with a sudden grin, catching one of Caterina's long red braids and tugging, "she can climb trees and play with Star all day and still an adequate dinner will find its way onto the table."

"Oh, Caterina," her Mama exclaimed after Christoph, a fresh greengage in hand, had taken his leave. "How on earth are you ever going to manage?"

No servants from home would come along. Christoph had insisted upon that, had been quite adamant that his own people could adequately attend them.

This had upset Lady von Velsen. She'd wanted to send one of the older servants along to advise Caterina. Of course, though none of them would have dared argue with their mistress, not one of them wanted to be exiled to far away Heldenberg either. When the word about Graf von Hagen's decision went out, there was much muted rejoicing in the servant's quarters.

* * *

The afternoon before Cat was to leave, a summons came from her mother. When she arrived at Lady von Velsen's room, she found it darkened. Her mother was afflicted occasionally by migraine and the silent, dim room attested to an attack.

"Oh, Mama," Cat whispered, approaching the bed. "I'm sorry. Is it very bad?"

"Rather, my darling. But don't you worry, it will pass." Lady von Hagen was pale, prone, her dress loosened, her stays opened. A maid beside the bed was wringing out a cloth in a basin of cold water.

"Hanna, dear," Lady von Velsen addressed the servant, "please go out now, but don't go far. I'll soon want you again."

As the girl curtsied and retreated, Cat stepped into her place. "May I help, Mama?"

"Yes, please. Do as Hanna was doing while I talk to you. It's a very serious talk too, Caterina, so please attend."

There was a pause, a tinkle of water as Cat wrung out the cloth and applied it to her mother's white brow. Finally her mother said, "There are a few last cautions I want to give you, my angel, especially about your husband the Graf's housekeeping arrangements."

"Yes, Mama." Cat was demure, thinking it was going to be another lecture about lazy servants or counting the hams.

"Caterina, as I believe you are aware, Christoph kept a mistress at Heldenberg for many years."

"Yes, I know," Caterina shifted uncomfortably. "Wili told me."

"This spring when your husband returned to marry, he told your father and me that this lady had married another man, a captain in his regiment, and that she had gone to live in Vienna with her husband and their new baby. But now, from something Uncle Rupert said to your father, I am not so sure this is the case."

"What?" Cat dropped the cloth into the basin and stared at her mother with dismay. "Surely you and Papa don't expect me to live under the same roof with a—a—concubine!"

"Has your husband talked to you about any of this?"

"No."

Lady von Velsen seemed to be waiting for some enlargement, but no more was forthcoming. After the wedding morning, Christoph had politely kept his distance. The most uncomfortable part of every day was when they

66

were left alone together in the bedroom. Every night her husband, docile as a lamb, climbed into bed by himself and went off to sleep. Except for the cousinly kisses and caresses which happened in public, he never offered to touch her.

"Well, Christoph had talked to Wilhelmina about this woman and they'd come to some sort of agreement. I know because she told me a little, but I certainly wasn't entirely happy about it. Wili, of course, was always willing to believe him, even his tale that although the woman stayed on at Heldenberg, he hadn't shared a bed with her in several years."

"Why are you telling me this now? I thought you believed in his miraculous reformation."

"Caterina," her mother hissed, her red brows contracting in a wave of pain. "It's all I can do to talk, so just hush, please, and listen. I'm at my wit's end myself, but perhaps the reason he hasn't spoken about her is that she really is gone. Heaven knows there is no reason to rake up trouble, there's enough as it is. What I particularly want to say is that I don't have the feeling that she's been gone for long. As a result, the servants may resent you, may feel that you have driven her out."

There was a pause while Caterina wrung out another cloth and applied it to her mother's brow.

"The only advice I can give you, as your husband so unreasonably refuses to let you take an experienced servant of your own along, is to keep your eyes open and your opinions to yourself, at least until you see the lay of the land. Don't trust anyone too quickly. It will take a long time to sort out who your real allies are in the house. And you will need allies, Caterina. A noblewoman, isolated in a place like Heldenberg, is in great need of friends."

Caterina stared at the pale long form of her mother stretched out on the bed. Was it all going to turn out to be a lie, this reformation? And was her husband's reticence based, not upon the impropriety of bedding her so soon after he'd lain with her sister, but upon the fact that his heart still belonged to a mistress?

Lady von Velsen lifted a hand wearily to her forehead. "Perhaps she is gone, but if not this will be the first test of your woman's bravery. You must control your temper, Caterina, at least for awhile until you understand the situation. Don't jump to conclusions. Try to trust your husband, but keep your eyes open. Above all, my angel, remember your duty to your family."

"Yes. Oh, yes! My heifer's duty! To be leapt, swell up and calve!"

"By the Blessed Brigitte!" Her mother, two red patches flaring on her cheeks, raised herself unsteadily on one elbow. "I endured it myself, Caterina. I wasn't much older than you when I was given to Theodor's father, Herman von Ployer. I shall not detail his abuse of my trust and person, his many cruelties, both large and small, but on the day I gave birth to Theo and Valentin—"

Theodor had had a twin, another half brother whose face Cat could not for the life of her remember. Valentin had died sometime during her fifth year and Cat distinctly recollected watching with dry eyed curiosity while Theo and the grown-ups had wept over his not very large coffin.

"—Upon that day," Lady von Velsen was saying, in the flat monotone of someone speaking of things she'd far rather forget, "Herman von Ployer congratulated me by saying that I had turned out to be a better brood mare than I looked. That very night, contented with having sired two sons, he returned to his townhouse in Passau, to the arms of the creature he kept there. From then on, thank The Blessed Mother, I was spared any more of his—attention."

A thrill of horror went through Caterina. She had never heard her mother speak like this, although she'd had a strong sense that Lady Albertine hadn't liked her first husband. As a child Theodor had lived much of every year with his von Ployer grandparents, but that wasn't an unusual occurrence when a widowed noblewoman remarried. In fact, by law, her late husband's family could have taken Theo away.

"Listen to me, Caterina. I want you to go to Heldenberg with Christoph and find out what the truth is. I think that in spite of all his wanderings, he is by nature too warm-hearted and imaginative to be like my brute of a first husband. But—" Lady von Velsen clearly in pain, rubbed her forehead hard and subsided into the bed again, "if your personal honor cannot endure what you find at Heldenberg, ride Star home and I will do whatever I can to protect you."

With those astonishing words, Lady von Velsen collapsed into the pillows. Caterina started to speak, but her mother waved her hand imperiously.

"Open the box by my bed and take out the golden chains. They can be broken apart by hand, and used as money. Utterly astonished, Caterina silently did as her mother directed.

"Good," said Lady Albertine, watching Caterina settle them around her neck. "Now, not a word to anyone. Call Hanna and go out. My head feels as if it's going to shatter."

* * *

"Mama says that she has heard you still have a mistress at Heldenberg."

Her husband paused on his way into bed, raised a dark eyebrow. Clearly he had been taken by surprise. Still on edge from talking with her mother, Cat stepped forward and blurted, "Is it true?"

"No, Caterina, it is not." His denial came without hesitation.

"I will not stay if she's there."

"Caterina, in the first place, I am done with mistresses, as I have already told you. And in the second—do you think I'm out of my mind? You, I think, are going to be quite enough for me to deal with."

As if this settled the matter, Christoph threw off his morning gown and climbed into bed. As he settled in, he said in an encouraging tone, "I know you're going to love Heldenberg, just as I do. It's a horseman's paradise."

His eyes had brightened. "Would you like to ride out there instead of driving? You and Star could both get some exercise."

"Oh, could I?" Cat cried, delighted at the idea.

"You don't think it would be too hard, do you, after all the time you've been kept out of the saddle?"

"Too hard?" Caterina, imagining a splendid summer ride of many days, was well on her way to forgetting how the conversation had begun. "My backside might get sore, but that's nothing to worry—" Her voice died away, apprehending the oncoming joke.

"In spite of the Landrat's attempts to educate you to womanliness, you still prefer astride, don't you?" She was relieved when Christoph avoided the obvious.

"Yes."

"If you've still got a pair of trousers, go ahead and ride that way. I've always thought it stupid to hobble a talented rider with side saddle simply because she's female."

"Papa thinks he cut up all my trousers, but I do have one pair that he doesn't know about."

"Good." She caught the sudden flash of his smile. "I anticipate a splendid ride to Heldenberg with you."

"Oh, Christoph! Thank you." After her long confinement, a five day's ride would be an exciting challenge.

"You are very welcome, little wife. It will be like the old days when we were playmates."

With that, he leaned over to blow out the bedside candle and just as always, Caterina heard him settling down to sleep. In the soft late summer darkness, she stretched out upon that couch that had been her bed for the last five weeks and prepared to do the same.

A few minutes later, she was upright again. She had forgotten to practice with the protector. As she sat there, listening to his steady breathing with the little knife in hand, she felt the stirrings of uneasiness. In her joy at the idea of a long ride, she had completely forgotten the important discussion she'd initiated.

* * *

The journey day dawned clear and the bride went out in a caraco jacket and tricorne. Although her parents looked cross, she also wore the secret pair of leather seated men's breeches.

On the first day her husband was very easy and charming. On the second day of their journey, however, he withdrew. As his big bay paced beside Caterina and Star, he was unusually silent, apparently lost in thought. As they made their way steadily into choppy foothills, Caterina said something about the changes in the land. Christoph emerged from his preoccupation to talk about where they were going. More of that land, he explained, was occupied by pastures and hay, by oak forest and orchard, than by the extensive plantations of grain, vines and root crops that were so characteristic of the warmer, flatter river valley.

"There are longer winters and a far less good soil than our papas have to work with. It's been a tradition in the von Hagen family for this piece to be the eldest son's, before he comes into the valley patrimony. If you can make ends meet up on Heldenberg, you can get the best out of land anywhere."

They were going slowly, the horses picking their way along a precarious cliff fall stretch of road partly washed out. "The first few years didn't go so well, but the secret seems to be, especially for someone who spends as much time away as I do—to get lucky enough to find a good bailiff. We're not doing splendidly, but well enough for me to keep too many horses. The fellow I've got now, Walter, has so far kept me out of trouble. And of course, the mountain forests have some good hunting."

"Too many horses?"

"Yes. I have a bay foursome, Hanoverians that should be taken to the Passau fair. If I don't have to go soldiering next year, I'll do it. With some training, they'll beat everyone all hollow, I'm sure."

"Oh! Are they big? May I drive them?"

"Well, the two mares are a perfect match at about fifteen hands. The two geldings are another hand taller, older and better trained. You may certainly drive the geldings, but the mares are young, an uneducated pair of bad girls. I've had them four in hand a few times, although it was rough work."

"Four in hand!"

Her husband smiled at her enthusiasm and reined Brandy closer. "We'll have to go driving often, especially you like it so much."

At the inns every night, they'd lodged in separate rooms. His big brother neutrality, securely in place most of the time was occasionally interrupted by remarks that might have a double meaning.

* * *

After three splendid, long days in the saddle, days in which they arrived hours before their baggage, they reached the foothills of the great gray mountains. The fertile Donau was now behind them.

That afternoon it started to rain. The clouds came suddenly, flowing down from the mountains like a ragged black skirt, trailing lightning and thunder. Inside the first five minutes they were drenched.

"Do you want to go into the carriage?" Christoph had moved Brandy closer to ask the question. Water was dripping in a steady stream from the brim of his three cornered hat.

"No. Why? I'm already soaked to the skin."

"Well, it's still a rough eight miles to the Black Swan. The host is expecting us and it's really the only inn in the area where we don't run the risk of getting lousy."

"Don't worry about me," Cat replied bravely. "I'll ride there. I've been wet before."

Evidently pleased by her resolve, he gave her a watery grin and tipped his hat, dumping collected water before pulling it down again tightly.

"Speak up if it gets to be too much, Grafin."

On and on they'd plodded, through wind and a steady rain. The road was now a mass of mud, the horses splashing and tripping through ruts now brimming with water. As they passed by an inn that didn't, from the outside, look so bad, Caterina's lips began to chatter. The rain was relentless, flowing down her back in an icy river and dripping out the toes of her boots.

By the time they finally reached their destination, Caterina was cold, soaked through and through. Shudders racked her thin frame. She was so stiff and numb that for once she didn't disdain the lift from the saddle her husband offered.

The innkeepers and servants came bustling into the stormy courtyard giving comfort equally to their noble lodgers, servants and horses. The room to which Caterina was escorted was comfortably furnished. It was not only clean, but she was overjoyed to feel how hot it was from a good fire, already set in the hearth.

"I'll have your trunk sent up at once, your Ladyship," said Goran, whose heavy blonde moustaches were hanging like a pair of limp rags under his long nose. Caterina thanked him and went to stand and shiver near the rosy hearth.

"Supper will come up as soon as we're dry." Her husband's tall elegance filled the door.

"Wonderful! I'm famished." Although she tried to stop it, her words were followed by a wrenching shiver.

"The innkeeper's wife wanted to attend you as you have no maid servant, but I told her that getting us dinner was far more important. I shall attend you. Sit, Caterina. First, we'll get those boots off."

She thought she ought to object, but she was simply too cold and too numb. Christoph knelt before her chair and helped her haul off the soaked boots.

"What happened to yours?" she asked. He was already barefoot.

"Goran has already appropriated mine."

Just as he finished the task, the landlady popped in with a huge pitcher of hot water and two large towels.

"Always the perfect hostess, Frau Schwann," said Christoph.

The sturdy goodwife smiled, bobbed, and went hurrying out again.

"You'll soon see that it was worth nearly drowning to get here."

Caterina nodded, managed a smile through her shivers. The people certainly were obliging and friendly.

"Now, I want no dramatic protests of modesty from you, young woman. You're going to get out of those wet clothes and I'm going to join you. We'll dry off in front of the fire like a proper husband and wife."

He had already taken off his wet jacket. As he hung it over the back of a chair, Caterina said, "Ah—Christoph..."

"Don't be silly. You're going to catch catarrh if you sit there much longer. Either you undress and rub yourself dry, or I shall do it for you."

Cat was too cold and uncomfortable to put much energy into argument. First, though, she hung her jacket and waistcoat on another chair back. Then, going behind, she began to undress, taking advantage of the small shelter this offered.

Christoph undressed with his usual matter of factness. The firelight played upon a sinuous rippling as he twisted and turned, first vigorously rubbing his wet hair and then his body. "Well," he grinned, dark, curls damply emerging from the towel, "What have you been doing? Watching?"

"Christoph!" Caterina flushed.

To her relief he turned and scooped up the robe Goran had already laid across the trunk. As he was putting it on, Cat took advantage of his lack of attention by edging closer to the cover of her chair and pulling up the soaked breeches which she'd been about to drop.

They were so wet that they stuck to her hips, so she didn't bother to rebutton them.

"Stupid stays," she muttered. "The leather has gone soggy and my fingers are so cold I can't get them undone." Knowing that she wouldn't have a maid for the journey, Caterina had worn a pair of leather front laced stays which she could take on and off herself. She had not, however, planned on being drenched in them.

"Well, come and I'll undo them. As you may have heard here and there, I'm an expert."

"Only if you tie your gown closed."

"If you insist."

"I most certainly do."

Smiling he obeyed, wrapping the sash around his waist. Only after he'd got that secured did Cat venture from behind the safety of her chair.

"Stand still." With great seriousness he bent his curly head close to her bosom to get a good view of the task. Caterina stood shivering and watched his big hands, astonishingly dexterous, work the leather laces loose without stretching or breaking. Outside the window a brilliant flash, closely followed by a roar, made them both start.

"If it's still at this tomorrow, we won't go on. The horses are tired out and I don't want you to catch cold." Then he raised his head. "There," he said with a big grin, "the gates of paradise are open." He gave the stays a tug.

"Christoph!" Both hands flew at once to the top of the stays, frantic to hold them in place. Underneath lay nothing but a fine, soaked muslin chemise, prettily raised, no doubt, by rosy cold nipples. As soon as she did that, however, he changed his strategy. In the next moment he was yanking down her breeches.

She tried to turn, to run, but the breeches, now dropped round her knees, were like hobbles. She began to fall, but great bear arms caught her.

"Now here's a pretty sight." Christoph laughed and swung her easily up against his broad chest. "A fair damsel in distress—and wet leather."

"You put me down!" She pushed at him, but this only opened the dressing gown and revealed his chest. Shamed by the tears of frustration that were rising, she punched the nearest thing, one imposing shoulder.

"What's this? Tears from the same Valkyrie who rode thirty hard miles today, more than half of them in that deluge? By God, only a wager, and a large one at that, would have kept your brother out in that."

His eyes caught, held hers. They were full of a delightfully sexless admiration—horseman to horseman. As he praised, he was obeying her, too, letting her down, although he did it in such a way that her slender wet body went sliding against his.

How hard he felt; how easily he'd held her, as if she were weightless. Without quite understanding, Caterina, rose on her tiptoes and impetuously gave him a kiss. His arms tightened at once. With his participation what had begun on impulse bloomed into the sweetness of savoring. Her skin was chilly and damp, but the hearth was roaring, cooking the flesh that fronted it. Crushed close, she felt muscles swell as she pressed wet muslin, cold raised nipples and Aunt Teresina's wooden locket against his chest. When the tip of an exploring tongue tentatively touched hers, she became alarmed and pulled her mouth away with a gasp.

"Have you never been kissed like that?" One arm held her tightly around the waist, the hand of the other came to recapture her chin. Cat found herself gazing into his eyes with their extravagant lashes. A green fire had consumed every trace of hazel.

"No!"

"Those stable boys of your father's really were a well behaved lot, weren't they?" A warm chuckle followed. "I shall have the honor of being first at absolutely everything with you, sweet Caterina Maria Brigitte."

Dismayed by the look in his eye, the look of a man who has gained a victory, Cat pushed him.

"No more." She tried hard to steady her voice, but the command had a quiver in it.

"A very prudent request." He seemed regretful, but he let her go.

"You know, angel, no one would believe that I've been sleeping in the same room with you for six weeks and haven't even got round yet to a thorough kissing of that big beautiful mouth of yours. Still, it's nobody's business but our own—is it?"

When she nodded, her eyes full of him, a dark warrior in firelight, he said, very softly, "Now, love, out of those wet clothes."

Cat, her body still humming from his caresses and a rushing, shameless feeling, seized the clammy bottom of the chemise and pulled it off over her head. At once there was the tingle of wet flesh meeting air, and the new, never before tasted pleasure of showing off her body, a pleasure that totally overwhelmed the fierce counter tug of the modesty she'd been taught.

Christoph subsided into one of the chairs by the fire, but his eyes never left her. A slight smile played about his lips. He was clearly enjoying the sight of her, wide shoulders and high gold dusted breasts.

"All of it," he said, a devilish grin barely in check. "Come on, Red." She had begun to blush, a blush that unfolded a bloom all the way to her nipples. "Show me. Only when you do," and suddenly he flicked away the other towel, flaunting his possession, "can you have this back."

"Damn!" Just when had he appropriated her towel? She lunged after, but he snapped it away.

"Take it off, little wife. I swear not to touch."

Cat, arms crossed in front of her breasts, stepped back and muttered, "Forgive me, cousin, but I don't find that particularly reassuring."

"First you tease and then you run. I didn't know you were such a chicken heart, Caterina!" He laughed, knowing that he had turned a favorite childish taunt against her.

Cat gritted her teeth. Turning to the side, she untied the thin strip that held the silk thigh length man's undergarment she'd worn beneath the riding breeches. She peeled it off and stepped out, one long shapely leg at a time. Her husband leaned back in his chair and let out a low whistle.

"Face me," he said, his voice ever so soft. "I won't touch, but after six weeks of marriage I'd dearly love to see."

She did as he asked. Later, in the cold light of the morning, brimming with guilt, Cat couldn't understand why she'd done any of it, beginning with the impulsive kiss.

Firelight dappled her long, slim form. The wet red single braid hung over one shoulder, while golden freckles gave her fair flesh an all over glitter. Her breasts, tantalizingly unfinished, were high with cold and excitement. Below, there was a perfect triangle of fine, red gold curls.

"Without a doubt, the finest piece of woman flesh from here to Istanbul." Christoph didn't move a muscle, but he did draw in a deep breath. The tiger's look in his eyes rose to meet the one in hers, the one which was, with a mad lack of restraint, daring him to make the next move.

Next, she nearly jumped out of her skin, for there was a sharp rap-rap-rap at their door. Caterina dashed for cover, flinging herself into bed.

"It's the Grafin's trunks, Herr Graf." Goran called from outside, "They're ready with supper."

The young Graf clapped his hands together, gave a shout of laughter and then cried, "Well, sir, enter!" Through the half-open bed curtains Cat could see that he'd slung her towel like a trophy over one broad shoulder.

The trunks came thumping in while Cat hid beneath the covers. After the parade of servants had gone stamping out, Christoph searched out Cat's morning gown and tossed it between the curtains. Just as she finished hastily slipping into it, supper arrived.

* * *

They sat at a small table by the fire and ate in an unaccustomed but pleasantly solitary state. Just as Christoph had said, the food at the Black Swan was wonderful.

A richly sauced venison pie, with its accompaniment of turnips and rotekraut, was delicious. Cat pursued it to the bottom of the dish and used chunks of bread to wipe up the gravy.

The meal was punctuated by comings and goings. Goran came to get orders for tomorrow; the innkeeper and his wife appeared too. Apparently they had played host to Christoph before.

At last the table was taken away. They had just settled down to a task that might have renewed their earlier, interrupted intimacy, for Christoph had begun to brush his wife's beautiful thick hair dry by the fire, when the host once more knocked.

"I'm sorry—devastated—Herr Graf von Hagen, but Herr Graf Thun's party has just come in, quite desperate to get out of the rain."

"And," Christoph finished with a rueful look at his wife, at the shining, wavy red mantle which fell over her shoulders and down her back, "You will need the ladies to sleep with other ladies and gentlemen to sleep with other gentlemen if you are to accommodate everyone. I understand perfectly, Herr Schwann. It's the luck of the road."

The plump innkeeper bowed nervously. "A dreadful occurrence in the middle of your wedding journey, Herr Graf, and I pray you will not be angry, but you have divined our needs perfectly. If the Countess Thun and her daughter, who is great with child, sir!—might room here with your wife, then you, the Graf Thun and his son in law could go to the west room."

After a torrent of apologies and explanations that rivaled the torrents of rain still blowing outside, the round faced host, bowing and bobbing, withdrew. Caterina began to get up, but her husband caught her hand.

"Just a moment. I want to remember how beautiful you look sitting there with all that fiery hair."

After a moment of studying her, her face, her lissome body wrapped in the morning gown, Christoph raised Cat's long fingers and in the most tender and humble manner, kissed them. Caterina, while experiencing that now familiar war of desire and doubt, allowed a thrill to pass through her.

"I am not accustomed to looking upon delay as a blessing, but in our case, my lovely wife, I believe it is."

Chapter Eight

There followed the tumult of two aristocratic families meeting and sharing small quarters. The servants bustled and their masters and mistresses offered each other congratulations and sent greetings to family members. Gossip from Court was passed by the Thuns, who were traveling home from Vienna for the birth. They discussed the abominable state of the roads and the equally abominable state of the weather.

The next day the intimate happenings seemed like a dream to Caterina. Dressed in a pair of her husband's pants which blossomed around her slimness—although the length wasn't bad—Caterina consumed her breakfast in near silence. The size of the young countess's belly and her languid passivity were equally unsettling. Caterina was glad they would go on. It had stopped raining during the night and a chilly, autumnal wind had blown blue skies down from the north

It was during this day's muddy ride that the peaks of the mountains suddenly jumped into view. One mountain of the group began to loom, the broken, bald peak intermittently veiled by gray clouds.

"See, Mistress? Heldenberg," said Goran, reining his horse close to Caterina's. "She's in one of her dark moods."

"Oh, she means us no harm," said Christoph. "The old witch is just winking."

"Who was the Helden, the hero of the place?"

"Siegfried, I believe, the one who killed a dragon, and," Christoph shot a grin at her, "married a Valkyrie."

* * *

The next day the dark pine forest poured down the slopes like a black wave determined to engulf them. Soon they left the road and rode through some rocky pasture, by-passing a tiny group of houses clustered around a squat, ancient stone church.

"Heldenruhe," Christoph said, pointing. "Our nearest neighbor. There is a church, a mill, a smithy and not much else. Just an hour's ride and we'll be home."

"Why did we not ride through?"

"Because we'd be detained by everyone from the miller to old Father Leopold. I'll take you down to meet them after you're settled."

They left the last of the cleared land now, climbing the shoulders of the mountain. Here they entered the pine forest, which was as forbidding and chilly as it looked, and trotted down a curiously yellow dirt road. Caterina, used to the sunny open Donau lowlands, felt oppressed and shuddery.

After miles of unrelenting gloom they reached a place where men had been at work again. Here the forest had been trimmed and thinned, tamed into a park. Now there were groves of oak and ash, interspersed with islands of cheerful, sun filled meadow. A herd of deer, tails flashing, bolted from one of them.

"Now that they've seen me, they'll tell all their friends and by tomorrow there won't be one to be found anywhere."

Suddenly the climb ended and Caterina had a first view of her new home. Heldenberg Manor, with an ancient stone first floor and a newer timber-framed second, sat on a cleared, grassy south facing slope. It was a surprise, after the long ride under the forest canopy, to look back and see how far up the mountain they'd come. Above them, with perhaps only a mile's interval, the stony upper reaches began.

On the near side of the main house, level with it, was a great stone barn, but first they rode past a row of tidy cottages which her husband said belonged to the farmhands and servants who worked the place. There were neat little patches of garden, tethered goats, chickens and a group of tow-headed, staring children. In one place, two women sat and spun in the good light of a flagstoned entrance. They rose to curtsy to the passing riders.

Beyond the house she saw a long, low structure like a barracks. Christoph explained that this was exactly what it was. He kept a small contingent of soldiers and their families at Heldenberg. Along the front of the manor, taking advantage of the southern exposure was a well tended garden filled with herbs, flowers and vegetables.

Their progress towards the house was noted. By the time they dismounted, servants had come and were lining up to meet them. Everyone was neat and clean and looked well fed. Their eyes, Caterina noted at once, seemed wary.

First to greet their master and new mistress was a somberly dressed couple, the woman younger than her graying husband. They were, Christoph explained, Herr and Frau Walter, the bailiff and his wife. "There isn't much Herr Walter doesn't know about my land and tenants. His good Frau manages the house and an excellent job she does."

Caterina smiled. The smile was dutifully returned, but without any particular warmth. Men in uniform saluted and housemaids curtsied one by one as she passed a crowd of faces and names. Then she met the head gardener, who was credited with the handsome and practical garden.

"It must have been work to make anything grow on this ground," Caterina observed.

"All the hay and manure from the barn for a good many years," the man said proudly. "The garden is more for the kitchen than for flowers, but you might want to change that, Lady," he went on in a thick Bavarian accent.

"Oh, no, sir," Caterina replied, happy that he, alone of the rest, seemed pleased to see her. "It looks like a wonderful garden just as it is. But, my Lady Mother has some nice roses. If you wanted a few hardy ones, I know she would be happy to send cuttings."

The man seemed pleased by that and backed up, tugging at his forelock politely. Was she imagining it, or were the house servants glaring?

"Well, here's one person," Christoph was saying, "who'll be glad that you aren't too interested in flowers. She likes cabbages better." The cook, a round, homely woman, stepped forward. "I've had cooks from Passau. I've had French cooks too, but by God, give me Frau Ute's cooking over all of them. My father says we eat like peasants up here, but it is right for us, isn't it, my dear?"

He pinched the cook's full red cheek, which caused her to dimple. Emboldened by his obvious affection, she said, "You don't get to eat enough of what I cook, Herr Graf."

"And you, my darling, eat too much of it," he teased, poking at her round belly, "so it works out."

Then, followed by all those wary, curious eyes, they went inside. Herr Goran went first, opening doors. At every other step his wooden leg made a hollow sound on the slates. Caterina had decided during the journey that she liked Goran, although she wasn't sure what he thought of her. He was utterly devoted to his master. As a body servant he was rough in manner and eccentric in dress, but she'd learned that he'd been a common soldier in Christoph's regiment, a Croat by birth, whom her husband had grown to value. After Goran had received his crippling injury, his commander had offered him this job, and Goran, although proud, had accepted. He could soldier no longer and had no home village or even a family to return to. It seemed that all had been lost during an attack by the Croat's hereditary enemies, the Serbs.

Now he, long moustaches drooping, opened the door of a long room decorated with battle flags and trophies of the chase. Somewhat to Cat's surprise, he didn't follow, simply shut the door behind them. Christoph led Caterina to the head of a lengthy trestle table and pulled out a chair for her. He seemed, suddenly, rather ill at ease.

"We'll sit for a moment, Caterina," he said, his usually musical voice echoing in the room. "They will bring us water and something from the kitchen."

He didn't sit with her, just went to gaze out of one of the high narrow windows that looked down the mountain. Caterina stared around her, noticing that while the battle flags made a welcome brightness against the gray walls they were badly torn and singed.

"I see you have the family arms displayed, the von Hagen's, and those of our great grandfather von Velsen and of the Mecklenburg's, but the devices on those two are odd."

Cat indicated the ones she meant. "Where did they come from?" It seemed to be something to talk about.

At once he turned and smiled, a man taking pleasure in a woman's interest. It was a ray of sunshine in that cold ceremonial room.

"They are Turkish, taken at the battle of Isvestia from the troops of Pasha Selim, one of the Grand Turk's Lords. He was commander of the flank that I broke."

"Aren't such things the property of the Emperor?" Caterina continued to gaze, thoroughly impressed.

"Usually, but his Highness was gracious enough to honor me with these at the time he awarded me my title."

"When you were wounded."

"Yes." Christoph's expression grew solemn.

"A great honor, Herr Graf." Cat gazed at his trophies with respect.

"God was pleased to give my men and me a great victory over Pasha Selim and then to spare my life. For a soldier," her husband said thoughtfully, "it would have been no bad end to make a brilliant exit that day, to go to a grave heaped high with honors in the service of the Emperor."

"Wili spent all that winter on her knees praying that you would be healed."

"The irony is not lost on me." The sunlight went from his expression as soon as Cat spoke her sister's name. "Wili was a good and devout woman. Far too good, I have come to think, for the likes of me." With that he turned away and returned to gazing out the window, as steadfastly as if she had vanished.

Cat wished she hadn't said anything. His humble mention of God earlier, this quick turn into dark mood was nothing like the man she thought she knew. She hadn't meant to upset him—or herself, for that matter. The mention of Wili had occurred naturally. Riding towards the manor Cat had sadly imagined how different this wedding journey would have been for her sister.

When, only a moment later, water came in, two pitchers and two salvers and two towels, carried by the thick arms of two lumbering servants, Cat heaved a sigh of relief. She and Christoph washed their hands and faces and dried them upon the toweling.

Next came big breasted Ute with a tray upon which sat a wonderfully fragrant coffee pot and a dish piled high with an odd light repast which Christoph explained was favored by some English lords he'd met in Vienna. It was a meal with which you might punctuate a night of cards, taking in your hands these two slices of bread filled with beef slices and a hearty dollop of mustard.

The cook stood at the end of the table, ready to wait upon any further needs they might have, but Christoph dismissed her.

"This will hold us until supper"

Sitting in solitary state and wordlessly they ate. In spite of her depression, Cat was hungry and took care of her share of the meal. She'd decided that it might be best to be silent for awhile.

Christoph seemed completely engaged by his own thoughts. She wondered if he would open a conversation, but he did not, except to urge food or more coffee upon her.

When the plate and pot were both emptied, Christoph arose, took Cat's hand and led her out of the hall. The peremptory way he did this, as well as his manner during the meal, made her feeling uncomfortably like a child left in the care of a disinterested adult.

The feel of that strong hand holding hers brought to mind their encounter at the Black Swan, an encounter where she had experienced his emotion and strength in a different way. That night he had treated her like anything but a child!

Was he, she wondered, just as confused as she was?

"That's the coldest room in the house, but it's where I've always eaten for some bachelor's reason. Probably," he admitted, "because that was where I first found a table. It's not so bad with a big fire and a bowel of punch and a pack of friends after a hunt, although it's been a few years since anything like that has gone on up here."

They were again in the hallway. From here a steep, ornately carved wooden staircase rose, something that had been added along with the second story.

"I want to show you your room," he said, smiling as they went up together. Food seemed to have lightened his mood.

The room to which he led her was down a long dim corridor. It faced south, nicely illuminated by three abutting windows. Servants were busily hanging green velvet curtains upon a newly erected bed. Although this was very long and wide, it was something of a maidenly affair, painted with pink and white flowers etched with gilt. A door on the left through which he led her opened into a large L shaped room. The smaller part had a southern window too, but the longer ran the entire eastern side of the house. This room, Christoph explained, was his.

The L contained a standing desk and several chairs. The main part of the room had a fireplace, several wardrobes, and wing chairs and finally, by the east wall, a large walnut bed with embroidered hangings.

It occurred to Caterina as she looked at this bed, that it, like the one now being set up in her room was outsize, the longest she'd ever seen. Both, she realized, must have been made to accommodate the height of her husband. Upon his bed an enormous black cat reclined, golden eyes staring. Christoph broke into a happy smile at the sight.

"Katter Furst!" He slowly approached the animal. "Hello, Wilde Bubbe. Katter Furst! Remember me?"

The cat gazed with an expression of amber eyed unconcern that verged on hostility. Just the tip of his plumy black tail thumped the bed.

"You can see how long it's been since I was here," Christoph explained to Caterina. "He's on his dignity while he tries to figure out who I am."

He knelt beside the bed and then extended his hand, so the cat could nose it. When this was accepted, he began to gently scratch its chin then moved to a vigorous rubbing of the massive head and thick furry neck.

"Ah, Furst. My handsome Furst," he crooned. It took awhile, but finally his effort was rewarded with a roaring purr. His careful approach and need to have the cat accept him touched Caterina. She already knew that her husband was partial to cats, for he had always been affectionate with Wili's. Holding a tiny kitten cupped in his big hands, his strong expressive face became almost motherly.

The preference of this red blooded giant for the feline had always seemed incongruous, but to anyone who challenged him, Christoph would say, "Dogs are loyal servants, excellent for hunting and guarding, but for a companion who is a fellow nobleman, get a cat. They don't love from need like dogs, but because they choose to."

When, at her husband's urging, Caterina extended her hand, Furst turned disdainful golden eyes upon her. Slowly he arose. After haughtily flicking his tail in her direction, he made a dignified retreat that led him across the bed and then down and underneath on the far side.

"Oh, ungracious fellow! Such bad manners, Furst." Christoph turned a smile of amusement towards her. "He puts on a big show, but he's really soft as butter. He'll learn to like you, I'm sure. One near stranger making free with his sacred self is probably all he can tolerate for one day."

At that juncture Caterina focused upon the embroidered hangings of the bed. Although the sides were pulled back, the head and foot sections were fully extended. The work was exquisite, covering the entire surface of each section. It was the most colorful, the most artistic, and also the most shocking, needlework she had ever seen.

How had she not noticed earlier? Across the expanse of those hangings, curvaceous naked nymphs and lecherous fauns wantonly disported themselves. Caterina's green eyes widened as they took in the various activities portrayed.

"They're French, far too dear to dispose of, Lady von Hagen, so you'll just have to put up with them. I confess to hoping they'll put some naughty ideas into your pretty head."

Cat felt the blushing start, but Christoph was quite gentlemanly. Once again he simply slipped an arm around her waist in his warm and easy fashion and led her away from the bed, back towards the adjoining room, the one that was to be hers.

At the door in the L, he paused to ceremoniously pull the key from the lock.

"You have my solemn word that I'll never pass through that door except by your invitation," he said. "But, of course, please consider yourself free to come through mine and join me in my bed if you ever become so inclined."

Cat who was still scarlet from those salacious bed curtains, looked down and felt more color bloom in her cheeks.

"What I don't want," he continued, "is for you to get in the habit of locking your door when I'm on the other side of it."

"I hope you are not judging my chastity by yours?"

"Not at all," he replied evenly, "I want you to learn that you can trust me."

She shifted uncomfortably as he slipped the key into his pocket.

"Now, if you'll excuse me I've got to run over a few things with Walter before we sup. It sounds as if they're out of your room now, so why don't you go there and I'll have Fraulein Elsa Heerbrand, the young lady who will be serving you, sent up. Get acquainted, do some unpacking.

I'll returned and take you down to one of our very dull suppers."

He opened the door that divided their rooms and formally bowed her through. Caterina, chin high, retreated. Just as he'd said, the housemaids had gone out, so she went to the window and leaned on the sill, studying her new surroundings.

* * *

Fraulein Elsa was nervous but full of shy smiles, a marked change from the rest of the staff. She seemed to be about the same age as Caterina.

"I know how to help you dress, Mistress, and I'm very good at arranging hair. I like to do that," she said, her voice dying away bashfully.

She was rather like Caterina in a way, very tall, yet not finished growing. Her thin face and long nose gave a naturally sweet expression a solemn cast. Her skin was clear and her teeth regular, her hair light brown, her eyes a shadowed blue. When Caterina asked her about her family, she poured out an entire tale.

"My papa left us a few years ago," Elsa said, "so Mama came to live with her uncle, Father Leopold, who is the priest down in Heldenruhe. Mama died last winter, Lady Caterina," she said sadly, "and I would have kept house for Uncle Leopold, but he wrote to Herr Graf von Hagen about me and here I am. I pray you will be patient with me because I've never been trained for service."

"I don't require anything fancy. All anyone ever does for me is to help me lace up, braid my hair and—" Cat had a sudden hopeful inspiration, "do some sewing."

"Oh, I love to sew! Everyone says I'm very good at mending and embroidering." She seemed delighted that she could be useful to her new mistress.

"Hurrah!" cried Caterina, blissfully clapping her hands. Sewing had been one of those womanly accomplishments for which neither her mama nor Frau Pluncke had ever been able to instill. "I mean," she tried to retrieve a semblance of dignity, "that pleases me, Elsa. As to my hair," she changed the subject ingenuously, "Sometimes Mama puts it up like this." She indicated a circlet

"Such red hair you have, Madame," said Elsa. "And it looks beautifully thick."

"Yes, it is, so I hope you won't pull it. I hate that. One of the servants at home always pulled it."

"I promise I'll be very careful."

"Um, well, you've got to pull a little, I guess, or the brush won't go through."

"My Lady," Elsa asked hesitantly, "why—why didn't anyone come with you from your homeplace?"

"My, um, husband," Cat stumbled over the word, "didn't want..." A tremble that seemed to come from nowhere entered her voice.

"I know how you must feel, my Lady," said Elsa with deep feeling, "to be away from your home. Up here at Heldenberg Manor every one snaps and snarls so. I don't think they wanted me here."

"I don't think they wanted me either," Caterina replied slowly. "We'll just have to help each other."

Elsa bobbed a curtsy, flashed a sweet shy smile. "I will do my best, my Lady."

* * *

Supper was served in the cold gray great room. After a perfunctory speech to her about the fine hunting and riding, Herr Walter involved Christoph in a long discussion about a stand of trees he wished to cut and how the unreasonable, superstitious peasants were resisting the idea. Frau Walter studied Cat, but didn't speak to her, except to coldly offer food. That woman, Cat thought, dislikes me, sight unseen. She would give, she thought, a great deal to know why.

Usually confident and outspoken, Cat felt herself sink. Every reply to her attempts at conversation came back framed in as few cool words as possible.

The food, two large pies, one of green apples, the other of pork, a tray of bread and country cheese, and a big, savory bowl of greens, was soon consumed.

A spare table indeed, Cat thought.

"Why don't you go up now, my Lady?" Christoph suggested. "Walter and I have talked for an hour before dinner and all the way through, boring you and Frau Walter to death and still have not managed to come to the end of Heldenberg's troubles." His tone was light, but she could see weary lines on his face.

Embarrassed, Caterina put down her napkin and rose. Everyone at the table followed suit.

"Ah, Herr Graf," she hesitantly ventured, "I would like to go to the stables to see Star."

"Not tonight, Grafin." His counter formality, the feminine of his title, rang oddly in her ears. "Star is in excellent hands. Believe it or not, probably the best horsemaster in the empire serves in my humble and remote stable. I shall introduce you tomorrow." The Walters obediently nodded. The gesture was emphatic, but some disapproval of this mysterious horsemaster, was observable in their pale eyes.

"But, sir," Cat persisted, "My Star is so temperamental, as you well know..."

Before she could finish, Christoph put his arm around her, began to walk her away from the table. "Go up, Cat. Do me the courtesy of not arguing in front of the servants. You may go to Star as soon as you wish tomorrow and you will see that she is well and that everything is just as I say." His tone was weary, parental.

Cat swallowed hard and inclined her head. At once Frau Walter clapped her hands and a maid standing by the door stepped forward.

"Light Lady von Hagen upstairs, Josefa. I'll just go and see if the Heerbrand girl has a ghost of a notion about what she ought to do."

Cat didn't like to hear Elsa spoken of like this, but she held her tongue. This place was exactly as strange and uncomfortable as her mother had predicted.

As they started up the stairs, Josefa said, "Watch your step, m'Lady."

Cat, more to hear her own voice than in expectation of conversation, said that she was "sure footed as a goat." When this homely simile drew a slight smile, the first she'd seen on any of the servants besides Elsa, she ventured, "It's been awhile since this house has seen any company, I'll warrant."

"Not really so long." The smug tone of the reply set Caterina aback so much—not the words, but the 'I've got a secret' tone—that she didn't venture another word until the door to her room was opened.

What a relief to see Elsa already there! She was just getting up from lighting a fire in the fat white wall stove which straddled the wall between Caterina's and whatever room lay next to it.

"Frau Walter is wondering where you are right this moment, Miss," Josefa said.

This too, Cat understood, was meant to intimidate, but before she could intercede, Elsa flashed back, "Herr Goran told me to come directly up and get ready for the Grafin."

Josefa sniffed. "Frau Walter is in charge of the household staff, not that old cripple. You'll pay attention to her if you know what's good for you."

Cat stared. Not only the insult to Christoph's valet but the fact that Josefa was daring to scold Elsa just as if Caterina weren't there. Before she could think of what to say, Josefa, without even a curtsy, had sailed out the door.

Worn out with growing uncertainty and a large portion of homesickness, Caterina at once began to think longingly of bed. She was not usually one to hide in sleep, but tonight it seemed the best refuge. Perhaps tomorrow after she'd seen Star and the stables she would feel better.

"Who does she think she is?" Cat gestured at the closed door.

"Oh, she's Frau Walter's little sister," came the answer. "She grew up here. She was the one who should have had my place."

"She's rude, whoever's sister she is."

Elsa nodded.

"Don't pay any attention to what she says. The plain fact is that I'm the only one you have to mind."

"That's what the Graf told me—and Herr Goran too."

Cat sighed. Perhaps this explained some of the chill she was experiencing. Still, she was already glad that Christoph had chosen Elsa.

"Do you want me to sit with you?" Elsa asked, as she worked at unbuttoning Cat's back stays. "The fire's well started and we could sew or read or whatever you would like to do."

"I think I'm ready to sleep. I've been riding astride for the last four days and I was badly out of practice, so everything hurts."

Elsa carried the stays away, folding them before laying them away into a mostly empty drawer.

"Where do you sleep, Elsa?" Cat suddenly asked.

"Well, I have been sleeping downstairs with the other maids, but the Herr Graf has ordered that I sleep there now, right beside you." The girl pointed thin fingers at a door opposite the one which led to Christoph's bedroom.

Curiously Cat went to lift the latch and peer in. Elsa's room was long and narrow, dominated by a bay window and the bulging backside of her own wall stove. It looked, she thought, with a sudden quiver, like her own nursery, with the communicating door and stove shared by the larger bedroom of her mother. Now, except for a pallet bed with a prettily pieced quilt and a battered trunk and one old chest of drawers topped with a pitcher and basin, it was quite empty.

"Of course," Elsa said, peeping in behind, "it's too fine and big for me, but it is the Graf's orders."

"Why do you say it's too fine?" Cat closed the door and asked. "It is proper for a lady's maid to be near her mistress."

"Um. Ah—"

"Who says it is not proper?" Cat insisted.

93

"Frau Walter. She, ah, she—well, it makes her angry that I should sleep alone in this fine large room, Mistress. A room with a window—and a stove."

"And what business is it of hers? If the Graf orders you sleep there, that should be enough for her."

"Yes, Mistress."

Cat took a seat at the dressing table in front of the mirror, tossed a heavy red handful over her shoulders.

"Come and brush my hair, Elsa." At once she wished she hadn't sounded so imperious, for the girl ran to her side like a rabbit. "I'm glad to see that you'll be so close," she said by way of atonement as the girl picked up the brush. Then she wondered if she were violating the rules her mother had given her, but she felt that if she didn't confide in someone she would burst. "Don't tell," she whispered, leaning her head back into the strokes of the brush, "but I was a little afraid of sleeping up here all alone."

Elsa paused in her work. Two pale girlish faces gazed at each other in the mirror.

"I would never tell, Lady Caterina. The Herr Graf told me that everything you and I talk about is always a secret, especially from the other servants. He says that is the most important rule for a lady's maid."

Cat experienced a warm rush of gratitude toward her husband.

"I think he's right, Elsa."

"Oh, he must be always right. He seems very kind and he is so very tall and very handsome, too." The girl's impressions all spilled out in a rush. "But Mistress," Elsa said, after a few more strokes at her mistress's hair, "why should you be afraid? You will not be alone."

The pale eyes in the mirror looked down although Cat could see the flush making its way up Elsa's neck.

"He is such a great soldier, the Herr Graf," Elsa murmured. "Um, won't you, ah, won't you be with, with him in his room?"

The only response Cat could manage was a nod and a blush of her own.

Chapter Nine

The next morning when Elsa came in carrying the breakfast tray she found Caterina alone in the maidenly bed, her red braids trailing out from under a demure lace nightcap, sniffling into one of her new linen handkerchiefs. Putting the tray down, she hesitated. Unsure, but wanting to help, she climbed onto the featherbed to join her mistress.

"Oh, Lady Caterina, please don't cry. Graf von Hagen says that if you are sad, I am to comfort you. And you know what? Even that mean old Ute didn't give me any trouble about breakfast this morning."

When Cat didn't speak right away, Elsa asked in a tiny little voice, "Are you crying because the Graf did not ask you to his bed?"

"No!" Cat jerked upright and glared. Then, catching herself she added, "We were, um, together, but, but—he, ah, got up early and I came back."

Elsa gave her a grave look, then whispered. "Is he angry with you?"

"Neither of us is angry today. I think."

"Oh, um, then," Elsa persisted after a short anxious pause, "are you missing your girl friends?"

"No," said Cat. "I didn't have any girl friends. Girls are mostly stupid."

"No girl friends at all?" Elsa, it appeared, hadn't taken the remark personally and proceeded to settle, with an incredulous expression, cross-legged in the bed. "I have a girl friend down in the village. Maria, the miller's daughter. I miss her a lot. We told each other everything."

95

"I guess my sister Wili was my friend," said Cat, wiping her eyes fiercely. "But now that she—she's dead—I guess my best girlfriend came with me."

"She did?"

"Yes. My mare, Star."

"But—um—you can't talk to a horse."

"I can and I do, too. I tell her all my secrets."

Elsa pondered that for a moment, then replied gravely, "But, Mistress Caterina, she can't answer."

Caterina sighed. It was, sadly, true.

"Elsa, can you ride?"

"I've never ever been on horseback in my life."

"Oh." Disappointing, but more or less expected. Riding was for aristocrats. Commoners might travel in horse drawn vehicles, but were just as likely to go on foot anywhere they had to go. "That's too bad. Perhaps I could teach you."

"Oh, I'd be too frightened. But I saw you yesterday. I swear I've never seen a woman sit a horse like that!"

After Caterina had collected herself and risen, Elsa brought her the morning gown and then busied herself laying out breakfast upon a sturdy small table. There seemed to be a lot of breakfast—heaps!

"The Graf says you are to be fed like a plowboy, so Ute gave me a lot," she explained.

"Really?" Cat had never thought of herself as having a large appetite. "That's more than I can eat, I'm sure."

"Well, m'Lady, he says you aren't done growing." Elsa went on, her voice dropping so that Cat could barely hear her, "And, my Lady, I put on extra so that—maybe—I could have some too. Here in your room, where they won't see."

Cat studied the girl's earnest face. She certainly didn't seem to be the kind of person her mother, during all those housekeeping lectures, had characterized as "greedy".

"Don't they feed you enough?"

"No, Mistress," Elsa said plaintively. "They give two pieces of bread and some tea for breakfast. At dinner I am given cabbage and potato. Supper is tea and bread again.

96

I've been here for a month and I'm always hungry. As poor as uncle is, we always had a little meat and fruit every week."

At once Caterina was boiling mad. "Who ordered such meanness?"

"Frau Walter said that was what I was to have."

"Did you tell your uncle?"

"Yes, once I got a note to the village, but he wrote back and said that they were trying to make me to go home, that they wanted Josefa to have the job, and that I should bear it until Graf von Hagen came and then ask for his help. He's so important and so busy, though, and he trusts the Walters so much, I don't dare. You seem so kind, Mistress, that I thought that perhaps this way I could have more food and not make trouble."

"Those miserable bastards." Caterina swore as vehemently as her father. Elsa gave an inadvertent start of surprise.

"Well, then," she said, "that's exactly what we'll do. You'll eat your meals with me—um," she amended, "whenever my husband isn't present. But when he is, we shall find another way to get you plenty."

"Oh, thank you, Mistress." Elsa had grateful tears in her eyes. "Downstairs they are all saying that you are so wild and spoiled that no one wanted to come with you, that at your home they were all glad to be rid of you, but it certainly can't be true."

With her mother's words sounding in her head, Caterina asked Elsa to sit down beside her and handed her a boiled egg. As she watched the girl eagerly peeling it, she said quietly, "Go on as you've been doing and be a mouse around them, dear Elsa, but, please, from now on, you are tell me everything you hear."

* * *

After eating, Cat dressed. Soon, good as his word, her husband came to take her to the barn to see how Star was managing in her new home. Here she was introduced to yet another intimidating servant, the horsemaster, Herr Rossmann, who walked them over to Star's stall.

The mare was discovered shiny and at ease. Cat was thoroughly surprised that the usually fractious animal had allowed Herr Rossmann, a perfect stranger, to groom her. Although she saw Rossmann's thin, intense face light up while they were discussing the blood lines of her beautiful mare, she found his taciturn manner and hard, pocked-marked face dismaying.

Herr Rossmann was of medium height, wiry, and quick in movement. His skin was so pale that at first Cat wondered if he might be consumptive. His eyes were black and penetrating and he wore long black moustaches in the same style as Hauptmann Goran's blonde ones. His clothing, blousy shirts and breeches, long jacket and sash, resembled Goran's too.

On the way to the barn, Christoph told Cat that like Goran, Rossmann had been born in the lands beyond the eastern border of their Hapsburg emperor's land. His name was a German alias for something unpronounceable and foreign. It was soon apparent that her husband had given a great deal of thought to how much time Cat and Rossmann would be together.

"My wife, Herr Rossmann," he said, making a formal introduction, "is a lady who, despite her sex and tender years, is very knowledgeable about horses. When she is not attending to her duties in the house," and here he flashed a rude wink at Cat, "you will see her about the barns. Allow her anything you would allow a skillful horseman, except when you are concerned for her safety."

As her husband spoke, Rossmann's black eyes flicked towards the tall, slim figure of his new mistress, away and then back again, like the flicker of a snake's tongue. This odd behavior was repeated many times in the course of the interview.

* * *

98

"Herr Rossman scares me," Cat said later, as they sat alone at dinner. "He's got a hard face, like a felon. And why does he move his eyes like that? Whenever he thought I wasn't watching, he stared like he's never seen anything like me before."

"I'll warrant he hasn't, Red Caterina." Her husband beamed and raised his glass in her direction.

"But, really, why?" The admiration in her husband's beautiful eyes was, as always, unsettling.

"Well, you have to understand that he's different. It's hard for those easterners to look directly at a woman. Of course, in his land you would never raise your eyes in his, or any other man's, presence. As perhaps you know, the Muslims veil their women and the rich ones who can afford to do so lock them up. Their neighbors, the Russians and the Serbs—Rossman is a Serb—are Christians of the Eastern Rite, but they have caught some Turkish habits. They keep their women wrapped from head to toe in black dresses, more like sacks than anything else. And there you stand, in a dress that fits, your face bare. Even with a shawl and a cap to cover your hair, to him you're practically naked." He paused and smiled at her obvious discomfort. "Therefore, little wife, as I know you will often be playing in the barn, I have decided you are to go dressed in this."

Christoph summoned Elsa and then sent her out after something. When the girl returned again, she had a loose one piece garment, like a black tent, draped over one arm. "Ugly, but, I'm told, comfortable. Just be sure to always cover your hair. Rossmann probably finds a woman's hair as stimulating as a bare breast."

"Is this eastern dress?" Cat stared at the strange garment.

"Yes, as near as I could explain it to the women who sewed it. As you can see, everything is left to the imagination. Wear breeches under if you wish to ride, belt it with a scarf and Herr Rossmann will know, beyond a shadow of a doubt in his savage mind, that you are a chaste, modest woman." Christoph's grin turned wicked. "And all things considered, it would be ironic if he made any mistakes about that, wouldn't it?"

When her green eyes widened, he grabbed her hand and gave it a comforting squeeze. "I'm rotten to scare you, Kitty Cat. Rossmann is quite trustworthy, but I do want to make the point about the dress."

Cat nodded. She didn't care much about clothes and the sackish thing did look as if it would be comfortable to work and ride in, at least, once it was belted. Besides, Rossman's cold eyes gave her the horrors. She wouldn't, she thought, put much past him.

"Did you know that Muslims believe that only men have souls?" Her husband continued. "To them, it's entirely possible that a good dog or horse might have more value than a woman."

The events of the last few months had brought her status as chattel sharply home to Caterina. To her proud mind it hardly seemed possible that there could be a lower state than the one in which she was expected to live.

"The grooms are afraid of Herr Rossmann." Uneasily she stirred the remaining noodles on her plate with a fork. She had only been in the stables for a short time, but that was obvious.

"And so they should be, the way they talk behind his back. But let me tell you a story about Rossmann," said Christoph, "that I think will begin your conversion. A few years ago, the campaign before last, my Brandy went lame. I, and everyone else I talked to, thought he'd never be fit to ride again."

"Brandy?"

"Yes, but Rossmann looked at him. He said I was not to worry and began brewing things up. Some were for Brandy to drink and others he used to bathe the leg. Every day he led him down to our stock pond, tied him to a row boat and then made him swim. Swim, by God! And in two months Brandy was fit again. Good as new, although I've never seen a horse recover from such an injury. I thought he was bound for stud and pasture, but he's quite well now, and strong as before. Frankly, after that, Rossmann will have to murder someone before I dismiss him."

"Well, he is awfully strange. Papa says that old soldiers often do terrible things because they have got used to doing them during wars. And Rossmann—well, the way he looks at me—or doesn't look at me—whichever it is—"

"You haven't been listening. Maybe you'll listen better from here." A strong hand seized her arm.

"Don't!"

Caterina twisted out of his grasp and began to run, but Christoph was on his feet even faster. In her father's house flight usually terminated unwanted conversations, but her husband seemed intent upon teaching her that this would not work here. His interception sent them spinning around wildly, a dark god intent upon the capture of a tall, half grown nymph.

"Whoa, runaway filly!"

Cat resisted, but her husband was more than a match for her. In an instant, he'd picked her up. Carrying her back to the table he took his seat again, Caterina firmly in his arms

"Let go. I'm not a baby." His hand passed up and down her back, messaging affectionately. Although she was embarrassed, it felt annoyingly good.

"Schone Jungfrau, don't quarrel. You are my baby. Humor your poor husband in just a few small things. You're so pretty to look at and you smell so good," he whispered, nuzzling against the tender back of her neck.

"Christoph," she protested, squirming as a tingle ran through. "What if a servant comes?"

"This will support our tale of wedded bliss." Nevertheless, he stopped. "Now, little one," he said shifting so he could look straight into her green eyes, "just remember to comport yourself modestly around Herr Rossmann, as befits a lady and my wife."

"I am both." Cat was emphatic. It was hard to feel any dignity in his lap.

"The first, sweet Red," said Christoph, catching her chin and tilting it up, "is true by breeding, if not quite yet by manner, but I'm confident that blood will tell. A little schooling and I believe you shall certainly achieve it.

His mouth grazed her forehead. Cat closed her eyes and endured both kiss and reproof.

"The last," her husband ended with a sigh, "is a fiction we maintain for the sake of our papas."

"I know how to behave."

"I rely upon it. Now, don't believe everything you hear the grooms saying and especially don't listen to dear Goran. Rossmann is poison to him."

After a last warm pass of his hand down her back, he released her. Caterina then discovered that some shameful traitor inside didn't really want to get up. Instead, this renegade self was longing to stay, to lean against his big chest, to accept his petting and relax into his strength and affection just the way black cat Furst did when Christoph picked him up and laid him across his shoulder.

"But aren't Rossmann and Goran both Slavs?" she asked. With as much dignity as she could muster, she got off his lap and slipped back into her own chair. "They even look alike. At least their huge moustaches and their clothes do."

"You better hadn't say that to either of them. What you need, I think, is a short lesson on the different, warring peoples who live on the eastern borders of Emperor Joseph's land." He settled back in his chair and regarded her thoughtfully. "And I believe I better begin at the beginning. Do you know anything about the Romans, Caterina?"

When she nodded, he smiled. "Very good. Did you allow your poor governess a moment of peace in which to bring them up? Those few times she wasn't smacking your palm with a ruler or hunting you out of the barn?"

Caterina stuck out her tongue. "Frau Plunke couldn't ever catch me to hit me," she declared. "And of course I know all about the Romans. They are after the Greeks but sort of like them, except fiercer. They conquered everyone, even us, and they made roads everywhere and all the hot springs into spas."

Christoph laughed, a cheerful sound in that cold room. "A most learned summation, my Kitty Cat. Now attend and hear a little more. The Roman Empire fell when wild men rode in on horses from the east, out of where the Bylorussians and the Ukrainians live today. Some of those wild riders were Hungarians and Magyars, some were Slavs."

"I know about Huns," Caterina said. "They traveled with herds of horses and cattle and their leader was Attila."

"Yes. Rossmann and Goran are from a land where many different tribes of Slavs settled. These days their land is divided between the empire of the Ottoman Turks and our Hapsburg Emperor. Their homeland has been overrun so many times, for the last several hundred years by Turks, that things are always troubled. They fight each other, too, those tribes. There are Serbs, Slovenes, Croats, Macedonians and a whole crowd who have become Muslim. Some Muslims, you see, are as white as you and me, although others are brown, like the people of North Africa."

There was a brief interruption while a servant came in bearing a bowl of brown speckled pippins. Plates were removed and a rough cutting board upon which sat a soft cheese in solitary state was placed between them. Cat picked up a knife and began to cut a up the fruit. She loved apples and cheese.

"So," Christoph continued, reaching for an apple, "Goran's village and all his family were killed by Serbs. No one can blame him for hating Serbs where ever and whenever he finds them. When I first took Rossmann on, I worried about one murdering the other. Lately, Goran's taken to putting it about that Rossmann's a Muslim, which certainly brings everyone to his side who wasn't there already. I'd never dare to leave the two of them alone at Heldenberg."

"But wouldn't your Hauptmann Goran know a Muslim when he saw one?"

"It is a fact of life that Goran is a Croat and Croats hate Serbs as much as they hate Turks. When I was fighting out

103

there, they were killing each other constantly, even when they were supposed to be fighting on the same side. There is just too much bad blood over too many years. Some Serbs side with us, others with the Russians, with whom they share a religion, but many live on lands which pay tribute to the Grand Turk."

Christoph cut his apple into sections crowning the slice with cheese. Another servant appeared, carrying a bottle of Moselle, which he poured into fresh glasses.

"It's hard to manage," her husband went on, "when the two servants I most rely upon want nothing more than to stick a knife into the other's heart. I've learned to take what one says about the other with a good deal more than a pinch of salt. And," he concluded, "it doesn't matter to me whether Rossmann goes to Mass or not, as long as he takes good care of my horses. Frankly, the fellow could have horns and a tail and wander around in a cloud of brimstone and I wouldn't dismiss him."

He smiled, but Cat had a last question.

"But why doesn't Rossmann go to Mass?"

"Because Serbs are Christians of the Eastern Rite, like the Russians. I wouldn't be surprised if it was a sin for him to attend our Mass."

* * *

After supper, Cat and Elsa continued with unpacking. Cat was startled when, without a knock, Josefa swept into the room.

"I'm to help you, m'Lady. Frau Walter sent me."

"That's not necessary." Cat straightened and tossed a braid over her shoulder. She didn't want this saucy creature butting in.

Josefa stood uncertainly by the door, surprised. Caterina was very tall and could project aristocratic command when she had to.

"Shall I go?"

"Yes, but thank you for coming and thank Frau Walter for her thoughtfulness." Caterina used a cool tone which would have done her mother proud, but in the next moment it was all undone.

As Josefa turned and put her hand on the latch, Caterina added, "Josefa, I suppose I ought to go down and speak to Frau Walter about the house." Belatedly, she'd remembered that a conference with the housekeeper was how her mother began every morning.

"What on earth for?" Cat was left staring at a whirl of skirts extinguished by the closing door. That's what I get, she thought, for showing weakness.

"Impertinent." She raised her voice, but the footsteps continued away along the corridor. "She's going to have to learn manners. Either that or she won't be here much longer."

"Oh, but Mistress," Elsa whispered. "She's Frau Walter's sister."

Cat shook her head. "I don't care if she's the Queen of Sheba. She's not going to talk like that to me. I shall speak to my—husband."

Some day, she thought, I will not stumble over that word.

It didn't take too long to finish the work. Elsa oohed at the sight of Cat's leather-seated riding trousers and her jackets and hats, at the high leather riding boots, at the gloves and cloaks. There was more of that than dresses, although Cat had been made, in the weeks before her wedding, to stand still for fittings. There were three new dresses, but more shifts, shirts and stockings in the trousseau than anything else.

"I pray to God," her mother had sighed one day, "that there is someone on Heldenberg who can sew for you, Caterina. In the meantime," she'd held up a shirt which she'd been embroidering white-on-white, "we'll work at getting you at least a year's worth of under things. Then we'll pray..."

When the last shirts were put away, they went into Elsa's room. Her maid had been sleeping with the housemaids before Caterina's arrival, so she too was just moving in. A nicked and battered chest of drawers, a chair,

105

and a washbasin were all the furniture. There were marks on the walls and on the clean but badly scuffed floors.

"This is exactly like a nursery room." The thought was spoken aloud. Cat's mother had always slept in a middle room too, accessible on one side to daughter and her nurse and on the other to her husband.

Elsa began taking clothing from the small trunk, kneeling to put them away in the chest. Suddenly she recoiled.

Something, Cat saw, was already inside. Elsa, alarmed, made a move to shove the drawer closed. Cat couldn't imagine what might be inside, but she realized she ought to see.

"Open the drawer, Elsa."

When Elsa, looking as if the end of the world had come, opened the drawer again, she saw a set of toy soldiers. There were foot soldiers with pikes, a cannon, artillery men and a set of cavalrymen mounted on a prancing horses.

Joining Elsa on the floor, Cat picked up a horseman and turned it round in her fingers. It was beautifully carved and painted, very much like the toys with which her father, over her mother's objections, had indulged her.

Her heart leapt into her throat. She was thinking of a thousand things, but chiefly of the night at the Black Swan, where she had stood naked before her husband, had asked him with her eyes to make love to her.

Oh, what if he had? What would she be feeling now?

"Elsa," she said, "Elsa, where is the child that these belong to?"

"I am sorry, Mistress. You must ask the Herr Graf."

Cat dashed down the stairs, passing housemaids with arms full of linen, on their way up. Skirt in hand she continued down the corridor, past the open door of the kitchen, bustling with the labor of autumn. Her haste, she knew, occasioned comment, but she didn't care.

When she reached the bailiff's quarters at the back of the house, she threw open the door without knocking. It proved to be a spare parlor. The men at the cluttered desk turned, surprised in the middle of looking over accounts.

Goran had been sitting near the door. He pushed himself warily upright with the stout cane he always carried.

Cat managed to drop a curtsy to the others, all the while fighting with fear and temper. "Herr Graf, Amtmann Walter," she said. "Excuse me, but I must speak to the Graf. This minute."

Christoph raised an eyebrow, but he stood, while indicating that Walter should leave. "I will send for you again, Herr Amtmann."

"As you wish, Herr Graf." Walter, with a look in Cat's direction, bowed. He began to gather up the papers.

"Leave it." The Graf's tone left no doubt in anyone's mind that an exit should be immediate. Helpfully, Goran opened the door.

"Of course," Walter muttered. As soon as he had gone through it, Goran started to follow.

"Herr Goran, please see that we aren't disturbed."

The Croat's balding head inclined as he closed the door.

Christoph waved her to a chair, but Cat strode forward and thumped the little cavalryman down upon the accounts. Her husband regarded it sadly. Then his long fingers came to take it up.

"Thank you for your restraint, Caterina."

"Where has the child gone?"

"Children, Cat. My two boys, fine fellows of eight and nine, who went this spring to boarding school."

"Did Wili know?" Caterina linked her fingers and squeezed, damning herself for every dot of emotion she showed.

"I had no secrets from Wili."

"But you kept secrets from Mama and Papa—and from me."

"Your father knew. As for you, we have enough to unravel, Caterina. I thought it best to take one at a time."

107

Cat gritted her teeth. Every response he made prompted more questions. It was hard to stay calm.

"Did Wili know you'd sent your boys away?"

"They are at the good Piarist's school in Perchtoldsdorf. I'm afraid that like you they prefer larking about on horseback to studying." A smile came to his face, a proud paternal look Cat recognized.

"What kind of father would I be if I did not see to their education? They went to school this spring not only because I would soon bring your sister here, but because it was time for them to start taking their place in the world. I will not slight the obligation of having fathered them." He looked straight at her. "The older is to go to the army. The younger, who has a gentle nature, I will help to civil service, perhaps."

"And Elsa's room was their nursery? And their mother slept in the middle room?"

"For the time she was my mistress."

The ferocious swing Cat launched was intercepted by a strong hand.

"How dare you put me in your mistress's room? How dare you?"

"Hush!" Christoph backed her to a seat in his chair.

After the attempted slap, his hands had fastened upon her wrists like manacles, so she struggled no further. Equally constraining was a sudden awareness that half the household probably had put an ear to the adjoining wall.

"None of your cowardly running before I'm done talking to you."

"I'm never a coward. Damn your black heart."

She glared. Finally, humiliating tears welling, Caterina nodded angrily, indicating that he could go on.

"Four years ago, during one of my long absences Barbara fell in love with a Hauptmann, a captain of my guard I'd sent up here to recover from an illness. Three years ago, just before their daughter was born, she and Hauptmann Ermler were married in Heldenruhe, with my blessing."

Cat stared. Somehow, this wasn't the narrative she'd been expecting.

"When I first found out about their affair, I was hurt, but I had to admit it was more my pride than my heart. I could never marry Barbara, so why shouldn't she fall in love with someone who could?"

"But she didn't leave Heldenberg until this spring?"

"No. She and her husband have been living here."

"Convenient."

"Caterina," her husband replied, "Hauptmann Ermler is attached to my body guard. Do you know how easy it is to kill the man by your side under cover of battle? As a matter of fact, he could have left me for the Turks last year, but he risked his neck to drag me to safety."

"Christoph, I'm not a fool. You are his patron. Papa says that poor men can't afford honor."

"Your father has many forcefully expressed opinions, but, as you know yourself, Caterina, he is not always right."

The chair into which he'd pushed her into was more than normally high. Cat considered, swinging one foot restlessly and staring at the squares of the slate floor. Only beneath Herr Walter's desk was the cold gray stone covered with a Turkey carpet.

"Caterina, I'm not a monster. I wish you had not found this," he said, turning his gaze back to the little horseman. "I had planned to tell you about the boys as soon as you had settled in a little. Wili and I talked over a lot of things that you and I haven't had time to go into."

He released her hands, and began to pace in front of the empty maw of the fireplace. Cat had no sense of this as a performance. Christoph looked like exactly what he was, a man of action who had been trapped by a tangle of circumstance that he couldn't cut his way out of with a sword.

"I swear to you, just as I swore to your sister, that Barbara and I haven't been lovers for a long time. Barbara stayed at Heldenberg because that was what she wanted. She helped her sister, Frau Walter, manage the house," Christoph said. "But, even if she hadn't made herself useful,

109

there were the boys, my sons, Caterina. There is nowhere so healthy for young children as the country. Wili understood why it was right for them to stay here with their mother."

"Wili would have believed the sky was red if you'd told her so."

"Wili said she could let the past go if I promised to be faithful. She also promised that if anything ever happened to me during their minority, she would see that their education was completed and suitable positions found for them."

A muscle in his strong jaw twitched, perhaps at the memory he was conjuring. Then he said, "This spring I told your sister that I was hers till death parted us."

Were those tears in his eyes? He cleared his throat and continued.

"When I put the ring on your finger, Caterina, I promised you fidelity before God and in the presence of our families. I shall honor my promise."

Caterina's head swam. There was a rising lump in her throat.

"If you were—were—honest with Wili, why haven't you been so with me?"

"I've explained. What kind of Blue Beard do you think I am?"

Caterina silently stared at her swinging foot.

"I'm sorry that this has upset you, Cat. I never intended for you to find out like this."

"You had six weeks before we were married. You never visited me once."

"Your father was absolutely against it. Frankly, I believe he thought you'd put me off and I'd refuse to go through with the marriage."

"And if you took another wife, his precious land would pass away from his blood."

"Yes."

Cat bit her lip. High handed, but just like her father…

"I hope you will be able to understand. As the boys are a part of my life, it's right that you should know about them, but I didn't intend for you to find out like this." His gaze returned to the cavalryman frozen in a motionless prance upon the papers, a man thinking about his sons.

Doubts and fears swirled. Again Cat remembered the thing Christoph had said at the Black Swan, about the "blessing" of delay. Had he been thinking of this?

Another black thought quickly popped in. Caterina blurted: "How many other children are there?"

"No others that I am obligated to as I am to Christian and Michael."

"Cuckoos in other men's nests, is that what you mean?"

"Perhaps, Caterina. No lady has ever taken me to task, but on occasion I've wondered. The fact is I've done a lot of things I've lived long enough to be sorry for."

Cat continued to gaze at the floor. So much to think through…

"There are no other secrets, Caterina. The past is past. As I told Wili, I want nothing more than to begin my life again. So," he ended, inclining his handsome dark head, "will you please stay? You must know by now that I have no intention of forcing you."

Caterina looked him up and down. "I promised my mother that I would try to trust you."

"I hope you will do more than try, but under the circumstances that is the most I can hope for." He took Caterina's hand up and briefly kissed it. "I shall not play the rogue with you." Dark eyes, gazing into hers, sent an alarming green flash, one that a subterranean something deep inside tugged to answer…

"There are a great many obstacles to our happiness, but I remain hopeful that in time we shall find our way. At the Black Swan we both had a glimpse of something beyond duty."

"Time will tell." Caterina severely quoted one of her mother's favorite maxims. Her heart, again heavy with doubt and homesickness, ached.

"Between us there has to be healing before anything can grow. Trust me a little, and I'll show you that a man can change."

111

Chapter Ten

At Heldenberg there were a few raw recruits for Christoph's company, young men from the farmsteads. There were also three officers and about fifteen foot soldiers from his regiment. These men always accompanied him into battle. They kept military discipline and so daily there were exercises and drills which her husband overlooked.

Christoph's days were full, for besides this and work with Walter, he took rides to survey his livestock and land. To Caterina's delight he always asked her to come. Those days were perfectly happy, the same cousinly fun they'd always shared. As they ranged over the broad shoulders of Heldenberg, Cat was able to enjoy herself, to let go of her fears and suspicions.

"You should meet my peasants. It's important, especially as I might have to go soldiering again next year. I want you to get a feel for the place and its problems. Your papa told me you were more interested in such things than women usually are and that's an interest I intend to encourage. If you have a talent for managing it will be useful, especially because I am a soldier and often absent."

Christoph talked with her about the people they met. He spoke about the livestock, about the few run down farms, the peasants who couldn't, for one reason or another, pay their tithe.

Cat loved these rides "on business." It was wonderful to be treated like a grown, intelligent person. It was also wonderful to get out of the house, away from all those cold eyes.

"Come on, Red," her husband would say when the business of the day was done. "Let's gallop."

And gallop they would, a breathtaking, glorious chase. She'd set her sights on Brandy's burnished rump and chase Christoph until they reached the high meadows. Then he'd slow and they'd ride knee to knee, gazing at the range of gray-headed sister mountains and down the long sweep into the valley.

"If you think it's lovely now, you should see it in spring," Christoph said as they rode by a herd of dun cattle. "It's a sea of Edelweiss, white and gold and green."

Peasants tugged their forelocks as they rode past, watching their master survey what was his. They recognized their young lord, but for the first time saw his bride, tall, slender and red haired, sitting her horse as easily as any nobleman.

* * *

Caterina, frequently left to her own devices, was in the barn a great deal. Here her path continually crossed the dreaded Rossmann's. One of the first things Cat overheard while she was in the barn were stories, the ones of which Christoph had spoken. The grooms called Rossmann names: 'Heathen' and 'Turkman devil.' It seemed that his Christianity, because he never went down the hill to the church in Heldenruhe, was suspect.

His temper was rightly feared. She saw a welt on one man's arm and learned that Rossmann was like to lay about him with a whip if his orders weren't carried out to the letter. Sometimes, in spite of her Russian drab, she'd feel eyes while she curried Star. When she turned, there would be the horsemaster, giving her the same sort of apprising once over he might give a new mare. As soon as her eyes met his, he would turn and walk wordlessly away. She knew it was the frank admiration of a man for a woman, but she did not dare to confront him.

In spite of the discomfort she felt around him it was next to impossible to keep out of the barn, for Cat loved horses and her husband's were no exception. There were four mares, a heavy, stately Oldenburg war horse, a long bodied Wurttemberg and two sturdy Hanoverians, all trailing foals or yearlings. There were also the bay harness horses, two mares and two gelded. Also in the barn was a pair of immense gray Percherons for farm work, as well as a hinny and two fat blonde mountain ponies. Brandy was the sire of most of the foals, but there was a new stud as well, a wild eyed silver Andalusian.

Cat was enchanted by him, by the agility and spectacular paces he displayed while loose at pasture. She thought he was one of the most beautiful creatures she'd ever seen in her young, horse loving life. She asked Christoph if she could ride him, but he said no.

"I don't think it would be a good idea until you've studied him for a time. That horse is not only crazy, but smart too. He has found a way to toss every man here, including me. Only Rossmann can stick on him. Why don't you go out on big Jack sometime while Rossmann's exercising him? That will start to give you a notion of what you'll be up against."

The Andalusian had been Herr Rossmann's pride and joy until Star had come. After taking in her conformation, her short back and long neck, her large eyed diamond head, all so true to Arab type, Rossmann had persuaded her to stand so he could count her vertebrae. The total, several short of the other horses, proved her ancestry to his satisfaction. "Yes," he declared to a small audience of grooms, "there's definitely Arab blood here. You Austrians don't appreciate how fine a little desert blood can be. You think that size is everything, but crossing will improve your horses, both in hardness of bone and in hardness of head."

It was Karl, one of the grooms, who told Cat. He added that the horsemaster was always stopping by her stall and crooning to her in his own strange tongue.

"She's scared of him, Lady," Karl said. "God protect her, just like the rest of us. You should see her, tossing that pretty head of hers, snorting and stamping."

Cat came upon it one day, heard the mysterious chant as she came through the gloom of the barn to Star's capacious box stall. She heard the strange words mingling with the sound of the mare's distress as she puffed and snorted, sounds punctuated by a nervous stamping.

"What a pleasure it is to have you in my stable, my beautiful red darling." Rossmann said.

Cat peeped around the half open stall door. Rossmann was running his hands along Star's neck, her withers. One minute the mare was issuing the stamping, eye rolling warning she gave when alarmed. The next she was standing, her sides quivering like sorrel jelly, breathing hard, but allowing the horsemaster's strangely long fingered hands to stroke her. They ran down her neck and across her sides; they lingered down the sensitive backs of her hind legs.

The sudden acquiescence and the terror that still seemed to sit in those round eyes sent every hair on the back of Caterina's neck erect. It was almost as if Rossmann was touching her!

"What are you doing?" She pushed through the door.

The spell was broken. At once Star gave a sideways hop, whinnied and reared. The horsemaster lifted a hand, said some quick distinct yet completely unintelligible words. Still quivering, the mare pushed her backside into a corner and stayed there. Her eyes showed white crescents and she continued to breathe hard.

Rossmann turned towards Cat. The look in his eye sent her backing up in a hurry too.

When they were both outside the stall, Rossmann wordlessly shot the latch. His face was pale. "What were you doing? You are supposed to know something about horses, but you were the one who frightened her."

"No." Cat trembled. "She didn't want you touching her. And—and—I don't want you touching her, if that's how she feels."

Rossmann's lip curled. Amusement, scorn, it was as plain as if he'd written it on the stable wall.

"Who will take care of her later?"

"I will."

"No," he insisted, "who will take care of her this winter, when the snow is over your head and you've got a belly full?"

Cat's jaw dropped. She couldn't have been more shocked if he'd slapped her.

"You want only the best for her, eh, Mistress?" A slight cold smile appeared. "Well, I am the best. The sooner she gets used to me the better. Don't worry. I know how valuable she is. I will do every little thing for her." He approached as he spoke, had come close. She found herself staring into his white face, into a pair of burning black eyes.

"You and I will be the only ones who touch her. You and I, and her chosen stallion."

Cat swallowed hard.

"She is well groomed, as you can see. Why don't you go and visit her now?" Rossman's manner turned off hand. Abruptly he turned and walked away into the gloom.

Cat went to the stall and peeped over the high wall. Star whickered a nervous greeting, tossed her head, making the blaze flash up and down in a blur. Slowly, as if she wasn't too sure of who Cat was, she approached, stretched out her ruddy neck and sniffed. Numbly Cat opened the door and went in. She stuck her hand into her pocket and came up with the fresh carrots the gardener had provided.

Then, while the mare munched her offering, she breathed in the good warm comforting horse smell and ran her hands slowly over the sorrel's shining neck and back. Star felt like a length of satin, for she was curried to a fare-thee-well, white stockings brilliant, her mane and tail prettily braided. Even her hooves gleamed. Cat thought ruefully that Star hadn't been in such fine condition since last autumn's hunts.

* * *

116

"Do you really know he's a Serb?" She asked at supper. "Goran says that Rossmann was in the Pasha's army."

"Yes, I know all the things Goran says," Christoph replied. "Some of it is probably true, but I also believe that Rossmann's personal honor is a sufficient guarantee of good behavior."

"But doesn't he make you nervous? You, who've fought so many times against the Turks, been almost killed by them?"

"No, not really. I see many reasons for their enmity, besides the hereditary ones. Herr Rossmann is learned, a thing which Goran, who was born a peasant, naturally mistrusts. Rossmann has books. He knows about the stars and about healing plants and medicine. The one thing I really do know about Rossmann is that in his own land he was a gentleman. Then something happened and his property was confiscated. After he came into my service, we passed through what was left of his village. He told me that the Turks had burned his family alive. They never take revenge by halves." Caterina shuddered. Once, as a child traveling with her family to Passau, she'd seen a barn burn, the flames shooting to the sky. There had been terrible sounds, the howl of the heaven piercing fire, the boom of collapsing timbers, the screams of animals and people.

Brave men had been in the barn, blindfolding horses in order to lead them out. Then the roof had come down. She would never forget the smell that had assaulted her, the hideous smell of burned flesh—man and beast together.

But this conversation wasn't going as she had hoped. She must complain about Rossmann. The house servants could play whatever games pleased them. The barn was where Star was, the place where she absolutely must feel safe, be respected.

"Until the day Rossmann shows me that he isn't a gentleman, a gentleman down on his luck, I won't treat him as anything less."

"Yes, but he still scares me. Today he, he—" Cat stammered to a stop.

117

"What?"

"He was most dreadfully rude."

"And what did you do to provoke him?"

Cat glared. "Why do you assume that everything is my fault? I tell you that your servant was rude to me and you start quizzing me?"

"I just want to know exactly," said Christoph, shifting around in his chair and regarding her somberly, "what Herr Rossmann did to offend you."

"It was what he said."

"Which was?"

Cat knew she'd sound foolish if she hedged further, but it was difficult to repeat those humiliating words.

"He was touching Star, um, gentling her, and, um, I could see that she was very frightened. You know how she is."

Her husband nodded understanding, encouraging her to go on

"And I told him not to do it because—because I could see she did not like it. Then he was rude to me."

"I saw Star just before I came in to dinner. She was beautifully groomed. Head and shoulders above the slap dash you've been giving her lately," said her husband, showing an eye for the details of life in his domain which she hadn't suspected.

"That's not fair. I haven't had time to do a good job since I've been traveling and—and getting settled—and—"

"Back to the subject, Lady von Hagen. I promise I shall take it very seriously if you tell me that one of my servants has been rude to you. What—his exact words, please—did Rossmann say?"

Cat bit her lip and lowered her eyes. "He said—he said that I should let him gentle Star because—because—when the snow came and when I had a—a belly full, I wouldn't be able to do it."

Christoph looked grave. He pushed his chair back from the table magisterially.

Then taking her hands into his, he said, "Sounds like nothing less than the plain truth, at least, as he sees things."

He pulled her first into his arms and then onto his lap. The maneuver was complete almost before she knew what had happened.

"Damn you!"

"Star ought to start getting used to him—and you ought to start getting used to me."

"Let go!" she cried.

"You are," he teased, "almost as beautiful as Star and exactly as temperamental."

He held her by the wrists, crossing her arms around her waist. He let her twist so that her back was to him and then pulled her close once more so that his lips could find the nape of her neck. As they brushed the feathery scarlet tendrils, Cat trembled. Just for an instant, she stilled, let the tremor run through her.

"Stop! Please."

"Do you know, Caterina, these last few months have been the longest in my grown up life that I've been without a woman?"

Cat raged inwardly, praying that he would loosen his grip so that she could get her hands away and give him the slap he so richly deserved. He did, but only a little, allowing her to turn to face him. Prudently, he did not relinquish his hold.

"Most men would say that I'm showing astonishing restraint with a beautiful young creature who is legally my wife." He was not teasing now, but serious. "And our papas would bellow in unison that I'm a damned derelict in my duty."

"Are you so quickly out of mourning?" She said it furiously, wild to hurt his feelings as he had just hurt hers.

Immediately she was pushed off his lap and onto her feet.

"Sitting you on my lap and giving you a kiss is hardly the same as dragging you to bed. You are a temptation, you know. Even—or maybe, especially—because I have lost a warm and loving partner."

"How dare you talk like that about my dear good sister?"

She was furious, not only because he'd dismissed her complaint about Rossmann. There was also a desire to erase the feelings his handling aroused. She moved out of reach, reflexively rubbing her neck, wanting to erase the tingles his lips had begun.

Her husband stood and shook himself like a dog throwing off water.

"I shouldn't have teased you," he said, "and I'll order Rossmann to curb his tongue. But what you aren't yet old enough to know about human nature—about me, or about your sister—or about yourself, for that matter, would fill a book."

He strode out of the room, calling impatiently as he went for Goran and the young soldier who stood sentry in the front hall. Cat went to the door of the dining room and peeped out. There she heard her husband giving orders for readying horses, men, guns, and his best hunting dogs.

In a few moments servants were bustling everywhere. The officer of the day put in an appearance, accompanied by an aide. Finally, gathering all her courage, she went out into the hallway among the men. As soon as Christoph saw her, he said, quite formally, "Grafin, I'll be away for a few days, hunting the oak woods for the boar that has been harassing the charcoal burners. Herr Goran will stay and look after you."

Cat, feeling red burning in her cheeks, knew that she should incline her head obediently and retreat upstairs. It was something of a shock to realize that Christoph was doing exactly what she'd seen her father sometimes do to her mother, go hunting in order to terminate a quarrel. She remembered how her mother had seethed.

She had to cross the room to reach the stairs, so she started as if going that way, but as she passed Christoph, she whispered, "I see you run away too."

He stared down at her and in his beautiful eyes she saw a spark. Laughter or anger, she couldn't tell which.

"Thank your lucky stars." He made a gracious gesture, bowing her to the stairs. A path cleared before her as she went.

Later, from her bedroom window, she watched unhappily as the hunters and a crowd of barking dogs trotted off to harsh accompaniment of horns.

* * *

For the days of her husband's absence, Cat did one of the things her mother had ordered her to do, which was to look into the kitchen every morning. It wasn't easy, braving those cold eyes and she didn't stay long, but even if she didn't know about cooking, Mama had said that she ought to look to see if everything was orderly and clean. Each time she entered the room everyone stopped what they were doing and stood there looking cross.

"Please don't mind me. She'd tried to sound nonchalant, but they insisted upon interrupting their work and stood doing nothing, standing at attention while she was present.

"Does your ladyship need something?" On the third morning the cook turned, showing a face that wasn't just red from the heat of her fire. She'd been in a bustle when Caterina had come in and clearly hadn't relished the interruption. "You can send Elsa down if there's anything you want. No need for you to trouble yourself with us."

The woman's tone was more than challenging. Caterina couldn't find her tongue. She was horribly aware of Josefa smirking in the corner. There were a few seconds of dreadful silence, all eyes on her.

When she didn't respond at once, the cook bobbed, threw up her hands in exasperation and turned her back.

"Excuse me, Lady! But the sauce will burn."

Caterina fled. Titters and hushing noises followed her retreat up the stairs. Embarrassed and angry that she'd let them best her, Cat set off to her room. She intended to don her black dress, have Elsa help her pin up her braid and head for her customary place of refuge, the stable.

As she plunged around a corner at a run, she dashed against the obstacle of her husband's chest. There was the smell of man, pungent with the chase. The beard that he

121

had started gave him an even more than usually dangerous air.

"What's the matter?" He caught hold and they spun in a swirl of dress and petticoats.

"Nothing! Nothing!" She pushed at the woolly material of his hunting jacket. "Just let me go." It was too humiliating to admit that she'd been driven out of the kitchen—her kitchen, when all was said and done!

"You're running, Cat, and that means you are running away from something."

"You run." She stopped struggling and glared.

"Never."

"Never? Then where have you been for the last week?"

"It was only four days, Caterina. I didn't think you much wanted my company. And it was more than high time I went out and took care of that animal."

Caterina looked up silently, tears of anger and frustration rising.

Men were so unfair, so dishonest!

"You know, Caterina," he said in a more gentle tone, "it's one of the things I don't understand about you. You're either in full scale attack or total retreat."

"So! I'm a—bitch—when I fight and a weakling when I give way? If I were a man, you'd be saying 'courage' and 'discretion'."

She went to storm away, but Christoph refused to let go. "Pax, Caterina," he said, offering the childhood pledge. "Your point is well taken. In fact, 'courage' is the word for you."

He bowed over her hand. Cat accepted his kiss, watching as the movement sent dark curls tumbling over one big shoulder.

"Let me get cleaned up, Grafin," he said, "and we'll talk more at supper."

* * *

He'd shaved, bathed and dressed again, and he looked splendid. Cat had to admit to herself that she had missed

122

him. They dined upon delicious venison from a young buck the men had taken, this with an accompaniment of buttery potatoes and turnips. When Christoph described the hunt, Cat was an interested listener.

Christoph had, in company with two of his men, held it with long pikes while the net was thrown. After a dangerous tussle, they'd managed to dispatch it. The creature had been a huge male, the body carried back to provide meat for the peasants.

"It seems they were cutting in a part of the woods that he felt was his. I always hate to kill a creature like that." Her husband wore a rueful expression, the first that Cat could ever remember seeing on any hunter, "the old fellow was just defending his territory, exactly as I would do if some strangers came upon my land. He gave us a good fight. I thought he was going to get his tusks into Heidelburg the way he attacked us from cover. He took five of our dogs and got a tusk into young Seibert's calf. I hope that will heal right…"

Finally, as their plates approached empty, Christoph suddenly said, "You know, you hurt me at least as much as I hurt you." When Cat looked up questioningly, he added, "Every time you say I didn't love Wili."

Feeling sorry, she watched in silence as he pushed his chair back from the table.

"I think, because we are in a unique situation, the problem is that neither of us knows how to behave. You can't see me as your husband and I have a hard time seeing you as anything but wild little Red."

Cat shifted nervously. This sounded right, although hearing that she was nothing more than "wild little Red" was something of a blow to that part of her that had just been surreptitiously admiring him.

"We need to have some rules. Therefore Grafin Caterina Maria Brigitte von Velsen von Hagen," teasing had intruded into his hitherto solemn tone, "since in every verbal combat we've undertaken, you've demonstrated a surprisingly lawyerly turn of mind, I think I shall start by explaining a point of law to you."

"A point of law? As pertains to?"

"Our marriage. As you know, I have the right to enjoy your body, a right which I am not exercising."

Cat looked at him warily, but he wasn't making any moves in her direction, just smiling at her, a smile which had developed a wicked edge.

"Therefore, it seems to me that in order to keep that right for some future time when it shall be more proper and more amenable to both of us, I shall begin to exercise a minute portion of the above mentioned right at least once every day."

"What?" Cat caught the drift, however, and this inspired her to try to get up. Christoph, however, had anticipated. He hooked his foot against her chair rungs and held it still.

"Which means that every day I intend to kiss you," he said softly, bending his dark head close to hers, "and pet you and generally take pleasure just an inch beyond that which is cousinly, and that you will patiently let me."

"Why should I?"

"Because, little Frau, it is a small prelude to our papas' desire, a small part of my right and a small part of your obligation."

The pompous declaration was accompanied by nothing more threatening than a gentle tug upon Cat's long single braid. "And, because I know what I am about, you and I will slowly but inevitably come to what everyone expects."

Cat blushed. Christoph nodded. Though the smile had vanished, his eyes were bright

"You're treating me like Rossmann is treating Star," Caterina muttered. She fixed her gaze upon her plate.

"Well, marriage is rather like that, isn't it? Slow, patient and gentle works with most horses, and I have a feeling that it will work here too."

"What a conceited brute you are!"

"Decidedly, but grant that this is a subject about which a wicked rake is well informed."

"Don't joke! All you've done—"

"Frankly," he interrupted, "I don't think I deserve the title. And I wish that you'd stop acting as if my intent were to do the deed against your will. As your papa would say, the stallion doesn't jump mares that aren't in breeding condition."

"Gottesblut!" Cat exclaimed, slamming her fist down on the table in what was a fine, crockery rattling imitation of her father. "That's disgusting! I will never submit!"

"Oh, I believe you will never submit, Caterina, but I also believe that you may do something that's a great deal more enjoyable."

"Christoph—"

"Have more venison. I won't pet while we are at table, but at some odd moment, I shall take you in my arms and nibble on your edible neck or," he went on, lifting his glass in her direction, "take a sip from that sweet mouth of yours."

* * *

Once Caterina was in her bedroom, Christoph left her alone so studiously that she soon felt quite safe there. At night, even if he were still moving around in his room on the other side of that unlocked door, she'd drop straight into sleep.

In the morning she'd lie inside the grass green curtains, listening to the chorus of birds in the pine forest, until Elsa arrived with the heaped breakfast tray and the luxurious, steaming bowl of hot chocolate.

She was surprised to be awakened one chilly fall morning by the heroic figure of her husband pushing aside the bed curtains.

"What are you doing?" She clutched at the covers. "Gott!" She exclaimed, as big arms closed around her. Her open hand slammed against his head.

"Ow!" Christoph sat back, clutching at the injured part. "Damn. That really hurt!"

"Well, it's your own fault," Cat retorted. She wanted to be tough, but seeing that she had truly hurt him, she

125

regretted her haste. "You shouldn't just climb into my bed like that," she ended lamely.

"The day will come," Christoph replied, rubbing his cheek with comic dignity, "when you will be delighted by my presence in your bed. But I didn't do anything, damn it, and I wasn't going to. Why did you hit me?"

"I—was—scared."

She still was. His body, covered only by a morning gown remained stretched beside her, boasting the supple muscularity of a cat.

"Well, it's got around that I'm never here and I thought I ought to remedy that. You won't have any authority at all if they think you aren't really my wife, you know."

Cat was suddenly sorry and was about to say so when he added, "I believe I was inspired by the love scene I saw last night with your pretty red mare."

"What?" In a flash she was on her feet, dancing furiously on the mattress. "What have you done to Star, you monster?"

Seizing a pillow, she began to pummel him, so hard that a blizzard of feathers flew. She kept at it too, until Christoph got hold of the other end.

One good yank and she tripped in the bedclothes and fell in a tangle of long legs, swirling down and shift. In order to keep her still, her husband threw himself across her and seized her hands.

"It wasn't me, you extraordinary little hellion," he panted. "It was Herr Rossmann, who has somehow gained the confidence of that four legged familiar of yours."

Caterina stared up into his beautiful green-flecked eyes.

"You're crushing me."

"That's the idea. You need more than crushing. And someday soon, by God..."

"What did Rossmann do to Star?" Caterina asked the question humbly, praying he would move before her ribs cracked.

"He bred her."

126

At once she was in tears. She had visions of Star, her feet and head tied, the stallion led in. It seemed so horrible; emotion choked her.

"She's not hurt." Christoph shifted to one side, although he still maintained a hold on her dangerous hands.

"How do you know?"

"I saw the whole thing. Rossmann has been leading her past the Andalusian's box and last night he, instead of trying to kick the place down as usual and scaring her, did some sweet talking over the wall. Rossmann put her into the little pen and then brought him to her. They trotted up and down together for a few minutes, then he got to it, smooth as silk, the greatest lover in the world. I was a little worried because Star's so unpredictable, but Rossmann believed that it would work. 'She likes him', he said, and he was right. You won't see a mark on either of them this morning, except for, hmm—" her husband's perfect mouth descended to Caterina's shoulder and delivered a kiss which grew to a nip, "a love bite on that snaky red neck of hers."

Caterina sighed, trembled. She wanted to scream, to cry—or, maybe, to kiss him back...

"Oh, Cat, everything's fine with her. And with you too." Sighing, Christoph sat up, drew her close and held her against his chest. Gathering a corner of the sheet, he wiped away her tears.

"What on earth am I going to do about you, Caterina Maria Brigitte?" He spoke softly. "It's definite now. In March I'm to go to my regiment. I've had a command from the Emperor. If the Turks advance, as everyone fears, I'll see battle again. I could be gone a year, maybe longer. And war makes widows, you know."

"I'll be alone here?" Cat shuddered. The whole world had fallen in on her head this morning.

"Well, we'll see." He rubbed her back tenderly. "I suppose you could go home if you wanted to."

For some reason she couldn't exactly fathom, this didn't appeal at all.

"Oh, why do you have to go soldiering again?" she asked, leaning her head against him. It wasn't just being

127

alone but the thought of him in danger... And, death was real. It had come to Wili and could come to anybody.

"You've been wounded, almost died already. Isn't that enough?"

"Well, it's not only honor and duty but the Emperor's command. I cannot disobey."

Cat nodded.

"If we are successful, there is a sharing of spoils."

"Spoils?"

"Yes. More than flags came home from that last campaign."

Cat's eyes grew wide. She understood the requirements of honor, but had never thought about this part of war.

"It's crazy, too, I know, but I—enjoy—danger."

"Christoph—"

"But you don't mean to say," he interrupted, smiling, "that you would you actually miss me?"

"Yes." She hid her face against his chest.

One big hand came to tenderly stroke her head. Cat stayed where she was, close to him, and enjoyed the good clean smell of his health, felt the muscles which might have overwhelmed, conquered and forced—might have, but never did.

"Let's get up and go see Star. Then you'll know that she's all right."

Chapter Eleven

A session with the supercilious young Lieutenant who taught fencing left the young recruits, not much more than boys, frightened, and sometimes bleeding. Herr Lieutenant Heidelburg was a martinet whose punishment for a mistake was made with the point of his épée. Heidelburg, who bore a few dueling scars himself, was of the opinion that a wound made a lesson less likely to be forgotten. The young trainees bore their injuries with a certain pride. Wasn't the swordsman who dealt the punishment a master? There was no shame in carrying a few scars from such an opponent. It was, in fact, the price of learning this gentleman's art.

One day Cat found herself watching her husband sharpening his skills against the dueling master. Although Heidelburg was highly skilled, it was only at épée that he stood a chance of outscoring the Graf. Christoph's strength, combined with phenomenal quickness made him a crushing opponent.

Watching the men laugh and flash out at each other, Cat found herself remembering a time when she and Theodor and Valentin had been playing together. The boys had been summoned away for their first fencing lesson. Cat had trailed along, interested and half expecting that she would be included. After all, couldn't she run faster than Theodor? Couldn't she catch better than Valentin? And wasn't she smarter than either of them?

But no, she'd been laughed at, taken away by her nurse. Later she'd been disobedient, played mock battles with the boys using some shepherd's crooks they'd commandeered. More than once, in spite of his training, she'd knocked the crook out of Valentine's hand, had done it until he'd grown so enraged that he'd finally hurled himself upon her and blacked her eye?

Now, watching her husband mop his brow, his face glowing with the pleasure of a hard workout, she experienced a resurgence of this long buried desire.

"Graf von Hagen?"

Christoph turned to her with a tentative smile, sensing that if Caterina had begun so formally, something extraordinary was coming.

"Could Lieutenant Heidelburg teach me fencing, too?"

When Christoph, a look of surprise on his face, didn't respond right away, she demanded, "Why not?"

"Women don't have the strength for saber, nor the endurance for épée. I respect your horsemanship, my Lady, but..." Heidelburg, clearly not relishing the idea, began a speedy defense.

"Some women are not used to physical effort and exercise, but I am," Caterina insisted. "That's just the same nonsense I was put off with when I was little and wanted lessons along with my brother. The Graf von Hagen knows that I'm quicker than Theo ever was or will be."

"In every way," agreed her husband, whose silent consideration of her suggestion had ended. "Well, Heidelburg, you are hardly overworked. If my lady wants fencing lessons, she shall have them."

To Caterina's undignified bounce of joy, he said, "Now, Grafin, you're going to be properly outfitted first. Then we'll have to agree upon times for your lesson. Lieutenant Heidelburg," he said turning to soothe his officer, "must not have his schedules upset."

"Oh, I want lessons every day, until I've got the drills by heart. Isn't that how you learn anything properly?"

Wearing a big grin of approval, Christoph threw an arm around her.

"Hear that, Heidelburg? An ardent desire to learn. And, sir," he added, drawing himself up in his most baronial manner, "if you lose that short temper of yours and put one mark on this beauty of mine, I promise you two matching ones."

* * *

Cat heard household gossip from Elsa, whose ingenuous manner threatened no one. She learned that there had been high and dashed hopes.

No wonder, Cat thought, that there was bitterness. She couldn't know whether her husband had misled them, or whether the whole thing had been wishful thinking.

She could imagine how it must have been while Christoph was gone, the pretty mistress and her sisters playing lady of the manor and having plenty of time to make themselves admired and pitied by everyone. And two fine healthy boys! It seemed Christoph had put aside a great deal to keep his promise to the von Velsens—and to Wili.

Josefa supplied most of the information, although she didn't seem to be aware of it. She was, Cat came to understand, very angry, and angry people, just as her father had always said, were indiscreet. It was Goran, however, who showed her the true well spring of Josefa's anger and disrespect. One morning, when Cat was splashing in the basin, hurrying to get to Star before breakfast, she heard a shout followed by a scream coming from her husband's room.

"What are you up to, hussy?" Goran cried.

"I've come to take away the water, Herr Goran."

Cat stopped washing and listened. She knew that Josefa brought water to Christoph every morning, and that it was received by his man at the door. After it was used and the Graf went out, someone else came back, emptied it and cleaned the basin.

"Come here, girl," Goran growled.

"I have done nothing wrong."

"Oh, haven't you?"

There was the sound of a rush and crash. Cat threw down her towel and rushed to open the door that led to her husband's room. Elsa followed.

The basin had struck the wide board floor and broken, sending soapy water everywhere. Goran had Josefa by an arm but she was fighting hard, trying, in fact, to kick the one good leg of the old soldier out from under him.

Rushing up behind, Cat caught Josefa by the glossy nut-brown braid that always trailed down her back. A hard yank elicited a shriek which pleased Cat, who'd been longing to have an excuse to do that for a long time.

"Thank you, Grafin," said Goran, for between the two of them they had quickly established control. "Now if you would put your hand into her bosom, you will find what she has stolen."

"I didn't steal it," cried Josefa. "I was taking it to wash as the Herr Graf asked."

As Cat hesitated, Josefa added with all the dignity of tone she could muster, "Just let me go and I will show you what I have."

"She does not do the laundry nor empty dirty water, Grafin. This one's far too fine for that," Goran's sneered.

"I wash and iron the Graf's shirts and stocks. All the time—whenever he is here," Josefa protested.

"Let her go, Goran," said Caterina.

When he did, Josefa shook herself and stepped back several paces.

"Croat dog!" she hissed.

"Enough," Caterina commanded. She had moved with Josefa, but had not let the braid go. Now, to remind her, she tugged again.

Josefa rounded on her in a swirl of skirt, ripped the braid free. Her brown eyes blazed. Cat stayed with her.

"Come on! Hit me! Try it!"

"Here," Josefa cried, hurling out the thing she'd concealed. "The Graf asked me to wash it." A rumpled white muslin neck piece trimmed in lace landed by Cat's feet. "He says that Hanna scrubs the life out of them and then no amount of ironing gets them right."

"A funny way to carry dirty laundry," Goran observed.

Josefa turned scarlet, and that was when Cat understood. "Go out, Hauptmann, and wait for me," she

132

said with an imperious wave. "Fraulein Josefa and I are going to have a talk."

Goran lifted a scanty brow, but he nodded and then thumped his way out into the hall.

"Um, Mistress?"

Cat had completely forgotten Elsa, who had watched the whole scene from the doorway.

"Go find someone who can carry a message to the stables," she said. "Have them ask Herr Rossmann to see to Star this morning."

Elsa went out the other way, passing through her mistress' room to a hall door. She had a perfect horror of her master's bedroom and wouldn't enter it for any reason, not even to retrieve sealing wax from his writing desk. Cat thought it must be the bed curtains. She herself had a hard time keeping her eyes off them—all that libidinous romping—whenever she was there.

After all the doors closed Cat said, "You are in love with the Graf."

The dark eyes flashed. Josefa's round cheeks went red. She was, Cat thought, quite pretty, just the sort of plump, dark haired creature her brother Theo fancied.

No answer to her question was forthcoming, so, lifting her chin, Cat bluntly asked, "Has the Graf had you?"

There was no answer to this either, but the dark eyes boldly lifted. An almost audible 'Wouldn't you like to know?' hung in the air between them. Somehow or other Caterina managed not to slap her, although the fingers of her right hand drew into a fist.

"I could dismiss you."

"I am the Frau Amtmann Walter's sister."

"And I," Cat drew herself up to every inch of her considerable height, "am Caterina, Grafin von Hagen."

"The Amtmann," Josefa replied, a quaver of uncertainty entering her voice, "is necessary to the Herr Graf. He would take it hard if I were dismissed."

"Ah, but you will not be dismissed," said Cat. Her mind worked furiously. "You will be sent to the house of—

of my brother," she said with sudden, cruel inspiration, "Herr Theo von Ployer of Passau."

"I—I do not wish to go to Passau, Grafin." The woman's voice quivered.

Knowing that she had Josefa on the run at last, Cat was inspired to continue spinning the web she'd begun.

"In Passau," she said with decision, "there are many noble families with servants who have comfortable and secure places. There are craftsmen and guildsmen too. It would be easy for someone like yourself to find a good husband there. I'm sure," she added, almost laughing aloud at the blow she was about to deliver. "The good Amtmann and his wife would be delighted to see you marry well."

There was a pregnant pause. Josefa humbly bent to pick up the crumpled stock.

"I really was supposed to wash it."

"Go do it, then. Bring it to me tomorrow morning before breakfast, ironed and folded."

"To you, Grafin?"

"To me, Josefa," Cat replied firmly. "Now go out and send someone to clean this mess."

"I will do it."

"No, send someone else. I don't want you inside the Herr Graf's room again."

The first proper curtsy Josefa had ever given her was dropped. Then the young woman, richly red faced, ran through the door.

There was the sound of Josefa's feet trotting down the hall and next came a baritone chuckle. Through the door which led to Caterina's room came Christoph.

"A wonderful performance, Grafin." Apparently he had been on his way to practice saber, for the weapon gleamed at his side.

"What have you done to her?" Cat swirled to face him

"Nothing. Nothing at all." He lifted his hands in denial.

When Cat made a face of disbelief, Christoph cupped both hands around the pommel of the saber.

"I swear on this sword," he said deliberately. "Not a kiss. Not a hug. Not a wink. Not even a pinch, although she does have a charming backside."

"You swear?" Cat thought it best to overlook his last remark.

"Yes, Grafin. On my sword. She has, however," her husband said, "on several occasions made her willingness known to me. I assure you, Caterina, I was not and am not interested."

"You liked her sister well enough."

"I did."

"Does Josefa look like her?"

"Not very."

While Cat turned this over in her mind, her husband remarked, "But this is the source of the trouble. Most women don't take a rebuff lightly, no matter how politely it is delivered."

"How did you know what was going on up here?"

"I saw Elsa dashing downstairs and she told me of the impending battle. I came through your rooms and got here just in time to hear that threat to send her to Theo. A witty solution."

"I'm ashamed of myself," Cat replied. "It's just that she has been so nasty to me from the very first day I came. It was high time she and I had it out."

"Well, Lady von Hagen," her husband said as he opened the door and bowed her into the corridor, "That was a performance worthy of your lady mother. Josefa took what I'd asked her to do as encouragement. From now on someone else will bring me water and for everyone's peace of mind, Hanna may beat my stocks to death with the rest of the laundry."

Cat gave him her arm. They walked to the stairs, very much the lord and lady.

"I will speak to Walter," Christoph said. "I know that he has had a matrimonial offer for her from a widowed cousin of his, a master mason of Passau."

"Oh, no," Cat exclaimed, halting their progress. "I would hate, I would never be one to force—"

135

"A marriage?"

"Yes." Cat met the knowing humor in his eyes with determination. "Walter is crazy if he thinks a pretty girl like that will settle for some old pot belly."

"I am inclined to agree with you, but not every woman is as lucky as you, Grafin."

Cat confined her commentary to a roll of her eyes. Chuckling, he tightened the arm around her waist, gave a quick squeeze followed by a kiss on the cheek.

"Are you certain you haven't done anything to her?"

"Neither to her nor with her," he said, once more halting their progress down those steep stairs. "And how often do I have to say it? Whatever you've heard, the simple wearing of a skirt is not sufficient, even if Josefa is a pretty woman. Even at my worst I have never been, as you once so delicately put it, a dog who jumps every bitch he gets near." He let go of her hand. "Now, excuse me, Grafin. I want to get this talk with Walter over."

He went down the stairs. At the bottom, he moved briskly towards the Amtmann's rooms, not once looking back. Cat knew her distrust hurt him, but she also knew that it had been necessary to her to provoke and to witness his reaction.

* * *

Cat loved to drive the trotters. She had at last convinced both her husband and Rossmann that she was competent to handle them. At least once a week she and Elsa would drive them down to Heldenruhe and back. They were never allowed to go alone, but always went with a young cavalryman riding behind. Cat couldn't believe that the forest was so very dangerous, although there was much talk of robbers among the servants. The village was a destination which delighted Elsa, who loved to visit her friend Maria and her great Uncle Leopold, but Cat was bored. It was the drive and not Heldenruhe which delighted her, the strength, skill and concentration it took to handle those two frisky horses.

Every now and then letters came to the Kleine Post in the village for the manor, letters for Cat from Lady von Velsen, or from Oncle Rupert or the Landrat for Christoph. Twice there were letters from Christoph's commander, General von Reischach.

One day, on their way back, the cavalryman asked if he might try his hand with the trotters. Having often admired his skill with horses, she agreed.

"Only if you take it slow, Herr Schenk," she said with a knowing smile. "If we have a wreck, it will be my head as well as yours."

"Never fear, m'Lady." The Ensign smiled and happily received the reins.

The naughty mares, feeling a change of driver, acted up at once, but Schenk, with little difficulty, soon got them under control. Cat leaned down to pick up the mail pouch. Looking in, she saw an astonishing quantity of letters—four!

Idly she turned them over to see the covers. Although the steady swaying of chaise made it a bit wobbly she could see that all were for Christoph.

She recognized the handwriting of three of the senders, but the fourth was a mystery, although the script was unmistakably feminine, round and down sloping. It said "Only for the eyes of Herr Graf Christoph von Hagen."

A chill shot through her. Carefully, surreptitiously, praying that no one would see, Cat slipped it into her pocket.

* * *

Later, sitting in the gloomy great room with a fire and a tray of tea and cakes before her, Cat carefully worked a small knife under the seal of the mysterious letter. She had seen her sister once do this when they had been visiting the von Hagen's, an occasion when jealousy had got the better of the otherwise charitable Wilhelmina.

Cat knew she had to lift the seal in such a way that she could put it back in one piece. The seal was ornate, a figure of some antique god holding a lyre. Cat heaved a sigh of relief as it came up intact. Swiftly unfolding, she saw the same childish hand that had written the address. It was dated almost six weeks ago, the usual turtle's pace from Vienna. The message was brief and cryptic.

* * *

A Saint's Anne's boy, Dear Sir.
~~With Respect, Konstanze

Cat pondered. She knew Saint Anne's day was close to the end of July. It was now almost October. The woman had apparently kept her own counsel for some weeks after the child was born, and then, suddenly, had decided to tell Christoph. And why should he care about a birthday—unless—he was the father?

A noise in the hallway brought her back to herself. Elsa, who she'd sent off on an errand, might return at any moment. Picking up a stub of red sealing wax and a fine bit of reed, Cat set about getting the angle right. Next she fired the reed from the candle and heated the wax, praying that coordination of hand and eye would carry the hot blob to just the right spot. As soon as the drop fell, she gently pressed the seal down. A little of the new wax spread out brightly on either side, but the delicate original did not entirely melt.

Not perfect, but good enough! After giving it a moment to set, Cat lifted the other letters in the pouch and set the letter from Konstanze carefully beneath them.

Saint Anne's... For a moment she lingered, not doing anything, although she ought to be hiding the sealing wax and putting the charred reed into the fire. Instead she was counting back nine months, remembering that Christoph had been in Vienna briefly just before that last, nearly fatal battle. She remembered Wili's chagrin that he had not asked her to meet him there and how her sister had grieved when the terrible news had reached them that Christoph was wounded, hovering between life and death.

Now here was the fruit of his selfishness! The baby had been born this year, not seven weeks after he should have married Wili. Cat could feel her skin tightening, feel all her blooming affection for him wither like flowers in frost.

Still, she thought, I must give no sign, for he will read the letter tonight. If I seem angry or upset, he will suspect I have opened it. Forcing herself to get up, she tossed the reed into the fire and pocketed the sealing wax. For one mad moment she imagined burning the letter, but instantly rejected the notion. Cat felt sudden pity toward this mysterious Konstanze with her round girlish handwriting, pity that another fly had fallen into the spider's web.

As Cat leaned there, feeling the heat sting her face, listening to the delicate crinkling of cinders, she was surprised by tears. They fell one by one, hissing as they struck the searing lip of the hearth. What would Wili have done? Would she have wept and then expressed that innate charity that had been her definition? Cat had always thought it weakness, Wili's enduring love, but now, today, she felt uncertain.

Whirling about, she ran to the tea table. Picking up the pretty little teapot in both hands, she smashed it onto the slates. There was an instant of relief as it shattered, but it didn't last. When Elsa came in a few minutes later, Caterina was still standing by the table, staring down at the wreckage, at the tea which, because she hadn't bothered to move away, had splattered all over her dress.

* * *

Christoph did not come back until almost dark. He had gone off and closeted himself with Walter as soon as supper, a meal for which Cat found no appetite, was over. She went up to her room, tried to read and failed, while Elsa sat nearby, sewing. Finally, wishing that it was morning so that she could ease her misery with a long ride, Cat got into bed.

Here she tossed and turned, thinking of the letter, wondering if it meant what it seemed. She thought about Wili and shed a few tears which she prayed didn't have anything to do with her own feelings for Christoph. Finally, hoping she could sleep, she did her exercise with the protector and lay down.

Listening to her husband prepare for bed was another distraction. How she wanted to run through the door to confront him, but knowledge of how angry he would be at her spying kept her from it. Cat thought she'd never be able to get to sleep. Still, somehow or other, eventually she wandered off into that strange realm.

* * *

There was Wili, sitting in the window seat. Her sister, blonde braids demurely crowning her head, was deep in embroidery, a piece stretched on a frame.

Cat ran to her, the letter in her hand, the letter from Konstanze. Wili gazed up at her with a serene expression.

"Wili! Read this!"

With deft fingers her sister ran the needle into the cloth. She took what Cat offered and studied it. Her skin, always pale, had a kind of shine beneath the surface. She looked up, shook her golden head, and without comment, handed the letter to Cat.

"I don't cry anymore." The soft gray eyes that Cat remembered so well were full of nothing but a profound calm. "It's your turn to cry."

Coolly picking up the needle, Wili continued embroidering.

* * *

Someone was inside the bed curtains, someone with gentle hands, whispering. Strong arms picked her up and Cat's wet face came to rest upon a freshly laundered nightshirt which covered a hard shoulder.

140

"There, there," a male voice comforted. "Wake up, Red. Wake up."

"Christoph," she gasped, understanding at last. Her body tensed

"You were having a bad dream."

To push against him would bring nothing but frustration, so she didn't, simply accepted his tender embrace.

Why hadn't Wili advised her? Why had she been so cold? Was it because she knew Cat was in love ...?

Her husband continued to hold her. One hand soothed, while the other cradled. She let her tears drench his nightshirt. His lips brushed her cheek on one side, tenderly.

"Wili." Cat whispered, telling the only part she dared. "I dreamed of Wili."

Christoph heaved a sigh. "She was on my mind tonight too."

How easy it was to cry herself out against his strength, to feel his hand on her back, upon her hair! His chest moved against hers as breath went in and out. She could hear his heart, an even drumbeat.

"Are you better now?" He sounded supremely weary.

When she murmured, "Yes," he released her and got out of the bed.

"Elsa. Elsa! Come at once."

Cat sat still, trembling with all the warring emotion she felt. A tall skinny figure joined his by the bedside, illuminated in the rippling light that came from the open door of his room. "Elsa, dear, you must sleep with the Grafin tonight. She's having bad dreams."

"It's not necessary," Cat said, but she had to move back, for Elsa was already joining her.

"I think that it is." Christoph began a retreat towards his own room. "Please stay, Elsa, no matter what."

"Yes, Herr Graf," whispered Elsa.

"Thank you," he said. "Good night, ladies." Gently, he shut the door behind him.

* * *

141

Silently Cat lay back. She felt beyond strange. "I don't want to talk," she said softly. "I'm upset but I think I just ought to try and go to sleep again."

"As you wish, Mistress, but you know," Elsa spoke after a pause, "you can trust me."

"Yes, of course." It was pitch black and Cat couldn't see a thing, but she knew that her maid was bursting with questions.

Suddenly, she ached to confide. Maybe not everything, but something.

Finally she reached out, took Elsa's hand and whispered, "The Graf never takes me to his bed."

"I know," was the whispered reply. "You are always so angry and sad."

"We are both angry and sad."

"It is because of your lady sister, is it not, Grafin?"

"Yes." Elsa's thin fingers pressed hers, but Cat was grateful when she didn't speak again. Christoph, she thought, had clearly been disturbed by the letter, maybe as much as she had been. The last thing she heard was him adding more wood to the fire.

Chapter Twelve

As Christoph prepared for his journey to Vienna, Cat was inspired to ask to come. She didn't like the idea of him traveling with the wildly enamored Josefa, who was, in fact, being sent into service at the Mason's home.

She didn't like the idea of him being easily able to visit the woman who'd written the cryptic letter. There was also the anticipated discomfort of being left alone on Heldenberg. These things loomed larger than any desire to see the great capital city.

However, the suspicion-evoking reply she was given was that he had too much business to attend to and that she'd be better right where she was.

"Besides," he'd added unkindly, "as soon as you opened your mouth in front of my Viennese friends, I'd be teased about having become a nursemaid, not a husband."

"You will be alone with Josefa and then you will visit Frau Ermler." The words came blurting out. "And, even if you are telling me the truth about them, there is—" and here she almost blurted out "Konstanze", but managed to change it to "those other Viennese women of yours."

"Cat! I warn you; I'm nearly dead from this unhealthy abstinence, but I shall keep my promise to you, although there are times, like now, when I wonder why I bother."

"Well, go on then! Tell all the heifers I say they can have you. Start with Josefa. I don't care! Why should I?"

"Your mouth, little girl! Get out of here before I take you over my knee. I'm done talking. Scat! Scat!" Scowling and looking purposeful, he strode towards her, raising a hand as if she were Furst and he intended to cuff her for the high crime of scratching the chairs.

Cat took off, beating a hasty retreat to the stables. Star, as always, welcomed with a soft whicker and the moist touch of her velvet nose.

Burying her face against the warm smell of the sorrel's neck, Cat cried a little. For the thousandth time she asked herself: Why did Wili die? Her sister would have unreservedly loved this man—this wicked man—who was probably going to Vienna to see a whole crew of mistresses.

For comfort, Cat did what she always did. She saddled up and rode into the forest, cantering along a trail that led up the mountain. As she rode ever higher, the trees shrank and shriveled, as if they'd come under an evil spell. Soon, she knew, they'd disappear, and she would be on the rock-strewn high meadows. She would ride straight across to the western cattle path. Then, in waning light, she'd follow that back down to the manor.

* * *

After a glorious gallop in the cold bright sun, Cat felt better, although still melancholy. Was it, after all, entirely reasonable to expect a man to remain faithful to a wife who wasn't really a wife? I know exactly what Papa would say!

She felt a little hungry, for it was close to supper, but she was unwilling to go back to her troubles just yet. It was a beautiful warm afternoon, a mingling of gold, brown and rust in the forests that spread out below. The sky over her head was blue. The view of Great Heldenberg and her companions was spectacular, even if the peaks were obscured.

There'd been clouds up on the mountain all day, a gray mass which moved as if it were alive, expanding and contracting across the strange lifeless zone of rock and castle sized boulder that shouldered the beige, late fall

144

meadows. She'd often seen the peaks hidden in this strange shroud.

In the stables, Cat had heard tales about these clouds. They said they sometimes came down to blanket the upper pastures for days, leaving the herders and their animals in a situation where they hardly dared take a step. Hidden within it, wolves, trusting to their noses, came from the forest and carried off unlucky strays, or, sometimes, dogs or small children. After a time, Cat slowed Star to a trot. The sun was low and she didn't want to miss the cattle path. It was dangerous to do so because of the ravine which lay about a half kilometer beyond. She had turned slightly south and had just entered one of those depressions with which the mountain side was pitted, when she felt a cold wet breath on the back of her neck

In an eye blink, the world she'd been moving through, the world of valley and mountain, of brilliant colors and rosy, waning sun, disappeared. Star snorted, half-reared and then stood stock still.

They were enveloped in fog. The air inside was cold and wet and queer smelling, like the exhalation of the ancient bog they'd been skirting. Stifling a shudder, Caterina dismounted. "Come on, girl," she said to the mare, rubbing her sweaty neck. "Maybe it will go back up the mountain again. In the meantime, we'll walk."

Holding the reins, she began to move in a direction that felt like down. Surely, if they just kept going as they had been, they'd soon hit the cattle path. "If not," she whispered, "You and I will be spending a miserable night together."

Of course, being out in the weather was the least of her worries. Cat racked her brains, trying to orient herself, trying to remember the location of the huts shared by the local herders. She walked on, staring at the ground and praying not to miss the worn manured path the cattle made.

Fog poured around them like a river. Sometimes she could see a few yards ahead, sometimes she couldn't even see her feet. She hoped to keep the high meadows on her left, but the grass, when she could see it, seemed sparser.

145

Was she actually going back up the mountain? It was impossible to tell. Worse, she kept hearing strange sounds, a smothered wailing.

Shepherds? Or—a scouting wolf?

Fear gnawed at her. Without the sun, her sense of time seemed lost as well, and it soon seemed they'd been in the fog forever.

* * *

Star's ears pricked. Then, she reared. If Caterina hadn't had a good grasp on her bridle, she would have bolted, perhaps to break a leg or fall into the dreaded ravine.

"Whoa! Whoa, Star!" She threw her arms around the horse's neck. Clinging to the mane with all her strength, Cat desperately sought to find, somewhere in the turmoil, thoughts of calm to send.

The mare hopped from side to side, but Cat managed to hold on. At last Star stood, brown eyes rolling, nostrils quivering.

Looking around, Caterina strained to see what had so frightened the mare. As one of those intermittent breaks flowed past, it let in a rosy shaft which told of sunset. Close, in that light, she saw a familiar landmark: an ancient stone, roughly pillar shaped, perhaps eight feet tall. The shiny gray surface was covered with a moving carpet of sparkling droplets.

This pillar, she knew, sat near the herdsmen's huts, at the very upward end of the cattle path. With a chill, she realized that if she'd gone much farther, she would have ended near the awful ravine.

But, which way was down? She peered at the ground, but now her feet—and everything else— disappeared again. Matching her spirits, everything turned into ghastly gray. Hoping not communicate her fear, Cat stroked Star's sweaty neck. At the same time, a long shiver coursed along her back.

What to do? Stay by the stone?

As she patted Star and wondered what to do next, a giant, a man of cloud, stepped out of that gray on gray. Water beaded his clothes, silvered his dark head and clung in beads to his flesh. Cat started, and Star reared again, nearly pulling her off her feet.

"Thank the Trinity, the Blessed Mother, and every demon on this mountain!"

The otherworldly man grabbed her horse's reins.

"The peasants say this thing is a lodestone which keeps people from the ravine, but I never believed it 'till now."

"Christoph!" Cat had never been so glad to see anyone in her life."

Easy, Star," he said, holding the mare, who was still shying and backing. "Easy, girl. It's only me."

When they finally got her quieted, Christoph slipped an arm around Cat and offered a watery kiss, which she, her heart welling with relief, accepted.

"Can you find the huts?" She was a little breathless from the enthusiasm of his embrace. Their quarrel suddenly didn't seem to matter.

"Yes, like Theseus in the labyrinth." He bent, plucked at a cord which extended away into the nothingness. "I was just coming to stake this behind the stone. The Schafmann's are stretching another just below their homes. Anyone who crosses will know to follow it to safety. You aren't the only person caught out here today. Their men are still high up with the sheep."

"Lost?"

"Stranded. They know how to deal with it. They have spears and dogs, so wolves shouldn't be a big problem. The cord is just to keep them from getting too close to the ravine." He'd found the upright, and secured the line. Then they began to go back, leading Star and following the cord. Around them, a twilight chaos swirled.

"How did you know where I'd be?"

"I could say that I'm good at catching foxes, but the truth is I watched you ride out."

"But I went east, through the pines."

"I knew you'd be in the mood for a long ride, and that you 'specially like the high meadow from east to west, but I beg you not to do it again, at least until I return from Vienna."

"This fog was way up on the barrens. It looked so far away—"

"Well, that's the danger. I saw which way you went, and then I couldn't take my eyes off the mountain. After a half hour of worrying, I decided that I wasn't going to get anything done anyway, so I saddled Brandy and rode over here. A good thing I did, for I'd barely reached Scafmann's when it came down." His strong hand squeezed hers.

Wavering before her eyes there were suddenly sheds and huts, low heaps of turf and stone. In one, empty except for a few chickens and a strong smell of the sheep, Cat unsaddled and secured Star beside Brandy.

"A good thing she's already bred."

Cat nodded. A pair of half grown boys appeared and began to help, stealing curious looks at their master and their young mistress. Settling in took awhile, getting hay for feed, wiping the horses down, drawing water for them, all of it done in that weird shifting twilight, like a game of blindman's bluff.

"Is your father out in the fog?" Cat asked one of the boys.

"Yes. All the men are." His fair skin reddened beneath his tan, perhaps because he was not yet considered one of them. "Mutter and Tante are in the big house with the little ones while Franzi and I and the Herr Graf put the lines out."

In the family "big house," which was a single, dirt floored room, they discovered two women, six children, an orphaned lamb, and a sheepdog bitch and three yapping puppies. It was hot and noisy, although the tumult did die down somewhat after the unexpected entrance of their lord and lady.

Caterina had one of the two chairs in the house forced upon her, so she sat and ate what was offered, a bowl of

148

bitter rye porridge with a thin coating of sheep's butter. It was gritty but hot, and she swallowed it gratefully.

As she ate, she studied her hostesses. The women were probably not old but it was hard to tell, for their faces were lined and leathery from exposure. One squatted by the hearth and nursed first an infant and then a toddler. She expressed gratitude that her master and his sword were to be there tonight.

"I always fear bandits when it's like this. They come in the fog, like wolves."

"Don't worry, Gute Frau. They'll get a surprise if they visit me." Christoph patted the short sword he always carried.

It was agreed that Caterina and Christoph would shelter apart in a small room that currently held much of the family's treasure of wool and sheepskin. After thanking the women for their hospitality and promising that he'd have a shoat sent up to them tomorrow, to "give them a change"—a promise received with delight—Christoph took a burning stick and went with Cat out into the thick night. The stone and turf room they entered shared a wall with the one they'd left. By trailing their hands along the stone, they found the door.

Both husband and wife had to duck. Inside, the smell of sheep seemed just as strong as before, although the smell was cleaner, emanating from a pile of market ready skins and washed wool that half filled the place.

By the meager light of the burning branch he carried, Christoph started a fire on the hearth, using some pine branches piled there. Caterina watched as he crouched, expertly nursing the first sparks with handfuls of twigs. Soon the sharp fragrance began to rise.

"I'll have to see these folks get more hardwood," Christoph said, selecting a chunk of wood from the heap by the door, "and, since you'll be here while I'm in Vienna, Cat, make sure that they get any and all autumn lambs for themselves. Frau Schafmann told me that for some reason, Walter took every one last year."

They pulled a pair of hides close to the fire and sat down. As these were going to market, they had been washed clean of dirt and ticks.

"They have so many children," Cat said.

"Not much else to do here at night."

Her husband moved logs closer to the hearth. "We'll have to sleep in these clothes, but if we can get some heat up in here, it shouldn't be too bad. Especially," he added, turning a smile upon her, "if you let me put my arms around you."

After he'd built up the fire and made a pile of wood handy, they lay down together. Cat was exhausted and melancholy, subsiding against him without a word. It was good to be away from the manor tonight. Her thoughts kept running toward Vienna, but whatever he did or did not do there, she had to finally admit to being in love.

The night would be one of dozing, for he would have to keep tending the fire. Husband and wife settled down together like two spoons, their damp cloaks bunched behind to bank the heat. Christoph kept one arm around her. She could feel his breath against her hair.

* * *

Soon she was dreaming, a dream that began in an erotic tickle and then swelled into a forbidden delight, like that which she gave herself when alone in bed. In the dream, a hand was between her legs, gently making love among the curls.

Cat swayed between two powerful desires, one to continue sleeping, the other to respond. Penetration was going on as well, a delicate and gradual entry. At each stopping place, little circles were drawn and drawn again. When each filled with wet pleasure, a further subtle incursion was made. Through the fog of sleep, Caterina began to move, wanting to deepen and widen sensation.

She came to consciousness gasping in wild release, like a snapping shower of sparks. She was still lying in front of the fire on that bed of fleece, but her husband's

150

hand, which had started the night guilelessly upon her hip, was now inside her trousers.

Gently, skillfully, for who knew how long, he'd been playing the burning secret. A luxurious slow circling of his fingers went on in the liquid benediction that had answered her bliss and his prayer.

Feeling her ecstatic sigh and shudder, Christoph rolled her over, began to devour her with kisses.

"You were going in glory...Now let me show you another way." Big hands took hold of her trousers.

"Not fair!"

In the next moment her long legs felt air. Then, half naked, she was thrust back into the wool while all the hard muscle of him crowded between her knees. Pushing her shirt up, he fell ravenously upon the sweets of her high, freckled breasts.

"I know your game," she gasped, still trying to fend him off, if not with her strength, then with words. "As soon as I love you, you won't want me anymore."

He raised his dark head and gazed deep into her eyes.

"God and the devils of Heldenberg gave you back to me just for this."

She felt him against her, pressing against the innocent opening. Fire and shadow rippled over his powerful body, while darkness gathered around his head like a crown. For one astonishing instant she thought she saw horns among his curls. Her hand rose to the spot, touched only thick hair and the honest skin of his forehead.

"Christoph," she made a final entreaty, knowing that she was lost, heart and body, feeling the hot pressure of his urgency, "Don't hurt me."

From his position of absolute command her husband came to seize her mouth with his, a kiss both hungry and absolutely tender.

"Oh, my precious Red! I'll take good, good care of you."

Curls spilling over his shoulders, he breathed her in, ran his tongue across the sensitive mounds of her breasts in an ecstasy of tasting, ending with a deep draught from her mouth. As he sampled her essence he was entering, a progress obtained with remarkable ease through the hot liquid breach he'd made.

His beautiful face shone as he paused to whisper. "Think of the hunt. You only get hurt when you fall; you only fall when you don't go with the horse."

Cat gasped as he, holding her easily against his powerful body, began a tentative rocking. Quick, shallow thrusts grew harder, went deeper. Casting an arm around his neck she began to move with him, to follow his lead and return his love, so long hungered for. As he rode harder, a savage joy surged through her.

"By God—and this Devil Mountain—I'll love you forever!"

Then it was all sensation, his hardness, the working muscular back to which she clung. The long defended citadel of her body was in flames. Reflexively her hips rose and fell. He knew exactly what he had to do to carry her with him, to keep her circling in fire. Hot liquid bloomed, splashed.

Kisses were lavished upon her. The pine fire howled and hissed, sent showers of sparks flying onto the flags. Heat crowded the tiny hut, poured over them in a monumental wave. Crimson rippled and flowed over their bodies, over Caterina's beautiful upraised knees, as her husband deeply, relentlessly, engaged.

"Oh, so good she is! Go my red angel, go again for me!" His powerful body rode a burning trail, thrust her deep into the ancient consciousness while her young body answered with abandon. Male and female, matched in height and strength, on a tide of that so long denied desire, strove to wrestle their way into yet another explosion of delight.

* * *

Afterwards, fingers tracing the expanse of his chest, she whispered, solemnly wondering, "Mama said the first

152

time would hurt. But it was all—all—ah—nice." Her body still hummed, while the all over blush flamed.

"My pleasure." Her husband smiled joy into her eyes, and then, meditatively ran his lips across her freckled, smooth shoulder. "A benefit of giving your beautiful self to a rogue who's had ample practice. And, just imagine, sweetheart. It can only get better."

Then there was an exhausted descent into unconsciousness, locked in his arms, his words of love echoing in her ears, his body so close, so protective and tender. Night and the mountain's huge silence enclosed them.

* * *

Daybreak... Cat opened her eyes to find him dressing beside her. On the hearth fresh branches made a chorus of crackling.

"It's just dawn. We'll saddle up and start down the cow path."

"Is the fog still here?" Dizzily, she sat up.

"Yes, but not as thick as yesterday." Carefully neutral, he handed her the wrinkled riding pants.

"Christoph..." she hesitantly began, twisting and shyly drawing her knees up in an effort to hide.

"Hush, sweetheart." He bent and dropped a kiss on the top of her head. "Just get dressed now. We'll have plenty of time to talk on the way down." As he went out, bending through the low door, she caught a glimpse of the veiled light that comes just before dawn.

* * *

"Give me your hand."

They walked, leading their horses, eyes carefully trained upon the trampled muddy trail they were following. Obedient as a child, she put her hand into his.

"You—seduced—me." Her body still hummed with what they'd done, but this morning the fear was back.

Afraid of what she felt for him, afraid because she knew they were walking down a path that would lead him away and straight to the temptations of Vienna.

"Yes, but the woman beside me knew what she wanted. And every word spoken last night is true. I love you, Cat—and you love me." He sighed. "Damn it, woman, I knew you'd wake up fretting."

Despite her confusion, she didn't pull her hand away. She couldn't.

"I—I do love you. I guess you know anyway. But you—you made something happen I wasn't ready for."

"I was afraid last night when the fog came down. I thought I'd lost you, just as I lost Wili." He raised her hand and kissed it. "We're mated now, Caterina."

As he spoke the cloud stirred. Next came an icy gust. All the mist remaining went rolling backwards in a sighing rush, almost as if the mountain had inhaled it. Now, there was an up and a down—an eye-watering burst of color.

The sun floated on a distant blue horizon. Spread at their feet was a blanket of yellow and gold, here and there patched with somber pines. For a moment they stood motionless, his hand warm upon hers. Cat blinked fiercely against stinging tears.

Chapter Thirteen

She didn't tell Elsa what had happened on the mountain. She hardly knew what to make of it herself. Her body was engaged; she wanted more of that—yes! But, in her mind, well, she had expected some great change from losing her virginity, but here she was, exactly the same as before. There hadn't been pain or show as she'd been told. It was all very curious.

She fretted sometimes and then was actually glad he had gone. What was it about the thing they'd done that made a part of her so weak, so vulnerable? Cat wished that she had someone older she could talk to—

Even my mother!

* * *

While Christoph was away in Vienna, Caterina had planned to spend as much time as possible on her horse, but this strategy was ruined by an early blizzard. Glumly, she sat with Elsa and stared at a blowing, a whiteout storm that lasted for days. About 6 hours in, it became very cold inside the manor, despite the great fires. Then the curtains had to be closed, just to barely keep warm. Candles were lit to see and the downstairs became a cavern. Caterina retreated to her room.

Mountain life had reached the shut in time, and the days were still shortening. It was hard just to wade to the barn. Thrown back on herself, there wasn't much to do but brood about what Christoph might, or might not, be doing in Vienna. She tried not to think of it, and her mood flew back and forth

Cold kept its grip on Heldenberg, but at last there was no more wind and snow. Cat rejoiced when a track to Heldenruhe was reopened by the long slow work of sleighs and ox plows. Daily she took a hard ride in that direction, though if she'd gone so far as to reach the hamlet, she wouldn't have been able to return until the next day. Most years, they didn't bother working so hard to clear the big drifts, but this year their master return.

* * *

It was just before Christmas, during the daily lesson with Lieutenant Heidelburg, that Cat dropped her guard. He treated her as he would one of his cadets and put a long, fine slash through her shirt into her forearm. It bled a torrent. Heidelburg was brusquely apologetic, but the wound looked deep enough to end the lessons for some time.

Cat, crossly suspecting that he'd struck her in order to get a Christmas holiday, was on her way upstairs. Her arm ached and the dressing they'd applied was swiftly reddening. Behind her, she heard the now familiar tap of a leg. Turning, she saw Goran.

"The Graf is home, Grafin. He wants you to come to him in his study. He's brought a gentleman back to meet you."

Desire leapt like a pup on a leash, although prudence tugged her back. She'd put a lid on all this emotion by returning to her original stance—that what had happened had been only the first close engagement of what might be a long war. Losing a battle did not mean she was utterly defeated.

"Am I expected to change?" Thinking of the visitor, Cat gestured at the men's clothes she'd been wearing. Cat was slender, but these days, even in trousers, there wasn't much doubt about her sex.

"The gentleman won't mind and neither will the master," Goran had a twinkle in his pale eye. "Oh, what a

156

brave fellow is that Lieutenant! Here, my Lady, let me see this."

Cat extended her arm. "It's not bad." Before him, she wanted to be brave, even though the wound was throbbing miserably.

Goran took her arm in his calloused hands and examined the bandage.

"He may be a master duelist, but he's a bad surgeon. Let me retie this before you go up to the Graf."

Another length of bandage was brought and they sat in the long hall. There in the cold and candlelight, Goran quickly redressed Cat's arm.

"And that's how it should be done," He tied the last knot. "And, Lady Grafin, you should know, though it sticks in his craw, Heidelburg says you're one of the quickest pupils he's ever taught."

Caterina beamed, pleased to her soul. Just as she'd always imagined, she enjoyed fencing—even after this.

"Who is the new gentleman?" Cat asked as Elsa helped her on with the morning gown she'd come carrying.

"You'll pardon me, Lady, but that's for the Graf to say."

Damn! Cat had learned to fear this prelude.

In the study she found her husband still in his dusty traveling clothes, but already eating one of those gambler's repasts of bread and meat. He had a companion sharing his meal, a short, blocky man, modestly dressed in a black suit and stockings. A thin bit of white lace at his throat made the only contrast.

"Ah, here you are." Christoph and the gentleman stood. "Lady von Hagen," this is my friend, Herr Stocke. He has agreed to spend a few years at Heldenberg."

The man bowed. Caterina, because she was still in breeches, bowed in return. There was not so much as a flicker of amusement in the strange gentleman's gray eyes.

"Herr Stocke is a learned man, one who didn't hesitate to give me some excellent advice when I was a boy. He was even so kind as to spend the last couple of winters up here trying to teach my thick-headed sons."

Caterina felt her heart sink. Was this dour man a school master?

"Yes." Her husband nodded in solemn answer to the unspoken question.

"Herr Stocke is your new tutor, Madame. Heldenberg steers a straight course without a wife's hand on the tiller, or so all my servants are busy assuring me, and as you can't spend all your life in the saddle or foil in hand, I have hit upon this to fill your days. As your good parents were so apologetic about the gaps in your education, I have devised a remedy. Herr Stocke will be able to devote full time to instructing you in accounts, French, history and geography."

During this speech, Cat experienced a burst of rage.

"What is the use of bringing this gentleman? I don't need a tutor. I can learn all I need to know by going about the place with you and Walter, just as I did with Papa and Herr Longenecker."

"Herr Stocke," Christoph said evenly, "would you leave us for a moment?"

Before the door had finished closing behind the upright black figure, Christoph said, "Didn't your mama teach you not to sauce your husband in front of learned professors?"

Caterina winced, for in catching her arm his hand had gripped the wound.

"Ow!"

"What's this?" Christoph, holding her wrist in one hand, pushed back the loose sleeve with the other and revealed the bloody bandage.

"Ah, poor Cat! I see that Heidelburg's been teaching you not to drop your guard and that dear old Goran's been bandaging you."

Cat tried to disengage him, but her husband had got an arm around her waist and was steering her towards his chair.

"Don't. I'm not a child. Especially now."

"Yes, angel, but you will listen best right here." He sat and pulled her onto his knee. "Now, haven't I said that I shall be gone most of next year?"

"But why should I have a schoolmaster?"

"My brave and beautiful Valkyrie, there are lady's maids who are better educated. If you cooked or sewed or knew anything about housekeeping, your lack of French and everything else might be overlooked by a gentleman, but you're ignorant as a yearling colt."

"That's not fair. I know all sorts of things."

"You do, but most of those things are about horses. You need more than one string to your fiddle. So, Caterina, its lunge rope and saddle for you. You will learn about keeping accounts, about where you live on this round world and a little French conversation, or by God above I'll leave orders that you aren't to ride until I come home."

"No one can keep me away from Star." This was certainly not the way Cat had imagined his home coming. "Why are you doing this? I don't need a tutor, I need time to ride the manor. I know how farm things should be. And," she ended, meeting his eyes, "haven't I—done my duty?"

"Splendidly." He touched his lips to her shoulder. "But tutoring is not punishment. Learning should not be confined to childhood."

He was so close, a bit whiskery and dusty from the road, but the smell of him, the touch of his hand, rekindled all kinds of memories, not only of the mountain, but of some tenderness between them on the morning he'd gone away. She felt a thrill at the touch of his mouth.

"There, there, my cat woman, please stop scratching. I was thinking about your sweet backside every other minute I was away."

"You must excuse me, Herr Graf," Cat muttered, head close against his great chest, "but I'm really getting cold and my arm hurts."

"My poor Caterina," he said, shifting to a warm rubbing of her long back. "Damn Heidelburg. Is it deep?"

"Herr Goran says I'll live."

"Well, then, you will. He kept telling me that last year when I thought I was dying, swelled up and covered with pus and leeches and attacked every other hour by surgeons with sharp knives." He pushed back the sleeve of the morning gown to look at her bandage again. "We'll undo this before you go to bed and I'll look at it again. I've grown to be a pretty fair surgeon myself."

With as much dignity as she could muster, Cat started to rise. "I would like another kiss before you go," Christoph said.

"You shouldn't have got the first. You did—what you did—before you left and then you come back and treat me like a child! Why do you want to waste my days so that I won't be able to ride and watch over your land as I should?" Frustration built with every word until she shouted: "I hate this dreary snow pile and I hate you."

He did not let go. Because the hand he held was attached to her throbbing arm, she couldn't bring herself to jerk that away, either.

"I think I'm right about bringing Stocke here and I hope that in time you will understand why. Come on, dear little Cat. Just for a minute pull in those claws."

She found herself against his chest again, cradled in his arms, her mouth repeatedly and softly kissed.

"I've been on fire for more of those sweets I stole on the mountain. Why can't you believe I'm in love with you?"

"Because you say it too easily." Nevertheless in the next instant she was kissing him back with answering warmth.

Not only did it feel good, but Cat was beginning to understand that his wanting bestowed upon her a kind of power...

"Our marriage is in its seventh month. Must we go into the New Year quarreling?"

"Yes." In spite of his words, in spite of the warm excitement she experienced in his arms, she still felt cross with him.

"By God," he chuckled softly, "the next time we see your papa I'm going to tell him this is no red filly he's married me to, but a tough little red mule instead."

Chapter Fourteen

That night, although she was partly apprehensive and partly desirous, her husband did not enter her room. Cat had not been able to make up her mind what she would do if he did although the glowing embers of the pleasure shared on the mountain was an inducement to her body, she was still afraid that he only made love to get the better of her.

She was surprised the next day at how cross she felt, deprived of the stimulation of either love making or a quarrel. While they were breakfasting together, Christoph suddenly winked and said, "Were you disappointed last night?"

"About what?"

He laughed then returned to buttering his rye bread. "Never mind, then."

Cat, upset and unsettled, had wanted to find release in a ride, but starting that day, she was, as she put to herself, "imprisoned" in the school room.

Herr Stocke was a much more intimidating teacher than Frau Pluncke. As a courtesy, Elsa was set to studying, too, but Stocke rarely took his eyes off Caterina, so she had no recourse other than to work. Initially, the teacher spent a lot of time patiently trying to find out exactly what she did know.

Days passed, with Stocke continually sighing and shaking his head, as if her case were hopeless. After a week, he set Caterina to work at accounts problems, all of which, the teacher explained, he'd derived from the books of the estate. The columns of numbers, the many entries, swam before Cat's eyes. Besides this, there were histories to read, geography to study, lists of French verbs to memorize. Dutifully, Caterina worked, swallowing her pride whenever she had to ask for help, trying bravely to ignore thoughts of the barn.

When she was dismissed, she rushed to change her clothes and go to exercise Star, or if new snow had fallen, just brush her. Then she'd return to the manor, half frozen in the winter darkness. After awhile, Stocke delighted her by suggesting that she tend to her horse in the morning and come to school when she was done.

"You're working hard, my Lady, and besides," he said with a twinkle in his pale eyes, "a restless pupil never learns much of anything. I've taught long enough to know that."

Needless to say, Caterina liked him far better after that. No matter how tired the barn work made her, she tried to do her best in the schoolroom. As time passed, she found she actually enjoyed the things Herr Stocke taught, especially history. Christoph was more than once pleased to find her sitting by the fire with a book open in her lap in the evenings after supper.

Winter held the land in a death grip. The peak of the Heldenberg was lost for days in howling storms. Ice underlay the snow, so that even with cleated shoes, the horses couldn't be safely ridden. The barns grew dirty and were full of the sounds of restive animals, kicking and picking fights with their neighbors. Some of the horses cribbed, groaning unnaturally as they tore U shaped holes in the stalls. Whenever there was a thaw and Cat could get out, she rode lanky, tall Jack, a Wurttemberg from her father's house. Star's belly was growing and Cat didn't want to take any risks with her.

She also spent time with the Andalusian stallion, grooming him. It was slow, even for her, to make friends, for the gray was truly dangerous during winter confinement. If Brandy started kicking and trumpeting in similar frustration, the gray was sure to join in. The barn

162

would echo with the screams and drum beats of the two studs as they punished their stalls. At first the ever alert Rossmann was anxious when Cat went in with the Andalusian, but after awhile he changed his mind, deciding that her "touch" made it safe.

The Graf watched his young wife's involvement with the horses with a combination of amusement and admiration.

* * *

Christmas came; the least splendid in Cat's memory, for her father's house was always been crammed full of neighbors and family. At Heldenberg, they celebrated in snow bound isolation.

Bed time usually found mistress and maid sitting cross legged in Caterina's bed talking over the day, the green curtains drawn back to get the benefit of the fire. After they had washed, standing on towels before the hearth, sponging their tall slim bodies, they'd put on their nightdresses and then take turns brushing and braiding each other's long hair. Sometimes Elsa played her mandolin and the girls sang softly together. Since the nights of Christmas had begun, they'd changed their usual late night cups of chamomile tea with bread and butter for the less digestible indulgence of wine and sweet kuchen.

Since summer, Elsa had become the perfect spy, for among the kitchen workers was a brawny-armed farm boy, Ekkehard, who had fallen in love with her. While they hid and held hands in some dark corner of the house, in delicious closeness, he'd tell what he'd heard below stairs. At first, however, Elsa had accepted the young man's courtship only at her mistress' urging.

"But, my Lady! I may be poor, but I'm a gentlewoman. Ekkehard was born in a stone hut up on Heldenberg."

"Oh, but he's a pretty fellow, Elsa, so blonde and strong! His papa is not a serf, he's a free farmer, and a good one, too."

Now, several months later, Elsa had forgotten that she'd ever disdained the handsome youth. Just before Christmas, Ute had been ill and Ekkehard had been among those set to cooking. He'd risen to his chance with surprising skill. Cabbage and noodles, roast meat, glazed turnips and potatoes, all well prepared, arrived in a timely fashion at the master's table. Elsa and her sweetheart had begun building castles in the air about the day he'd be head cook in a big kitchen in a big house maybe in Passau, or maybe, even, in Vienna!

New Year's Eve found the young women tête-à-tête in bed, long legs crossed beneath night gowns, whispering about love. Cat was still keeping her secret, so in both cases their tales of romance were almost done as soon as they started.

Happiness, combined with a glass of the delicious sparkling wine, had tonight made Elsa so bold that she'd just told her mistress that, in her opinion, she should forget all these sins and sorrows past and become, "for true and all," the Graf's wife. The wine had worked on Cat, too, rendered her incapable of reprimand. She felt loose, free, and confident.

"Sometimes," she sighed, shivering, remembering the hard feel of her husband's body upon hers, remembering the irresistible rush of his kisses, "I want to do exactly that."

That was when the door between her husband's room and hers—the door that was never locked, the door that was never opened—did just that. There stood Christoph, dark locks over his shoulders, wearing his brocaded burgundy gown. After gazing at the two surprised young women intently for an instant, he smiled.

"A pretty sight indeed. I'm sorry to interrupt you, young ladies, but I'm afraid that for the last few nights I've been sitting on the other side of that door, hearing you sing and whisper and feeling left out. Tonight it occurred to me that this is an odd way for a husband to feel..." Eyes big, Elsa belted her loose gown tightly. Then, mandolin in hand, she crawled backwards out of the bed.

164

"Yes, I think that tonight, the eve of the New Year, my wife and I will be alone. You may go to your own room tonight, Elsa, but first come here to me." The tall girl obeyed, clearly nervous. Now, in such alarming undress, the master seemed very deliberate.

"Stop looking as if I were about to eat you!" Impatiently he caught Elsa by the hand and pulled her lanky and now visibly trembling form closer. "You have been good to my wife, and so I've decided that you should have a fine present at the New Year."

"Oh, sir!" Elsa blushed, lowering her eyes. She, like most women, found Christoph attractive. Proximity combined with the touch of his hands was heady!

"A certain young fellow from the kitchen has been so bold as to come to me and ask for my help- and I have agreed."

Elsa's big eyes started.

"I have promised he shall have the opportunity to learn his trade, Fraulein," Christoph said. "It may mean a time of separation for you both, but in the meantime, consider this the beginning of your dowry..."

A golden chain was lowered over head. For a moment, Elsa stood stock still, eyes bright, hardly daring to breathe.

"Oh, Herr Graf! Thank-you!"

"You are very welcome."

Courteously, with a hand on her waist, Christoph guided her towards the door to her room. "Now, dear, one last thing. Before you sleep, go knock at Goran's door and tell him that tomorrow they are not to begin breakfast until I call. If he's not in his room, go to Herr Stocke. Apologize, but ask him to relay the message downstairs. Under no circumstances are we to be disturbed before I call, but, listen! Don't you go downstairs yourself. I don't want you wandering about in your nightgown tonight when everyone is drunk."

"Yes, Herr Graf. I understand, but first let me..."As excited as she was, Elsa hadn't forgotten her mistress. Turning, she scampered back to the bed, leapt in and gave Cat a warm hug and a kiss.

"Oh, Mistress," she breathed, "Your husband is as good as he is handsome." Then, she was out of the bed and away in a flurry of night robe and long legs. As the door closed behind her, Christoph offered Caterina a hand to help her out of bed.

"If you don't mind, Lady von Hagen, come to my room."

"I think you've stolen her heart from me, sir, but that was wonderfully kind." Cat uneasily replied, feeling the heat in his strong hand. "Thank you for being so good to her."

"You, too, are welcome. She's been your friend, which has meant the world to me. You were so sad when you first came here."

With a courtly gesture, he pushed his door wide and bowed her through. Caterina passed him, nervously tossing a red braid over her shoulder. In his room, the fire was warmly flickering, somehow setting the amorous couples on the bed curtains in motion. In averting her gaze from those escapades, Cat's eyes fell upon the table by the fire. There was an opened bottle upon it.

"It seems proper we should welcome the New Year together."

Casually, as if there was nothing much on his mind, Christoph let go of her hand. Going to the small table, set handy to a capacious wing chair, he poured wine then handed her the first glass.

"Oh, but I shouldn't. I had wine for dinner and Elsa and I drank a glass of what you sent to us too."

"As I hoped you would." Despite what she'd said, Cat felt so anxious that she took the glass he offered and began at once to sip it.

"Oh, it's the same you sent to us. So delicious! Is it French?"

"The finest, my innocent connoisseur."

"It is late, sir, almost midnight. What are we to talk about?" Cat asked, setting her glass down.

"Why, about us, of course." Raising his glass formally, he toasted her. "To the New Year and to our future

166

together, Red Caterina." He threw back his handsome, curly head and drank deep. "Now," he said, setting his glass next to hers. "We shall visit as a husband and wife should upon the occasion of the New Year." Then he made as if to sit and take her onto his lap.

"Don't. That makes me feel like a baby."

"Well, then, shall I treat you like a woman instead?" His arms encircled her waist. She was lifted, pressed against his broad chest, and thoroughly kissed.

How effortlessly, yet how gently, he held her! She could sense how entirely his strength was reined in. When his warm lips released hers, Cat felt weak. As she foundered in the tide of desire that washed through every fiber, he carried her to his bed.

On the mantel, the clock struck twelve as he lowered her, down onto the fresh, clean linen.

"A new year and a new life—let us begin tonight, my Caterina. Oh, my red angel, forgive me all my sins and let me become a new man in your arms."

He was in bed with her now, kissing her through the fine muslin of her gown. "I remember some skinny red headed brat telling me that the only husband she would ever accept was a fellow who could ride as well as she did?"

"Don't tease! I—I—"

"Didn't you tell me it was nice when we made love up on the mountain?" Above her he smiled, caressed. Then his hard body was upon hers, thrusting her back into the fragrant lavender bed linen. A practiced hand had somehow found entrance between the loose laces of her nightgown, gone to caress her breast. At the same time, kisses fell upon her mouth, her throat, her cheeks.

She began to respond and Christoph drew her onto her side, parted her legs with his. In another moment he'd swept up the nightgown, found the red gold nest. As she wriggled and caught at his wrist, fingers firmly but delicately went to work upon a tender dot of pleasure. After the first shock, there was a softening, a yielding, a flowing.

Wave after wave shot through her. She tossed in his arms, trembling, open.

"My sweet lady..."

How different this was from what Cat had long ago imagined, the act she'd seen in pasture and barn—a chase, a collision—and over! The last of modesty drowning in desire, she arched against him, her only goal to help him keep the pleasure waves crashing in.

She felt helpless, deliciously so. Sometimes she'd protest that this was another seduction, but, ever so smoothly, his beautiful smile mocking, he'd stop her mouth with kisses and when she was distracted, press on again.

All her half-hearted endeavors to escape became entangled with the thing his hand was doing, contributing ever more to the loss of will. Beneath that fine brocade morning gown, her questing hands, suddenly bold, learned that he was naked.

"Dear heaven. You're so beautiful." He bent his curly head to lavish kisses upon her flat belly. Then, with tigerish grace, he mounted.

* * *

Memories of night! That beautiful body of his, muscles illumined by the fire as he bent over the table pouring more wine, the way his dark curls fell over his shoulders as he carried a sparkling glass back to the bed.

She'd cried, conquered by her own feelings, by his skill, but he'd held her against his hard chest and caressed her, soothed her, as tenderly as if nursing a child.

"I've lost again."

"No, silly woman," he murmured, lips against her hair, "you've won. You're going to be both wife and mistress, Caterina." They sipped from the same glass and caressed ever more warmly until, somehow, she'd let him begin again.

Afterward they slept, his arms tight around her. Once she'd been awoken in the night by a noisy shower of sparks as he'd set a couple more logs on the fire. The assurance as he'd come back to bed, the possessive way he'd simply rolled her over and begun, matter of factly, to restart their fire as well, till their two strong bodies were coupled in another bout of that astonishing pleasure.

* * *

Embarrassed by what she remembered, Caterina hid her face in the pillow.

"Oh, no," he said, turning her over. "No more of that. All that happened last night was that I was your husband and you were my wife. Not a feather's weight of sin in it."

He was right, but she still felt shy, so he gathered her against his chest, let her hide her face there and contented himself running his hands over her curves. In the safe haven of his big arms, Caterina lay, her loosened red hair falling in a fabulous cascade across the pillow.

After a time, he shifted. "I'm going to call Goran, call for hot water and breakfast. But," he said, sitting up to pull back the bed curtains, "It's snowing hard again. I think," he said, turning a smile upon her, "that we shall stay right here while I shall engage you in the study of a subject I've badly wanted to teach."

Chapter Fifteen

The news that the Graf von Hagen had taken his lady to bed spread through the manor like wildfire. It could hardly be kept a secret, for good as his word, he kept her in his room and tended, for the first two days of the year to nothing but eating, sleeping and making love to her. Caterina was embarrassed, but, good as his word, Christoph showed her that joy could be found in every position on those instructive bed curtains. Only when the storm died down did they finally emerge, into a world in which the old guard was even more ill at ease than ever, although the usually reserved Herr Stocke had an almost merry twinkle in his pale eyes.

For most of the first day of resumed business, Christoph divided his time between Walter and Stocke, so Cat and Elsa were left alone. In the intimacy of a shared meal, Cat whispered to her pink faced maid that she now understood, (completely, utterly!) why sins of flesh were committed. They spent the day doing as brides and their maids everywhere did, blushing and whispering confidences. Elsa, of course, had been lonely, but she had a full complement of gossip to report.

Wolves and wind howled on Heldenberg. It was a shut in time, limited to that beaten track between the house and the barn, but Caterina hardly felt the confinement. Her husband was occupying her mind and her heart in a way she never would have believed it possible for a mere man to do.

Although summer had witnessed their marriage, the winter provided the perfect time for a most deliciously reclusive honeymoon. Christoph was absolutely tender, absolutely adoring. Caterina bloomed like a rose. There were no more of those dull, tense lord of the manor dinners attended by the bailiff and his wife, by the officers and Herr Stocke. Instead, in the peaceful haven of Christoph's room, Cat would recline in her husband's lap in that big chair before the fire. With the table pulled close, they'd nibble and drink, kiss and talk. Big Furst lay on the Turkish carpet, looking like a black feather duster, grooming himself or just basking by the fire, the privileged sole companion of those long evenings.

One morning near the end of February, Cat lay in Christoph's great arms, blushing as she hadn't in weeks at what he was whispering. The fact under discussion was that she had not used linen since October, a non event her worldly husband had noticed.

Although Cat couldn't really be sure, for she often skipped months at a time, her husband was certain that their very first night of love on the mountain had planted a seed. In the night time privacy of his room, Christoph never neglected to lavish kisses upon the still flat belly that might be nourishing the hoped for child.

* * *

March roared in on a sudden south wind and with it came a good thaw. After a few days of warmth, icy torrents began to come down, every stream that would merely trickle in summer now swollen to a huge, rock rushing cascade. Usually Cat was excited by the first mud season days of spring, anticipating a season of riding and new foals. This year, however, she knew that in late March, Christoph, in company with his men, would once again leave for Vienna. From there he'd travel to the eastern border of the empire to do battle with the Emperor's enemies.

Another unpleasant thing, and not a small one either, was that Josefa was in the house again. She had not pleased the von Beilers, had been moody and intractable, finally insisting upon being sent back to Heldenberg where she had arrived just a few weeks ago.

Her brother in law, Walter, was furious; his wife uncertain and upset. Christoph was first puzzled and then annoyed to see that his effort on her behalf had been, as he put it, "scorned." Herr Walter, it was said, had promptly begun a new correspondence with his widowed cousin. In the meantime Cat daily felt those same sorrowful jealous eyes upon her, could see the desperate, hungry way the Josefa watched her husband.

"Something is going to have to be done about Josefa. To have her moping and brooding around here is unbearable. And Goran told me that he caught her in your room just before dinner today."

"I know," Christoph replied. "But don't worry. She is to go to her cousin just before I leave."

"To be married?"

"For the present she is only to keep house. It seems that even this ardent gentleman has now cooled. He has heard tales about her odd behavior, tales that I think traveled from the von Beiler's."

"She really is terribly unhappy," Cat said. "Every time she looks at me it is plain how much she dislikes me, yet all I can feel now is pity. She seems to be even more obsessed than she was before she went away."

"All the more reason for her to leave. I had hoped that at von Beiler's she'd be able to let all that foolishness go. Their household is so big and always lively. Even Frau Walter, who I'm beginning to think encouraged this nonsense, is at her wit's end and has let her know it, so perhaps she will take her situation seriously."

"Christoph," Caterina said. "Tell me how it was with you and Josefa's sister."

He stared straight at her, considering, and then nodded, resolving to face the past. "That's where all the trouble began, certainly. Josefa always admired Barbara."

"Why didn't you just marry Barbara?" It was a question she'd been pondering for months. Christoph was an only child. And Barbara had borne him those two fine boys.

172

Whether or not Cat would do so was a perfect unknown. Not only the von Velsen patrimony, but that of the von Hagen's was at stake in their marriage. Until now it had been easy enough to play haughty noblewoman and say that Barbara was "not of equal quality," that there had never been any question of Christoph's marrying her. Now that Caterina was carrying a child, she found herself brooding on Barbara and her children more and more.

Where had his heart been in the matter? His honor? It was imperative to understand. "For several years that was what I wanted to do, but it would have been a difficult decision. On one side were Christian and Michael, on the other the long time promises made to your father and to Wili."

"But you knew all that when you started the affair."

"Yes. But love is a force, as I think you understand. Barbara and I fell in love and then had to struggle with the consequences of acting upon it."

"I have heard that you stopped loving her and that is why you went back to Wili."

Christoph's gaze did not waver.

"In fact, Barbara stopped loving before I did, although I'm sure Frau Walter could argue the point."

"And I have heard it said," Cat drew a deep breath and went on, using the hearsay she had gathered, "that you often quarreled."

"Couples quarrel. I had my notions, she had hers."

"It has also been said—" Cat, despite knowing she was treading on thin ice, continued, "that Barbara was a sensible woman and that she found another man and got on with her life when it became clear that she had no hope of persuading you to marry her."

"Caterina, I think Barbara grew up before I did. I was selfish, content to go on not making up my mind. Why should I? I was having my cake and eating it too. She made my mind up for me. Someday perhaps," he said, "you will meet her. She is a great lady."

Cat thought this over. Then she said, "How could she ever stop fighting to make her sons legitimate?"

"Even the best mothers sometimes think of themselves. Barbara followed her happiness. As to the boys' legitimacy, she knew from the day they were born that no matter whatever happened between the two of us, I would never let them suffer."

Cat had subsided into a chair, boyishly drew up her legs under her skirts and wrapped her arms around them. It seemed to help with the tension. Her husband looked down, steadily regarding her. He didn't look happy, but neither did he look guilty.

"It's not a heroic narrative." He said this into the ensuing pause.

Cat ran her long fingers down her braid, soothing herself with the feel of her hair. "So she truly loved her Captain?"

"Yes, and he risked his career to have her. When I came here after a long absence, I was greeted by the two of them hand in hand, asking for my permission to marry. She was already great with his child." A rueful smile appeared at the memory.

Cat looked up with surprise. She tried to imagine the reaction of Theo—or any other man she knew, for that matter—in a similar situation with a trespassing underling and a pregnant mistress. All she could come up with was— murder!

"To do that they certainly must have trusted you."

"I was angry at first. I felt a fool. And I was."

"Why didn't you marry Wili right after that?"

"It would have been the sensible thing to do, but my nearly perfect record of folly hasn't been marred by much." He carefully reached down to catch her hand and press the fingers. "Those days are over, Caterina. I should be punished for my past, but instead I have been given you."

Then he drew her up, out of the chair. Cat knew what he wanted, could see it in his eyes, could feel it in the way his arms came around her waist.

How far we've come, she thought, as his mouth descended to hers. I've heard the whole story now, from these very lips so warmly kissing. And I believe him, love him...

* * *

Cat tried her best to stay out of Josefa's way. At first desire to avoid trouble seemed to be mutual. The day of departure, both for the worrisome servant and for Christoph drew closer.

Then, late one afternoon as Cat was returning from riding, a curvaceous figure stepped from among the shadows just as she crossed the chilly, fireless hall.

"Something has come for you, Grafin," said Josefa, "but it's in the hall." Without waiting for Caterina to say anything, she turned and went through the door into the great room.

Cat, feeling a prickle of unease, followed. For an instant, she entertained a fantasy that Josefa was going to plunge a knife into her heart as soon as she followed. In deference to the notion, Cat passed through the great room door warily, but no one was waiting in ambush. There was Josefa, pale, plump and pretty, standing beside at the dinner table. The seven arm candelabrum was lit and her antagonist stood in the golden glow. The cold empty maw of the hearth opened shadowy behind her.

"Here it is. Something for you, Grafin." Josefa thrust a letter toward her. She did not walk to her mistress and offer it as was proper, but stayed where she was in the light.

The proffered letter seemed to glow, to swim inexorably in Cat's direction. She stepped forward and took it, feeling as if she were suddenly on the edge of that all devouring ravine on the mountain.

"Why, it's a letter from the Graf!" Caterina exclaimed, studying the cover "How did you get it?" Next she saw that the seal had been lifted. "And how dare you open the Graf's letter?" She lifted eyes of green fire to Josefa, but her anger was fearlessly ignored.

"It's a letter a wife ought to read before it goes to Vienna," Josefa said by way of explanation. She took

175

another step back and favored Caterina with a malevolent grin.

As if trapped in a bad dream, Cat opened the letter and read:

My dear Konstanze, This of necessity is to be brief, but I hope it puts to rest all the concerns in your last to me, the receipt of which was long delayed by mishandling. I will soon be leaving here, and should arrive at your door just after this arrives. Unwilling to let you go unanswered, I send a captain of my guard posthaste with this. You may take this letter directly to Herr Fassbender, the banker who is first floor at Unter Tuchlaben on the Judenplatz, and he will release immediately to you two hundred gulden, which should relieve the cruel importunity of your late husband's creditors."

"My sister says this woman had four hundred gulden from him last spring. As much as any musiker can earn in a year." Josefa said it contemptuously.

"Herr Walter says the Graf is crazy about this woman. More than any of his others. She is always crying poverty and he's always running, purse in hand." Keeping a safe distance as she spoke, Josefa smiled, a smile of mad triumph.

And this triumph, Cat thought with a dreadful pang, is over me.

Lowering her head to escape her foe's awful pleasure, she numbly scanned the last paragraph.

* * *

Dear Konstanze, never feel shame or fear to ask a favor of me. Did I not swear to continue as protector? You have suffered much; now take heart and look for my arrival. Christoph von Hagen, Graf Heldenberg

* * *

"You needed your eyes opened." Josefa shouted. "When he took up with this woman it drove my sister crazy

176

and sent her straight into the arms of that low captain! And now our noble Herr Graf makes love to his wife, but once you've dropped the son you've got in your belly, he'll forget all about you. Of course, he'll take care of you, exactly as he does my sister and all the others. He can't find you a new man to warm your bed, but I'm sure he'll see that you have plenty of pretty horses to play with. Perhaps that will provide sufficient consolation." Josefa's dark eyes blazed into Caterina's, filled with the exultation of hatred.

Cat, frozen by the words, didn't move, even when the Josefa suddenly darted forward and snatched the letter away. She simply stood motionless, her world crumbling around her.

It seemed as if a knife, one with a blade of pure ice, had been shoved into her heart.

Josefa letter in hand, went away, left her standing there, and a chilling vision came, one she'd not had since the hot joy of the New Year. It was a memory of Wili, pitifully weeping, prone on her bed.

"I always believe him. Always! Why am I such a fool? All he has to do is put his arms around me and I believe..."

* * *

"Grafin! Grafin!" Elsa was white-faced. "What has happened?"

"Oh, Elsa! Grosse Gott! I'm a fool!"

"A fool? Why—"

"Just like my sister and all the others! I'm leaving and I'm doing it right now."

"Leave? You can't! You mustn't!"

"Hush and help me," Caterina exclaimed, seeing the stricken look on the girl's face.

"Ach, Himmel! Where will you go? How will you get there? The roads are still so bad; a storm could come. What if robbers caught you? And the baby! Oh, Mistress, you must not go!"

Pushing past the frightened young woman, Cat flung herself upon her jewelry box. Yanking out the gold chains

177

her mother had given, she dropped them over her head. As needed, she'd break them apart and exchange them for whatever was needed on her journey home...

"I saw a letter that he wrote to his mistress in Vienna. Josefa showed me."

"Josefa? Don't believe her, my Lady! She hates you!"

"Yes, she does. But this letter was in my husband's handwriting. Oh, Elsa!"

Choking back tears, Cat gave her maid a huge, heartfelt hug. "Elsa, you must be brave. As soon as I can, I'll send for you, I swear it. Now you must promise not to tell I've gone."

"Oh, Mistress—"

Another objection was about to be made, but Caterina didn't wait. Tearing out of Elsa's arms she flew down the stairs, across the great room and out towards the barn. Knowing that because it was near twilight, Rossmann wouldn't allow her to saddle up, Caterina dodged and ducked through the shadows, collecting saddle, blanket and bridle.

There was mad elation in hide and seek. It was just like the old days of disobeying her father...

When she had what she needed, she slipped between the fence poles into a small, muddy barn side enclosure. A ride would surely assuage the awful thunder of her heart!

And here was deliverance. The Andalusian raised his sculpted silver head to stare.

"Come to me, my beauty." She focused upon her desire to the exclusion of all else. As she concentrated, she emptied her mind of everything but him. Calm, and the much needed control came, and so did the Andalusian, bobbing his head, in his customary dance of retreat and advance.

The instant he was within reach, Caterina caught his halter. In the next five busy minutes, she'd snapped on a lead, tied him to the fence and bridled and saddled him.

Usually he was difficult to tack up, but now he seemed to sense her urgency. All the hours she'd spent gaining his confidence this winter, Cat thought, were about to pay off.

In the next moment, she was up. There was a wonderful rush of excitement as she reined him away.

The Spanish stud obeyed her commands, rising straight to a rocking canter. It was ecstasy, the wind in her face, the drum beat of hooves resounding as the silver stallion took high tailed flight across the snow-patched, soggy pasture.

She rode a white whirlwind flying away from all her grief and trouble. She would escape! She would ride, ride, ride, until the pain, the shameful needing love, was hammered from her heart, her mind. She would hide at Aunt Teresina's ruined farm. Some of her Aunt's peasants were still on that land. They knew about keeping secrets...

"Caterina! Caterina!"

Alarmed, she looked over her shoulder. Behind, coming hell for leather, was a big dark man on a dark horse.

Christoph and Brandy! Once again, for the highest stakes, she was the fox!

As soon as she eased her grip on the reins, the Andalusian began a gallop, fairly flying toward the bottom of the pasture. There was a fence, of course, but Cat knew a place where the two top poles were down. Heading toward this, she urged him on with her heels and voice.

As he obediently gathered himself to make the jump, something darted, bolted, crashed away into the bracken on the edge of her vision. It was the headlong flight of a pair of deer who had been boldly mingling with the cattle, sharing their hay.

In this situation, her human eyes saw better than those of the horse. Although she, with all her skill, tried to signal confidence through her hands and legs, the Andalusian's attention was lost. His jump began off lead. There was a crash, then splintering, as the Andalusian's chest and legs hit wood.

"Gottverdammte!"

Snow and mud rushed toward her. From the bottom of her heart she was furious, furious at being caught, furious with herself for taking such a stupid risk with the horse. It

179

was the last thought she had before her head slammed into the ground.

* * *

When she came to, there were lights swirling. She raised a hand to shield her eyes, then groaned at the pain. There was pain in her shoulder, in her back, in her neck, in her knees, in her head.

Everything outside felt skinned. Everything inside felt broken.

"She's coming around."

"Are those idiots ever going to get here with the wagon?"

The arm that supported her could have belonged to no other man, the oak tree feel belonging unmistakably to her Christoph. He was looming over her, studying her face with fearfully.

"Christoph!" She caught at his jacket, "The Andalusian?"

"He's got a long gash at the point of shoulder, but Rossmann says it's not deep. There doesn't seem to be any leg damage, though why, the way he hit that fence, I don't know."

"Thank God and all the saints."

"Yes. Now we've only got you to worry about." He was angry, but there was also fear in his eyes, which she'd never seen there before.

"Damn it, Caterina! What in hell were you were doing?"

"I have to get away from you," she said, despite the shattering headache.

"To where?"

"To where you'd never find me again."

"We thought you were going to get there, too, when the Andalusian failed the jump. Straight to heaven—a place where you certainly won't be bothered by me."

There was a wagon ride back to Heldenberg, then, cradled in her husband's great arms, a painful journey to

180

bed. A drop of laudanum was administered by the Graf himself.

The next day was miserable, passed between pain and sleep. In the afternoon she was poked and prodded by the doctor who had ridden posthaste from far down in the valley. Like the Andalusian she was eventually pronounced "bruised, but essentially sound." Because she had hit her head and was enduring a relentless headache, she was ordered to stay flat in bed.

Elsa ran back and forth to the kitchen, carrying potions and broths from the hand of Ekkehard, clucking over her mistress like a hen. Christoph sat by her side too. He never left, not even while she slept.

"Elsa says you saw a letter I had written."

"Yes."

"And that was why you were running away?"

Cat, her face swollen and bruised, was lying flat as the doctor had ordered. Tears that she couldn't seem to stop were steadily coursing down her cheeks.

"Why, Caterina? Don't you think I can visit Widow Gottlieb, help her in her trouble and not make love to her?"

"That was a love letter. You said you were done with mistresses. You swore. To Wili! To me!"

"I am done with mistresses, and that was not a love letter."

"You visited her on your last trip."

"I did not. Her very talented and very improvident husband was ill. So ill he died just after I got back from Vienna. When she wrote of her difficulties, I had to help."

"Did I not swear at our parting to continue your protector?" Cat quoted the words that had burnt themselves into her memory, throwing them like a handful of rocks.

"The word is tainted, but I am no longer her lover. I wanted to give the widow entree to a banker as soon as possible. I will even show you what she wrote to me—"

Cat waved her hands in the negative, clenched her red brows. The very idea of adding to the nearly unbearable pain!

"My sorry past has left me with obligations, obligations I will not, must not shirk. This lady and her two small children, the youngest of whom, I confess, may be mine, are in danger of debtor's prison."

"The Saint Anne's boy?"

"What?" His eyes flashed rage, a rage which he mastered. He brought his powerful hands to his face and rubbed fiercely.

"A child conceived while you were writing Wili those penitent love letters on your way to fight the Turks!" Caterina accused him. "By Saint Brigitte, Christoph von Hagen," she cried, squeezing her locket, "I will not close my eyes the way you expected Wili to."

"It was my last, crowning folly, the jewel in my crown. Nevertheless, without my help, this lady will end in debtor's prison, along with her children. Consider it, Caterina. Or are you like all the other so called virtuous people I've ever met? Not a drop of real charity in you?" Feeling pity, yet fearing his maneuvering, Caterina began to sob. She didn't want to, but it was impossible to stop. Her head was pounding as if someone had driven a stake into it.

"I'm sorry that you have found this out because I knew exactly how you'd see it. As did Josefa."

"I've been fool enough to love you, even when I know very well that as soon as a woman does that, you are gone."

His handsome face darkened. "So, you believe that I have spent the last three months toying with you, like Furst does with those wretched mice he catches?"

Caterina, tears flowing like a river, nodded.

"Grosse Gott! Justice miscarries when she settles her scores with me by breaking your heart."

Cat, feeling nothing but stony disbelief, replied, "You've made a fool of me, just as you did to poor Wili. Go to your Viennese woman and leave me alone."

"In a few days, Lady Wife, I will. I want some time to visit with my boys and I've got to get to my regiment, or pay a stiff fine for being late. Beyond that, I've a responsibility to my soldiers. We're going to fight the Turks and we must have each other's confidence before we get there."

He leaned against the bedpost and stared at her.

"What a mess! And most of it's my fault as usual, but don't you see that you've a part in it too? God, Caterina, how I wish you could find it in your heart to trust me just a little. Since the day the Wili died, I've tried to do right."

"Go away. You're making my head ache. I want Elsa." Memories of his love making, of the helpless surrender she'd made of her heart and body, filled her mind. How shameful it seemed now, the memory of being rocked, over and over again, night after night, to that glorious annihilation. His pursuit of amorous variety, how he'd had her, always naked, in all those ways, his whispered teasing about her 'long, long filly's legs'...!

There was a pain in her chest that didn't seem to have anything to do with her injuries. It felt as if her guts had been pulled out and were being tossed into a fire before her eyes.

* * *

On the night following, Caterina awoke crying, crying with a new pain, one that swiftly overcame all the others. At the first sound both Elsa and Christoph were beside her. After some terrible cramps, the worst she'd ever felt in her life, a gush of blood filled Caterina's maidenly bed.

"Well, if you were thinking that I'd lose interest as soon as you'd produced an heir," Christoph observed miserably, after the servants had gone out with the bloody sheets and clothes, "the time has been postponed."

"It wasn't a miscarriage!" Cat shrieked at him. She felt like an animal harried to death, the quarry at the end of a hunt. "I was never carrying anything of yours! It's just another of your lies. To make me feel worse than I already do!"

Her husband arose from the bed beside her, his handsome face filled with despair.

"If you really think that, then God help us both."

* * *

Christoph stood by Cat's bed, dressed in his uniform. He looked anguished, but every bit as masterful and lordly as he had on the day on which they'd married.

"When you get up, Cat, you'll find that the house has been almost emptied, "from kitchen to the door keepers. Everyone who appears to have more of an allegiance to the past than to me has been dismissed. I've no time to find more staff and, frankly, my confidence in Walter has been shaken. Stocke will be sharing responsibility with him now, and if anyone new is hired, he will be the one to do it. We have a new woman to cook, one from Heldenruhe. Ekkehard will be leaving with me, to begin his apprenticeship in my Cousin Wagensperg's kitchens in Vienna. Fraulein Josefa will go to Heldenruhe tonight with her sister and from there to Passau. I have told them, and I think they understand, that her enmity has robbed me of the ability to do anything more for her. I cannot predict who she will next harm. I'm taking horses, so there will be fewer grooms. I shall sell the trotters and some of the mares and yearlings in Vienna."

"Your beautiful trotters?" This surprised Cat more than anything else he'd said. The removal of staff she'd been hearing about from Elsa.

"I'm a bit short of cash this spring, little wife. And four are an unnecessary bachelor's indulgence. I had intended to take the Andalusian along with Brandy, but now he's not fit. I'll get another war horse from my father on the way."

She felt sorry, knowing how proud he'd been of his matched pairs, so she stretched out her hand. He accepted it, tenderly kissed her fingers.

"It may be an entire year before I return. If, when you are better, you still think you ought to return to your parents, you are at liberty to do so. Herr Goran, whom I've left here to care for you, will accompany you."

Surprised, she opened her mouth to speak, but he reached down and rested the gentle tips of his fingers against her lips. "This is quite a long speech, so let me finish. I don't think that running home is wise, but do whatever it is you think you must. As long as you remain here at Heldenberg, you are the lady of the house and my wife. Perhaps you will decide to wait until I return. If you do, then we will try once again to regain what I hoped we'd found."

He sat down on the edge of the bed beside her. His eyes were sad, almost bereft of any but the darkest color.

"Now, Caterina, I intend to lecture. It seems to me that just as much as a man owes his wife fidelity and all his tenderness, she owes him trust. If you can't find it in your heart to trust me and believe in my love a little, I think it would be best if you did return to your father." He gently tilted her chin and brushed her lips very softly with his.

"Aufweidersehen, little wild cat. Apply yourself to your lessons. I've told Herr Walter that everything is to be open to you, particularly the accounts. If he is uncooperative, tell Herr Stocke. Please write to me often, tell me about Heldenberg. If worse comes to worst and the Turks finish me, you shall at least end as an educated widow."

"Oh, Christoph, don't say—"

"Perhaps these are words spoken to the wind," he interrupted, "but let me repeat one last time that I love you, Caterina Maria Brigitte."

Caterina couldn't believe it when the door closed behind him. Would he ever return? And would she be there to meet him?

* * *

Lying in her bed, head aching, surveying parts of herself where various swellings, cuts and bruises changed color daily, Caterina felt as isolated as if she were marooned. Elsa was poor company, all her thoughts on Ekkehard, now gone to Vienna. Not three days after Christoph and his entourage of soldiers, servants and horses left, another huge spring storm swept the mountain, blanketing the land in white and cutting them off from the

185

outside world again. The manor seemed eerie now, with its closed doors and silent passages. When she was up and around, the similar emptiness in the great barn and at the barracks surprised her as well. So many people and animals were gone.

Cat's headache resolved itself in a few weeks, but there was a month of aches and pains, as all the various stiffnesses and swellings subsided and abraded skin repaired itself. Herr Stocke immediately set Cat piles of work which she embraced without argument. Buried under dozens of arithmetic problems or deep in the study of some ancient back and forth wrangle between warring Electorates, Caterina could, for a little while, forget her heartache.

She did discover a new boon companion. Christoph's cat, Furst, made a sudden decision that Caterina was his. When Elsa and the new cook's girl carried up dinner in the evening, their parade was headed by the black tom, his bushy long tail waving like a battle flag. Furst spent much of each lonely evening on Caterina's lap. Most nights she fell asleep with her hand resting on the warm, fluffy belly which he, flopped in the bedclothes beside her, presented for rubbing.

Chapter Sixteen

Green began to crown the forest. Tall drifts in the lee of the pines sagged, crystallized, sending streams down the slopes. Later than in her Donau valley home, so that Cat was simply longing for it, came spring. Looking out the window at night, she could see the mares standing in the horse pasture, great bellies silhouetted by the moonlight. Among them was her Star.

Christoph wrote to her faithfully. He told her of Vienna, of the mustering of the troops. Later came tales of battle in the lands of the Croats and Slovenes, of skirmishes on the Hungarian plains. There was little news about the state of his heart. Caterina fretted that the letters which Elsa received from her Ekkehard, although short and badly spelled, were a thousand times more passionate. She tried to concentrate upon her studies, but when she couldn't endure sitting for another moment she went to the stables where a friend—no, an admirer—waited.

All through that lonely spring Cat's pleasure in the company of Herr Rossmann had grown. Now a white smile flashed whenever Cat came into view. Star too had grown to trust him while her mistress had been sick. Now, even if the mare was loose in pasture, she'd come when Rossmann whistled. Tossing her five point blaze like a high spirited filly, she'd cheerfully allow Rossmann everything. It was almost funny to remember that once Caterina had thought the horsemaster threatening and taciturn.

These days they had plenty to talk about. Mistress and man compared remedies for worms, bot fly and injured pasterns. He explained how he'd worked his cure upon Brandy, talked about training and breeding, and lamented the loss of so many fine horses from the Graf's stables. They rode out together and he showed her field and forest in another way than Christoph had. Rossmann's interest was in herbs peculiar to the mountain. He even paid her the high compliment of showing her secret places where delicious morels grew.

Suddenly, one day, the thought that Rossmann was actually rather handsome chased through her mind. His dark eyes were full of a high intelligence, and his slender, limber frame was strong and erect. Even his flowing black moustache, which had once seemed so sinister, appeared as fitting and manly, part of what she had come to appreciate as "eastern style."

It was obvious that he admired her, too. Their uneasy awareness of the boundaries that lay between mistress and man, Christian and Orthodox, Slav and German, sounded other notes of uneasy excitement. While Caterina was currying great bellied Star, Rossmann often leaned over the wall and visited. It was during one of those chats that she told him about the day when one of her father's stallions had taken a run at her.

"My friends were scared and I should have been," Cat explained. "He came charging across the pasture at us. He was a big gray Wurttemburg and he just looked so beautiful." Rossmann nodded, apparently imagining the scene.

"He came right up to us and began rearing, smashing his hooves down close to me, threatening and trying to get us to run, but I told my friends not to move a muscle and I stretched out my hand. Finally, he stopped his battle dance and lowered his head so that I could touch him. After, he snorted, whirled around and went high tailing away. Understanding horses is the one natural born skill I have." She paused to tug a burr from Star's creamy tail.

She was thinking of the way the accounting problems which Herr Stocke had set stubbornly refused to reconcile. "I'm afraid I'm a rather poor gentleman's wife."

Rossmann's eyes, jet black and lively, turned towards her with that new respect.

"You make a fine wife for a countryman, Mistress."

* * *

Doggedly, every day, Caterina returned to doing as her mother had suggested, going to the great room to approve while morning orders were given to the diminished staff by the new housekeeper. Later in the day, before supper, she'd endure her chilly company as she followed up on the progress of the day's work. In spite of the curt replies, Cat began to garner some understanding of the ins and outs of housekeeping at Heldenberg.

When warm weather came, she'd take Elsa and walk after dinner. She particularly loved to stand at the edge of the pasture and look up at the stars. The looming mountain, the pine scented air, reminded her of evenings with Aunt Teresina, who, on similar evening walks, had told her tales about the heroes, goddesses and dragons who battled across the night sky. When she was alone, Herr Rossmann sometimes joined her, always making a sudden, startling appearance at her elbow.

"A beautiful night, is it not, Mistress?"

"Indeed, it is," she replied, with more feeling than she'd intended. "There's the dragon," she added, hoping to cover how glad she'd been to see him.

"Yes. In my land it is called 'dragon,' too."

"Do you know the constellations? My Aunt Tanucci taught me a little, but I've forgotten most of it."

It turned out that Rossmann knew the sky intimately, although here and there he made groups differently from the way Cat had been taught. He even had names for single bright stars, explaining that the Spanish Moors, who had been a very learned people, had named them. They, he said, knew things about history, mathematics and healing that no other Westerners did.

It became a pastime on clear nights to stand at the pasture fence and stare up, Herr Rossmann pointing and

Cat sighting along his arm. Elsa would huddle at her mistress' feet wrapped in her cloak, shivering and yawning and wishing for bed. Nights on the mountains were always chilly, even standing in the warm exhalation of the barn.

It was often very late when Cat said good bye to Rossmann. On their way back to the house, she and Elsa would acquire another companion. Black Furst would emerge, a moving shadow, usually coming from the good hunting ground close to the haystack. He'd growl a throaty meow and wave his fluffy tail in greeting. Sometimes the meow was muffled because his mouth was full of mouse.

"Have you got all your business tended to, Herr Furst?" Cat bent to scratch his round head and give his blocky body a hearty all-over rub. Then the three of them would walk back to the manor together.

She sensed a general disapproval of this star gazing, particularly from Herr Goran. Predictably, Goran had been upset when his master had 'detailed' him to Heldenberg, making no bones about his opinion that Christoph's chances of survival were next to nothing without him. The Hauptmann was always moody and sometimes drunk. He'd go out of his way to pick fights with the guards. Without his master, he seemed at loose ends.

"Why don't you get Hauptmann Goran to give you fencing lessons?" Stocke had suggested one day. "He's not as spry as Heidelburg on that wooden leg of his, but he's far less likely to blood you to make a point. Besides, it would give him something to do."

"It's an idea, Herr Stocke." Cat had been sorely missing the exercise of foil ever since Heidelburg had gone away with Christoph. "But do you think he might be offended?"

"Ask him, my Lady. I have a feeling that he'd be glad of a task. I've heard he was a master of saber in his day."

When the proposition was first put to him, Goran cocked his head to one side and slowly stroked one of his flaxen moustaches with a thick hand. "Well, I'm no stylist, Grafin." Then, with a sudden grin he added, "But there's nobody like me in all of the Osterreich to teach you how to win a real fight."

At the time of Cat's first fencing lessons with Captain Heidelburg, Goran had been openly dubious about her ability, but, like everyone else he'd been impressed by Caterina's quick reflexes, her determination and her obvious athleticism. Besides, if his master felt it was all right for his wife to learn saber, it was not his place to argue.

Toweling the sweat from her face after the first lesson, Caterina said, "I think you're a far better teacher than Heidelburg, at least in my humble woman's opinion. I swear, I saw so many new things today."

"Thank you, Grafin." Goran too was sweating, his broad leathery face lit by a rare broken- toothed smile. "A woman, even a strong one like you, Grafin, or even half a man like me," he nodded ruefully down at his wooden stump, "will never have the strength to beat a whole man, but we can still sharpen up some tricks that could save our lives, even against a much stronger opponent."

Caterina's days were full. There was studying with Herr Stocke, making the rounds with the housekeeper, riding the land and now her saber practice.

* * *

One night as Cat walked back from the barn arm in arm with Elsa, who was lighting their way with a small lantern, she noticed a man leaning against a shed. It was a vantage point, she knew, that would allow the watcher a clear view of the little rise where she and Rossmann customarily went for their star-gazing.

"Come out," she cried, exercising those new tones of command she'd been practicing. "I see you perfectly."

The peculiar rolling gait as the man obeyed instantly betrayed who it was.

"Herr Goran, what is the meaning of this?"

With his wooden leg tapping over the uneven ground, he approached.

"I am watching over you, Grafin."

"Well, I've Elsa with me. Surely Herr Rossmann is protection enough."

"Begging your pardon, Grafin, but my orders are to watch you."

"Why?" Caterina experienced a wave of anger, for suddenly she thought she understood. "You are spying on me, aren't you, Goran? Skulking and spying."

"Oh, Lady Caterina..." A protest came from Elsa, who had a genuine fondness for the older man.

"Hush, Elsa. Hauptmann Goran can speak for himself."

Goran repeated, "I must keep watch over you, Grafin."

"By Mary and all the Archangels!" Inwardly Caterina damned Christoph. "Is this my husband's order?" Did he imagine she was as dishonest as he was?

"I am always the Graf's man, Lady."

"Indeed? Well, sir, I think your action insults me."

"Lady von Hagen." The command ringing in another male voice made both Goran and Caterina spin to face the newcomer.

"Do not be angry with Herr Hauptmann, Mistress. I have enemies here who would say anything to get me dismissed. As do you, still, Grafin." Rossmann, materialized out of the darkness, drawn by the sound of voices.

"I am not one of your enemies, Grafin," Goran rumbled. "No matter what this clever heathen says."

Elsa gasped, stumbled backwards. She saw, as her mistress did, the flash of Goran's steel. Next, as if in a mirror, flashed Rossmann's dagger.

"Stop it! Both of you!" Bravely, if not too wisely, she stepped between them.

"Of course, Grafin," said Rossmann, bowing and backing in order to keep a safe distance between him and the Croat. "Herr Hauptmann," Rossmann said formally, squarely facing his enemy, "you mistake me. I am saying that as long as you watch, no one will be able to tell the Graf any lies."

Goran growled, but slammed his steel back into the sheath.

"I'm sorry to offend," he mumbled.

Caterina could tell by his wooden tone that his feelings had been hurt.

"I do whatever I do by the Herr Graf's orders." With an awkward gesture of gallantry he waved her forward. "Will you go in?"

She looked around, but Rossmann had melted away into the night like a spirit, no doubt heading for his meticulously kept cottage. There was nothing else to do but walk on in silence.

Just as they reached the front door, Goran observed tautly, "Herr Rossmann is no company for you to keep in the night, Grafin."

"Why? Because you imagine he's a Muslim?"

"Grafin, I do not wish to quarrel. I know you admire his learning just as the Graf does, but you shouldn't trust him too much."

"And should I trust you more? You who watch me in secret?"

There was no reply to her jibe. At the door Goran stepped forward and opened it, bowing the two women inside. The doorman, who'd been dozing on the bench in the hall, leapt to his feet, groping for his sword.

"Is this how you guard the house?" Goran pushed past Caterina and dealt a blow to the man's head. "If I were a bandit, you'd be dead now, damn you! Here is the Graf's lady, safe and sound, no thanks to you."

"Hauptmann!"

"Discipline must be maintained!" Goran shouted back.

He was right, of course, and the doorman was rising to his feet without help. Cat knew Christoph would have been just as angry. To sleep on duty was to put the entire house in danger. The doorman tugged a forelock in Cat's direction, looking profoundly guilty.

"Herr Lenker, you must do better."

"Yes, Grafin. It will not happen again."

Putting away her dislike of such scenes, Caterina walked towards the stairs. Goran accompanied her. She knew he'd walk her to the door of her chamber.

193

At the foot she paused to survey the man beside her. In the light of Elsa's lantern she saw the lines that tragedy and profound reserve had etched. She was now ashamed she'd accused him of spying. No doubt it was just as he'd said and he was following her husband's orders—to the letter.

"Herr Hauptmann."

"Yes, Grafin."

"Outside—I misunderstood. I thank you for such attention to your duty."

"I follow orders." His fair, balding head inclined, but in spite of her apology there was absolutely no change in the severity of his tone or the disapproving expression in his eyes. He hated her friendship with Rossmann and that was all there was to it.

"I wish you could like Herr Rossmann better, Hauptmann. Like my husband, I need you both, your loyalty and your wisdom." Knowing that the stiff necked fellow wouldn't give an inch, she retreated up the stairs.

* * *

On the eve of Saint Brigitte's day the entire household went down to Heldenruhe to Mass and then to join in the feast and dancing. Caterina had a steer driven down, a gesture of largess towards the peasants.

Among the few who didn't go were Caterina and Herr Rossmann. Ordinarily, Caterina would have, for lately she'd been a regular church-goer. There was Wili to pray for and now the welfare of her absent husband. Of course, Cat would have loved to watch the dancing and bonfires, but on this May eve she suspected Star was about to deliver her long awaited foal. The mare had restlessly moved to the highest reaches of the north pasture and flatly refused to let either Caterina or Rossmann take her back to the barn.

"In this she isn't wise, my Lady. Wolves were seen here last week."

"Well, go get your gun and come back. I'll stay with her."

Cat was a little surprised when Rossmann, without a murmur of protest, did as she asked. For awhile she looked around, eyes straining beyond the circle of lantern light into the darkness.

Did the clump of boulders shining in the field below conceal Herr Goran? And did Rossmann know he was there and say nothing out of a belief that his watchfulness was a kind of protection for both of them?

After the night of the uproar, Cat had not detected Goran again. Nevertheless there was a constant prickly sense that someone was watching her.

* * *

Almost as soon as Rossmann was out of earshot, Star went into labor. Caterina did not waste another thought on anything else. About an hour later, the moon just rising over the dark shoulder of Heldenberg, a slice past full, the foal emerged. The mare had gone down to do it, and Cat, sitting beside her and stroking her head, was relieved. It had gone perfectly. A surge of joy shot through her as she pulled the foal's wet caul away and massaged her wet heaving sides. Star had made another filly!

As she did that, the mare staggered to her feet. Caterina gazed at her, silhouetted against the starry night. Trees loomed beyond the pasture; spines of mist like dragon's breath rose from the creek. The mountain made a rough black triangle beneath the waning moon. The mare was still licking the steaming gangly heap when Rossmann returned, leading one of the ponies. "A beauty, Grafin," he said cheerfully. "After she stands and nurses, we'll put her over the pony and Star will follow us back to the stable. I don't think she'll argue with us anymore."

Star's elegant head began to angle back and forth, nervously scenting a freshening wind. Her fine ears swiveled, then pricked. The night had been dead still, but now a cold blew down from the heights.

A strange sound, a kind of wailing, came with it. The forest shook and sighed. Caterina had felt quite brave, even

195

alone in the thin moonlight, but at this eerie noise every hair on the back of her neck stood up.

"Ready the gun!"

"No need, Mistress." Rossmann added something under his breath, something not in German. "Star will catch your fear. It's not wolves. See?"

He lifted an arm, pointed up the dark flank of the mountain. Cat, following his gesture, saw a slim rising tongue of fire.

"They won't bother us. It is hexerei. Witches."

Cat's jaw dropped, but Rossmann was matter of fact.

"On May Eve they dance. They sing and drink." Contemptuously, he spat. Cat couldn't tell whether it was witches who elicited his disgust or the notion of drinking alcohol. His abstinence made another strong argument for those who believed him to be Muslim.

"Real witches?" Caterina felt her knees tremble. "My father said there was no such thing."

"They are real and they are everywhere. In my country too." The mare was pushing the foal with her nose, trying to get it onto its spindly legs.

"Where is your country, Rossmann?" Cat had always wanted to ask. She'd heard so many tall tales, and now, alone, it seemed the moment to dare it.

"Far away east. Through the forests and then to where they disappear. By the Tisza River where the great Hungarian plains lie beneath the sky."

"Plains? All flat? All pasture?"

"Yes, but wider and drier than you, Mistress, have ever seen. The sky comes down to meet the waving grass. Horses and cattle roam there."

"Is that where you learned so much about animals?"

"Yes, Mistress. My family owned great herds."

Above them on the mountain, a strongly rhythmic, robust chant began. Rossmann looked away.

"On the mountain—they—sound happy," Cat hesitantly suggested.

"Well, magic is sometimes good."

"But the priests say they are bad."

196

"Pardon me, Mistress, but your priests are ignorant men. Hexerei pray for things peasant and noble alike need—for good harvests, for many lambs and calves, for strong children."

He was staring at her now, staring as if he had cat's eyes, could pierce the darkness to see straight down to the depths of her soul. Cat's skin prickled. She could almost feel his mind reaching to touch hers, just as he did with the horses. Suddenly she was not only nervous about wolves and witches, but about the mysterious Herr Rossmann too.

"When I was a boy," Rossmann said softly, "my grandfather took me to see a hexe. She lived in a cave in the one high place I'd ever seen. She did good sometimes and evil sometimes, but on that day she gave me a present."

"A present?" His confidential, whispery tone sent shivers along Cat's spine.

"The power over horses."

Curiosity instantly overcame her alarm.

"Is that why Star was so quick to let you handle her?"

"In the Cave of the Red Horse, the power was given to me."

"The Cave of the Red Horse?"

"A very powerful place, Mistress. The ancient ones painted many animals on the walls, many cattle and horses, many creatures that have gone away to far lands, many animals that no longer live on those plains, or anywhere else, I think."

The foal was up now, tottering on those long legs and nosing for a teat. Star, despite her skittishness with humans, was a surprisingly calm mother. She gently nudged the baby close.

"And where did you meet your hexe, Mistress?"

"What?" Caterina couldn't quite believe her ears.

"The one who gave you your power."

Her tongue became immovable, but Caterina felt the compulsion of his eyes. It was as if she were a horse he was talking into standing still for something that would hurt. Reflexively, her hand flew to the Protector.

"I've—I've—never met a hexe. My Aunt Tanucci taught me about animals, but it wasn't magic, it was just learning to understand their ways—" Her voice trailed away as she recalled, with a chill, the sacrifice her Aunt's peasants had made.

"My hexe gave me a mark," said Rossmann in a voice filled with soft persuasion. "It was a blue spiral. Do you have one?"

Cat knew this was wildly impertinent, but she could not control the surge of panic that followed. It was all she could do to keep from running away across the pasture.

"No!" she cried. Her hand gripped the locket. "What do you mean?"

"I apologize if I have upset you, Mistress." Rossmann's gaze shifted away, as if his question had never been asked. "It is a thing of my people. Ah, look! The foal suckles."

It was a welcome distraction, the sight of that delicate head tucked under her mother's belly. Cat rejoiced to see it, for this meant they could soon go back to the barn. There they'd be out of the darkness, away from the wolves, witches, Rossmann's weird conversation and whatever other mysteries lurked tonight on the shoulders of Heldenberg.

That was when a movement by that nearby outcropping attracted her eye. This time, instead of anger, she felt an enormous wave of relief. In spite of the lure of May Day festivities, she and Rossmann were not alone.

* * *

Not much later she was able to slip a lead on Star's halter. The mare was fidgety, but with her mistress' soothing, she allowed herself to be led, allowed Rossmann to pick up the long legged baby and put her across the pony's back. Caterina, who had already mounted steadied the damp, wondering creature in her arms.

"I've worried you." Rossmann spoke again as they set off for the barn.

Caterina didn't reply.

"I am sorry, Mistress. Sometimes I forget that I am not on the plains, that this is more—ah—civilized." Cat caught the tone. She had come to realize that he often spoke ironically. "That, up there..." She indicated the still visible flare of orange, "is not what I would call civilized."

"Perhaps, but many folk share it. Best you say nothing about what you saw. Many of your best peasants are on the mountain tonight and your priests still burn witches. And after the hunting of witches starts, no one—neither high nor low—is safe."

Cat nodded, only too vividly remembering the cruelties that had followed the burial of her aunt.

"They are mistaken about the nature of God, Mistress, but hexerei know many useful things. Where they are all destroyed, much wisdom is lost."

In this speech Caterina heard an echo of the rationalist professor Herr Stocke waxing philosophical, saying that the search for knowledge was the one eternal and unchanging goal of mankind.

"Some thought my Aunt Teresina was a hexe," Cat admitted as they slowly walked along. "After she died, the rumor brought suffering to her peasants. Believe me, Herr Rossmann, I know how to keep silent."

* * *

By the time they made their slow way back to the barn, pink fingers were tracing the east. Only a thin trail of smoke remained visible upon the mountain.

A couple of men were approaching, emerging from the cover of the eastern forest. Cat wasn't particularly surprised to see that it was Goran and one of the younger grooms. As they drew closer, she saw how tired they looked. Obviously they had spent the night keeping watch over her.

Goran played his part well, jesting about "staying to watch the pretty country girls dance at Heldenruhe". Then he solemnly congratulated Caterina on the safe delivery of her new "baby". She accepted his congratulations with pleasure.

199

After lifting the foal down, Rossmann and Cat led the horses to a box stall which had been prepared with fresh straw, a good feed of oats and a bucket of water. Star swiveled her ears and her dark eyes rolled.

She was rather nervous about all the people who came to look, but she let Cat lead her. The baby, already stronger, walked along beside her, whisking a stubby little tail.

Soon there was a small crowd as servants and the milkmaids came to admire Star's foal. Everyone looked tired, much the worse for wear. Wherever they'd been celebrating, down in Heldenruhe, or up on the mountain, they seemed cheerful, in spite of the fact that they still had a day's work to get through.

"I hoped the foal would be a white, like the beautiful Papa," said a young milkmaid. How pretty she looked with that wilted wreath of spring flowers in her hair! "But she's exactly like her mother."

"Exactly," A tall, lanky groom agreed.

They watched as the foal, her blonde tail waggling, began to feed. Star stood still, her elegant head turning from side to side, regarding her well wishers solemnly.

"She looks so proud."

"Just as any mother of a fine babe ought to be," said Herr Goran.

Caterina felt an edge to this. It seemed to her that everyone, from Elsa to the grooms, had lately been keeping up a constant stream of praise for motherhood. Suddenly, Caterina wished with all her heart that Christoph were here, standing beside her. She knew he too would be delighted to see this new, beautiful creature.

"What will you call her, Grafin von Hagen?"

"I think Mai would be perfect."

Everyone present smiled and nodded agreement, while Caterina fingered her locket and pondered all the queer happenings of the night just passed.

* * *

"My Dear Christoph," Caterina slowly wrote. "Star dropped her foal on the first day of May before dawn. Rossmann and I were ready for she seemed restless and insisted upon staying way up in the north pasture. Rossmann got his gun, but no wolves came down, thank heaven, and thank Saint Brigitte—and some others—who watched over us. We didn't get back until sunrise because the pasture is so steep and the pony he'd brought had to go slowly. I named the foal Mai for the day and she is so much like her dam. She grows more nimble and frisky every hour. I am down in the barn every day with them but Herr Stocke will tell you that I do not neglect my studies or attending to the business of your house."

Caterina hoped that was right. She was certain Christoph would be delighted to hear about Star's foal. Suddenly, she wondered if Christoph knew about the May Day fires on the Heldenberg, but decided that as Rossmann advised, the less said the better.

Now, she thought, for the hard part, the part she'd tried to write over and over again. From a pigeon hole in the desk she withdrew a paper, one covered with many blots and scratchings out, and slowly began to copy from it.

"I know that I am not a good housekeeper as Wili would have been but I am following the housekeeper although she does not like it and I am learning. Widow Lotz is nicer than Ute ever was and a good teacher too."

Cat sighed and studied this last part. Did it need commas? Then, unbidden, intruding upon her grammatical meditations, the terrible image of Wili's limp body appeared, the light gone forever from her kind eyes.

"Oh, dear Wili," Cat sighed the words aloud. "I know you forgave him. You always did. Now I must learn to do that and to trust him too. That woman in Vienna fell in love with him and I know exactly how it happened. Just like you always said, dear Wili, cruelty is easy. It's love that's hard."

Cat bent over the paper again, dipped the quill and tapped it on the edge of the well, praying she wouldn't blot the so far perfect letter.

"I shall trust to your honor and to your judgment and also hope you were able to help the lady through her trouble to whom you are obligated."

She paused and nibbled on the feather, wanting to get the words just right. Finally she copied from her practice sheet:

"If it is your wish that I remain at Heldenberg, I shall and endeavor to do my duty as your wife because it is the will of my parents and of my Oncle Rupert and also..."

Cat paused, consulted her heart and then wrote in a swift scrawl, "because it is my greatest and most carefully considered desire. Your wife, who prays every day for your safety and for your speedy return. Caterina, Grafin von Hagen."

Chapter Seventeen

She still couldn't believe what she saw when she opened her eyes. There was the same morning light, the same sun that shone on her at home, shining through the bars of a room that had become her cage.

Her past, the wild Heldenberg, her freedom—all of it gone! Lost to a chimera of wanting, a dream that she would ride to find her man, that this would prove her true, true love, this facing danger for him…and what had it brought? Nothing but death and destruction to those who had bent to the folly of her desire and will…

And Rossmann—that traitor! Everything Goran had said and more—who had encouraged her, who had ridden with her knee to knee, who had smiled and taught her from his store of knowledge, who had so completely gained her trust all through that lonely, fatal summer…

* * *

Images from the past weeks flooded her mind as soon as she came to consciousness. She'd traveled the long road to Passau, boarding the ship. Then down the Danube, the glitter of Vienna, where she'd left Elsa in the house of those Wagensperg cousins in whose kitchen Ekkehard labored, all of this passing like a dream.

No time to wait!

She must reach her husband—must have the joy of his arms around her! Days were spent watching the glittering water, nights almost too excited to sleep. They left the river and rode into Hungary, which had been nearly swallowed by the Turks at the time of their last incursion half a century ago. Over the last eighty years some parts had won free again. With armed men, with Rossmann and faithful Goran, they set a course for the camp where the last letter had come from Christoph.

Caterina was something beyond happy. She rejoiced in the freedom of traveling, in the strength in her young body, in her purpose. She headed east with all the determination of a migrating bird.

Rossmann, who had spent the summer encouraging her to make this journey, seemed to share her delight; he seemed almost giddy. Goran was anxious, angry that his advice had not been listened to and clearly worried about the danger into which they were going.

Graf von Hagen's main company was found at the camp when they arrived, but he and his cavalry were away on a raiding mission. A week passed of restless waiting. Caterina, encouraged by Rossmann, pursued the idea of riding out to find him. Everyone else she'd brought from home—and the commander of the camp—had flatly said it was a bad idea.

"You are in danger here, Grafin. Outside this camp the roads in every direction are filled with bandits and enemy soldiers. You should wait here for your husband to return." Goran heartily agreed. "Best we wait as the commander says. Be patient. The Herr Graf will return. Besides, we don't know where he'll come from. You could ride out and miss him, putting yourself in danger for nothing. Staying here is safer than a wild goose chase." But Caterina, feeling so near to her husband, had been on fire to push on. Rossmann was reassuring, saying that he knew the land here like the back of his hand.

"Of course Goran is cautious. He is a brave man, but he is from the mountains to the south, not so familiar with this territory as I am. But," he'd ended, his dark eyes sparkling, "what better way to show the Graf the strength of your devotion?"

After a few more days, over the objections of the commander, but accompanied by men he'd provided, Cat,

Goran and Rossmann had ridden east. She'd been scared but sure all would go well, that she would find her husband quickly. On the second day out, just as Goran had begun to insist they turn back, they'd been caught by a large Turkish raiding party. It had burst upon them out of dense thicket which lay on the north side of the road.

The soldiers fought like tigers, but there were simply too many. All around her men fell. Her escort, Major von Hoffmann, urged her to turn and ride, ride for her life, but then blood spurted from his mouth, spilling down his buff waistcoat. Looking surprised, he'd pitched forward onto the ground.

She had turned Star and ridden as fast as she could, calling for Goran. Together they made a run for it, but were cut off. There were so many! A crowd of them seized Goran's horse and forced him off it. He disappeared from view, a wounded boar disappearing beneath a host of dogs. The air was rent with shouting, and swords flashed and fell upon the fallen man.

When the Turks tried to catch Star's bridle, the mare reared and kicked. It took several men and foot ropes to hold her. From somewhere, Rossmann, the only one of her entourage left alive, appeared. Now he stood beside Caterina, waving and shouting something in a language the enemy understood.

"Don't do anything, Grafin. I'll keep you safe."

And he somehow had. As his talk was all in that strange language, Caterina didn't know why. Slipping to the ground and bowing, slave-fashion before his captors, Rossmann had apparently explained that the horse would only go with them willingly if they left the red haired girl on her back.

Caterina was trapped. She was sick with fear, rage—and guilt. Surrounded by barbarian soldiers, laughing and crowing to each other in their raucous tongue, a long march of days began. Curiously, neither of she nor Rossmann was tied and he was allowed to ride beside her.

"Their Ban, their head man, wants Star," he explained, "and I think he may want you too, but the Pasha will be the one to decide."

Caterina tried to hold back her tears, but, during the long days of travel, many fell. She wept for brave Captain Hoffmann and the men who had died trying to save her. She also feared for her husband, for Rossmann said that he'd overheard their captors boast of destroying an Austrian raiding party.

The greatest pain came with the realization that it was her fault. Despite what the soldiers—what the faithful Goran—had advised, she had been head-strong, had brought this disaster about.

Now, as they rode away, she saw that the Turks had taken fresh territory. There were gruesome burned villages, signaled long before they were seen by a stench that rose to heaven and a sky darkened by whirling carrion birds. Caterina hid her eyes from the heaps of splayed and bloated things that had once been men and women.

By night she could see the stars, see they were heading due east. Through forest and over a mountain pass they traveled, at last descending into a river valley. "The Tisza", said Rossmann. "It flows through those plains I told you about, past the place where I was born."

They had taken all her jewelry, the golden chains her mother had given her, the pearl earrings that had been a birthday present from Christoph, her wedding band. After she'd carefully opened the wooden locket and showed the picture inside, they had, to Cat's great relief, lost interest in that. Rossmann gave her a scarf to wrap around the lower part of her face and head which kept out the dust and also moderated the eternal gawking of the men. At first, she was simply glad for Rossmann's protection, but as they rode on, suspicion swelled into fear.

How relaxed he seemed, and on what easy terms with their captors!

Indeed, Rossmann had said he knew the country well, but as one day and then another passed, he never said a word about escape. When she put it to him, he said, "It's not wise to even talk about, Grafin."

"Why?"

"Because if we tried, I can tell you exactly what would happen. To start," Rossmann said simply, "They'd kill me and then they'd all make use of you. If you didn't die of their ill treatment, they'd sell you. There are, truly, fates worse than death."

She'd shuddered, but managed to ask another question.

"Well, why haven't they—done that already?"

Rossmann smiled again, the way a man smiles when he has a secret.

"I have told them that uninjured, you are worth a large ransom."

* * *

Upon the plain, the trees dwindled away until they were nothing more than bushy scrub. All around golden grasses hissed in an ever present wind.

Rossmann announced with ill concealed delight that they were on the plains of Hungary. It was his home place!

As they rode knee to knee, Rossmann began to tell stories about his past, about how his family had herded cattle and horses on these very plains. With a chill, Cat realized that all he said was clear confirmation of everything Goran—now a body left behind—had said of him. "I thought you said you were from the land of the South Slavs."

"I am a South Slav by blood, a Bogomil, but my people converted to the true religion—Islam—in my grandfather's time. He followed a war lord into Hungary in the reign of Selim the Great."

Rossmann smiled; Caterina felt her face pale.

"Ah, yes, Goran was right. Your husband knew, but he's not a believer. A non believer can never entirely understand the strength of those of us who do."

Caterina's head spun with so many questions, so many suppositions, but she dared not speak. Her rage and sorrow at his betrayal and her folly left her heartsick.

"The Graf von Hagen," Rossmann was slyly cheerful after they'd ridden for awhile in silence, "is a man who might have been happier had he been born in this part of the world."

"Why?"

Rossmann had been waiting for that, like a cat by a mouse hole.

"Why, Caterina," he said, all pretense of deference abruptly thrown aside, "because a rich man here may lawfully have as many women as he can keep."

"Here or there, he wouldn't wish for more than me."

Rossmann threw back his head and laughed, showing a plenitude of white teeth. "No man made like him, in our world or yours, remains celibate for a year, in the midst of a war or anywhere else."

Her thoughts whirling, Cat closed her eyes and rode, praying for the thousandth time that she would suddenly wake and find this all a dream, but there was no peace there either. In waking reverie as they plodded along, or in the unconscious night, the cold gray eyes of Goran haunted her, accusing scornful of her folly.

* * *

The fearsome soldiers kept their distance. Sometimes Cat understood they were talking about her, their eyes and gestures clearly indicated the offensive tenor, but no one tried to touch her. Clearly, she was to be brought unmolested to wherever it was they were going.

"It will be in the hands of their Pasha," explained Rossmann, when she, unable to bear her imaginings, began to speculate upon what her fate might be. "He'll decide."

"Decide what?"

"Whether he wants you or not. The Ban says that while it is true that you are very beautiful, the Pasha has never liked women with red hair."

208

"You were my husband's friend, Herr Rossmann. You must escape. You said you know the country! Find him, tell him how to find me!"

"Impossible. As soon as I was gone, well, I've told you what would happen. No, no, I must stay by your side."

Then he'd looked away, wearing that same expression of contentment he'd worn since they'd entered the plains. Caterina shuddered, but even the new fear of him didn't completely distract her from the idea that he had not yet told her the whole truth.

* * *

In the center of a heavily fortified town they were paraded, the captured horses, the arms, and Caterina. She and Star were much stared at. An enormous grinning soldier approached, offering to lift her from the horse.

The crowd laughed at how both woman and horse defended themselves. Star reared and kicked. Caterina slapped the soldier across the face with the reins.

While this was going on, a commanding black man marched forward. When he appeared, the crowd promptly fell away. At a clap of his hands, soldiers surged from all sides. They roped Star, head and feet. When the ropes pulled tight, the mare grew quiet. She knew quite well what would happen if the foot ropes were pulled.

With the mare hobbled, Caterina dismounted. At once the enormous soldier stepped forward. His burly hand caught her neck and forced her down, onto her knees and further, into a head on the ground obeisance. Her red braid fell into the dust.

Prone, she choked back tears. Once more scenes of battle came crowding into her mind, of the broken and bleeding bodies of the men who had died to save her. There was Goran, swinging his bright sword, trying to clear a path for her escape...

The dreadful reverie did not last long, however, for in the next moment, she was hauled upright for the inspection of a pair of lively dark eyes, eyes set in a round black face.

Having only a short time before seen her very first black man, Cat stared back.

His hand, fat and pink-palmed, oddly like a woman's, reached out and pulled the improvised veil away. To her chagrin, the plump fingers, fastening on either side of her jaw, forced her mouth open. He then proceeded to look inside, exactly as if he were buying a horse. She tried to jerk her head away, but the huge soldier now held a handful of her hair. When the black man, who was very richly dressed, finished with his examination, he spoke. Cat was astonished to hear German.

"Can this man of yours control the mare?"

He pointed at Rossmann, who from his knees replied, "Servant of the Mighty Lord Pasha, I am the lady's horsemaster, but am only too glad that the fortunes of war have brought me home to my own people and away from the sinful infidel. Accept my services in the stable, sir, for I know the commands that rule the red mare."

Caterina stifled the desire to spit at him, although she also prayed that Star, at least, would be well cared for.

"Sir! He can groom my horse and handle her, but she'll refuse anyone on her back but me."

The Pasha's emissary turned and smiled, revealing a mouth spectacularly full of beautiful teeth.

"Then he shall take care of the mare. With the Pasha's Arab stud, she'll drop splendid foals."

A wave of his plump, black, hand and Rossmann arose, bowed low, and then took Star's bridle. When she went with him quietly, the crowd having seen her battling wildly before, watched in wonder.

The pink palm made another gesture and Caterina was dragged away, across the bustling courtyard into a crowded market. As she was hauled along, Caterina saw rugs, jewels and cloth for sale—and human flesh.

They stood chained while buyers flocked around, looking in mouths, touching and prodding as if they were buying livestock. A group of fair skinned girls and boys were being pulled to their feet for inspection. A girl, close to Caterina's age, stood like a marble statue, her black robe discarded upon the ground, her face a blank, while a potential buyer handled her breasts.

This final tableau of degradation sent her senses reeling. She could barely recall anything of the rest of her journey through that terrible market, or of the imposing building she was taken to, or of the labyrinthine corridors she was hurried along. When Caterina was finally thrown into a small, dark room, she ran and crouched in the darkest corner, shuddering like some captive wild thing.

* * *

Time passed. After what seemed an eternity, there was the shuffling sound of feet outside. A jingle of keys followed, the squeal of a lock, and then light entered the room.

Two more black men, dressed in long white robes, stood there. At once she sprang to her feet, ready to use the locket, but another figure, black robed, veiled, and squatly female, made an appearance between them.

"Don't do anything stupid." Although heavily accented, again the ringing words were German. "You are in the Pasha's harem now. Nothing can harm you here—except your own folly."

Caterina took her hand away from the locket and stared at the woman. She felt herself shaking with fear and exhaustion.

"We've come to take you for a bath, Red One, and then you shall be clothed and fed."

"Bathe?" It seemed crazy, and for a moment Caterina's fear rose in a choking cloud, but the events of the past days had played her nerves almost to deadness.

"Yes."

The old woman's eyes, the only part of her face Cat could see, twinkled. "Even a dirty German barbarian like you can wash. Now take off those boots and put these on." Wrinkled, ringed hands held out a pair of high pattens, ornate, but basically the same kind of shoe that Cat was accustomed to use on muddy days walking in Passau. After

211

a moment's hesitation, she sat and began to tug at her riding boots.

"You are German?"

"Long ago. That is why the Lady Mother sends me to teach you, to make a barbarian fit to live in her son's house."

"I am not a barbarian. I am Caterina von Hagen, born to a noble family."

"And I am Ayhan, not 'you'. You will respect and obey me or you will end up back in the slave market. Did you see enough of that to understand what that kind of slavery means?"

"Yes—Ayhan." Caterina swallowed hard.

"As for who you were before you came here, best you forget. If the Lady Mother permits you to remain, she will give you another name."

"Who is the—Lady Mother?"

"That is how we speak of our Pasha's mother. Now, no more questions. There will be plenty of time to learn. By the way, these creatures," Ayhan said, gesturing at the two blacks, "are not men; they are eunuchs."

As Caterina stood now, she could not help but study them. They were shiny black and dressed in long, fine white linen robes. Although they were tall, they had the same slope shoulders, round hairless cheeks and soft, plump bodies as the Italian castrato singers she'd seen at the carnival operas down in Passau.

* * *

There was a dream quality to everything that followed. She was so tired, and had been afraid for so long. Now she was walking down a long hall, clacking along on the wooden high pattens. There were corridors and doors, torches and candles, but no windows. From unseen nearby rooms came the babble of woman speaking in languages she did not understand.

When the door at the end of the hallway was opened, a gust of heat met her. She'd entered a long room with stone floors, light entering through high, dripping glass windows. A thin sheet of water flowed over the tightly stoned floor, which was barely visible at first because of all the steam.

In the middle of the room was a pool. Two plump, fair skinned girls were sitting in it, giggling and splashing each other.

"You!" The old woman shouted. The girls started guiltily. Apparently they'd been so engrossed in their play that they had not noticed her entry. They turned, pink tipped high breasts buoyed by the water.

Ayhan shouted something and pulled a slender and pliant birch rod out of some hiding place within the elaborate folds of her robes. At this they both leapt, squealing out of the pool and dashed away through a far door.

The old woman glared after them while returning the birch rod to her sash.

"Undress and get in."

When Caterina simply stared, she shrugged, turned and said something to the two blacks. In an instant, they both descended upon her and began pulling at her clothes. She fought, struggling and kicking, but found right away that for all their look of softness, they were sufficiently strong to enforce their will.

"All that will happen is a bath!" the old woman shouted. "You stink!"

Just as one of those black hands seized her locket, Cat landed a punch, the quickest, hardest blow of which she was capable. The eunuch staggered backwards, blood spurting from his nose.

Ayhan and the other eunuch displayed not an ounce of sympathy. Instead, they both began to laugh. Sulmuh, you fool. She quickly interposed herself between the injured eunuch and Caterina, barked something that sounded like a warning, accompanied by a rapidly shaking finger.

Turning back to Caterina, she said approvingly, "A good arm and a good eye. The Pasha will certainly sire warriors on you."

"Make them leave and then I will obey," said Caterina, rubbing her aching knuckles.

"All right, Red One. But remember that Sulmuh would love to beat you now. Believe me, he knows a thousand ways of hurting and not leaving marks. If you don't obey me, I'll let him do it."

The eunuchs, now involved in a shrill quarrel, went out. Caterina sat upon a stool which looked like an upended wooden cage and began to undress. She was hoping that this demonstration would discourage any further attempts at taking her locket. As it was only made of wood, it wouldn't be, she hoped, as endlessly attractive as if it were of gold or silver. During the last week's captivity, Cat had thought much about the protector, but wasn't sure exactly what good use one little blade could be put to—unless, of course, she finally decided to use it upon herself.

Another woman arrived in the room, stout, dark and dressed very lightly in a loose tunic. She carried a pail and an enormous sponge. When Ayhan pointed and growled orders, she went to one of the spigots set along the walls above catch basins and filled the pail.

"You are to sit still while Zehra scrubs you."

The pail was set down beside Cat and the woman, with a cautious look, squatted down beside Caterina and began to work a fine, pale liquid she poured from a pitcher into the sponge.

"Let's see this precious thing," Ayhan suddenly rasped, stabbing a bony finger at the locket.

"It's only my Saint," said Caterina, keeping a tight hold on it. "My Aunt said I was never to take it off," she added ingenuously. She opened it for Ayhan's inspection, displayed the picture of Saint Brigitte.

"Heathen nonsense," the old woman pronounced sharply. Then in a softer tone she added, "If it is not a saint, just a picture, I don't need to take it from you. Do you understand, Red One?"

"I understand, Ayhan," Cat meekly replied. "It is only a picture."

"Good. The first thing you will learn is the true way of Islam. I shall begin your instruction tomorrow."

"I must become Muslim?"

"If you are to be an odalisque, at the rising of the next full moon. It is that or the marketplace."

A month or a year, thought Caterina, will make no difference, what I believe is what I believe. She thought of the peasants on Aunt Teresina's farm, wondered if in a month she'd be able to make the choice between martyrdom or survival...

"Ayhan, what is 'odalisque'?"

"Odalisques are slaves, handmaids of the kadins, the wives of the Pasha. They serve their kadin as a house servant does, but they also sing and dance for her. They bathe their kadin, just as Zehra is doing for you. You will learn to plait her hair, to sing or to play the songs she likes. Maybe, if you are very lucky, the Pasha will see you and make you one of his concubines."

For so many days she had been exhausted and terrified. Now, the heat and the awful feeling there was no escape left her weak, unable to even twitch. Caterina closed her eyes, and allowed the stout woman to lift her arm and scrub it.

There was the splash and tinkle of water. Ayhan was gathering up her clothes, the leather knee britches, the long drab jacket she'd been wearing.

"Ayhan, I must have clothes."

The woman muttered something in her language and then spoke in German, "These are filthy and immodest. Others will be brought."

Zehra said something, something that caused Ayhan to throw up her hands, shake her head and burst into a torrent of impatient speech. Cat didn't understand, but the gestures seemed to say, 'Why didn't you tell me that when you first came in?'

"I have to leave you now. Let Zehra wash your hair. The Lady Mother will whip us both if you bring lice into her house."

Ayhan growled something to Zehra, who cowered. Then she marched away, her squat form disappearing into the haze of steam. The penetrating heat touched Cat's aching bones. Mesmerized, she sat and allowed the ministrations of Zehra, who was alternatively soaping her with the sponge or scrubbing her with a strange scratchy fiber which looked like dried cucumber.

The heat continued to grow, reaching a point where Caterina felt she could hardly breathe. Large drops of perspiration ran down her body. It also fell from hard working Zehra, falling sometimes onto Caterina and sometimes onto the steaming floor. By the time Cat had had her hair soaped and rinsed in one of the basins set along the walls, in the magically endless flow of hot water, she was so weak she could hardly stand. Her lungs burned from the unaccustomed heat.

When she felt ready to faint, a large linen sheet was wrapped around her, and Zehra pointed to the pattens. With a sigh, Caterina stepped into them. With Zehra's arm around her waist, she walked through the same door that the two plump young females had used earlier.

Chapter Eighteen

They entered another large room. This one held another pool and a tinkling central fountain, but it was not as hot, nor as steamy. There were divans and Caterina was led to one. Feeling weak in every limb now, she subsided onto the sail cloth surface. A pillow was placed behind her head.

Here was Ayhan again, with a bowl and a rag in hand.

"This is to remove body hair," she said. "It will sting, but we will wash it off before it burns your fine white skin."

"What?" Caterina, horrified, tried to sit up.

"It is not only disgusting, but a sin for a woman to have hair on her body."

"Where will you put that stuff? On my legs? Under my arms?"

"You will lie still while I put it between your legs, too. Every part must be made smooth and soft and bare."

Apparently, the humiliations were to be endless.

Caterina bowed her head submissively. "Ayhan," she said, "I am very thirsty."

"And hungry, too, I expect. If you lie still and do as I say, a drink will be brought to you."

Caterina did as she was told, sitting up against the pillows.

"Now relax. Part your legs. After the paste is on, be still or it will get where it is not supposed to be and really hurt you. While it works, we'll cover you and you can rest. Zehra will get you drink."

While this final ordeal was going on, Zehra trotted away and then returned from somewhere carrying a cup.

"What is it?" Cat asked, as the girl knelt and raised it towards her.

"It is made of barley. Boza it is called," explained Ayhan. "It will strengthen you and quench your thirst."

With exquisite skill, Zehra fed Caterina sips of the faintly sweet, chilled drink. After the long fast and the enervating bath, it was heavenly. Boza proved to be cold, smooth, and thinly sweet and sour, with a delicate after taste of cinnamon.

When Caterina began to complain that the paste was hurting, Ayhan scraped it away with a mussel shell. Then she rinsed with very hot water.

"Ow! You're boiling me!" Cat tried to shield her already insulted private parts.

"We must get all the paste off, Red One. Either that or it will eat another hole in you," Ayhan said with a grim smile.

Cat could still feel the dreadful burning so she endured it, allowed the sponge to send scalding water over the tenderest places and down the inside of her thighs.

"The first time is the worst," said Ayhan. "Eventually you won't have to do it more than once every month or so. The hair becomes—discouraged."

She lifted Cat's arm and stroked the tender nakedness underneath. "Now, red barbarian, you begin to approach beauty. Ah, but what is this?" she suddenly asked, touching the spot that was always extra tender.

As she did, Cat felt a shock of terror strong enough to revive her. She could see Aunt Teresina leaning over her with a bit of ice wrapped in a towel, pressing it against the place where the spider had bitten, the place that had always afterward been marked with blue.

"It's a scar!" Fear surged to panic when abruptly the door opened, and a large, enormously fat black man came towards her, accompanied by the two eunuchs who'd escorted her from the small room.

218

Feeling dizzy sick, Cat crossed her arms over her breasts and clenched her knees together. She'd never been naked in the presence of so many people in her life.

"This is the Chief Eunuch in charge of the women," Ayhan announced. "He is a physician. He must see whether you are already bred and if you are healthy. Nothing else will happen. Now don't act crazy. Just lie still and it will soon be over."

Under the direction of this huge personage, apparently yet another of the black castrati that the palace seemed to be full of, the two men seized her arms and held her down upon the couch. The one whose nose she'd bloodied took a cruelly painful grip.

There was nothing else to do but submit. When the examination was finished, the huge man grunted to his feet. As soon as she was released, Caterina curled into a ball and hid her face. After saying a few quick words to Ayhan, the Chief Eunuch left the room. To her relief, he took the others away with him.

"It is all over now," said Ayhan, patting Caterina as she sat, trembling and rubbing her aching arms. "He says you are healthy and that you are not pregnant. You are to be kept and trained to be an odalisque."

Then she was led into a small antechamber with a dry floor, pegs on the walls and benches. Here stout Zehra had set out a complete set of new clothes.

First there were a pair of pants, very full, which reached to Cat's ankles, then a smock of a fine green silk gauze edged with embroidery. It had wide sleeves and was closed at the neck with a diamond button. Over this went a long flowing caftan which she recognized as the same sort of garment Christoph had had made for her. This one, however, was beautiful, of a greenish blue color and embroidered beautifully with winged horses.

"Do you like the Pegasi?" Ayhan asked. "It was thought to be most appropriate for you."

"Do you know about my mare? Where is she?"

"All I have heard is that the horse is wild and very valuable, more valuable than any barbarian would have the sense to know. She will be well cared for, just like you. And she is yours no longer, Red One. In the harem you own nothing, not even your freckled skin."

Cat swallowed the lump in her throat, stared down at the tiny winged horses, so skillfully rendered. For an instant she imagined herself on the back of one, soaring through the sky, back to Heldenberg, back to the arms of her husband…

Zehra was offering her the last piece of clothing, a waistcoat of a brilliant green, closed with jeweled buttons. Numbly, Cat put it on. Next she was told to sit so that her hair could be combed and braided.

"Ayhan…"

"What now, girl?"

"I thought Turks dressed their wives in black long tunics."

"What? Oh, the feradge is what you mean. Yes, that is how a woman, if she ever goes outside of the harem, must dress. If you ever see the outside of these walls again, you will wear the feradge and a yashmak, too."

"Yashmak?"

"Yes, a veil that covers your face and hair. I will show you how to wear it. In time I will teach you all you need to know in order not to sin."

"I will die if I cannot ride again," said Caterina softly.

"Then you will die."

Afterward, she was escorted back to the little room. She almost didn't recognize it, for in her absence a barred window had been unshuttered and a couch had been moved in, one covered with blankets and pillows. There was also a low table and a Turkey carpet. Upon the table sat a plate of something which smelled wonderful, a kind of stew poured over steamed grain. Beside that sat a basket of cherries and a pitcher that looked to be full of more of the delicious Boza.

"Go ahead, Red Mare Woman. Eat. Sleep. You will see no one until I come tomorrow to begin your training."

The door locked. As soon as she heard the soft scuffle of slippered feet departing, Cat hurled herself down on the

220

carpet by the table and began to stuff the strangely spiced stuff into her mouth with her fingers. Later, lying on the comfortable divan, stomach full of strange but excellent food, body clean and warm blankets wrapped around her, Caterina wept long and bitterly.

How long could she survive inside a cage?

How could she sleep when such images of horror crowded her mind?

After she'd cried for a long time, a profound lassitude arose, from the food, the hot bath, the skillful massaging of her body by the slave. It wasn't long before she found release in sleep, the most profound since her capture.

* * *

The sun was well up the next day when the door unlocked. There stood Ayhan. Behind her stood plump Zehra carrying a tray of breakfast.

"You will wash, and then you will have a lesson on how to eat properly. And no nonsense!" She indicated the door, outside of which Cat caught sight of the skulking, ominous Sulmuh.

Obediently, Caterina washed her hands and face in a basin. Then she sat down upon the carpet by the table.

"Sit like this. Cross your legs." Ayhan folded herself gracefully down beside her. When Cat reached for food with both hands, the old woman dealt the left one a stinging slap.

"That hand is unclean. It is to be used only for the call of nature. You may never use it to eat."

Caterina, who was hungry, repressed the urge to hit back.

"Watch me. Use your fingertips, just the ends." Every move Ayhan made in bringing the food to her mouth was astonishingly elegant. "Only three fingers. Don't gobble."

* * *

In the courtyard below the birds sang so beautifully that, for fleeting moments, she felt almost happy. Open to the sky, the area was only partially paved. The remainder was filled by a garden of dwarf trees and bright flowers. There were two sparkling fountains.

For a few hours every day, Cat watched a crowd of gaily dressed women and romping children enjoying the sunlit garden.

"All you see here, kadins, concubines, odalisques, children, and slaves of the Pasha." Ayhan explained. "Kadins are wives. Islam allows a man to have four, but if he is rich he may also have four concubines, as well as any number of odalisques, who are, as I've said before, slaves of the kadins. A man may take any wife's handmaid he chooses to his couch." Caterina shook her head, utterly amazed.

"In the west there is a custom of mistresses. All rich and powerful men have them. One way or another true male nature will express itself."

Every day Ayhan sat with her, teaching her the language and telling her stories about the ways of the harem. Caterina was an interested and often horrified listener, for the world Ayhan described was a web of conspiracy, betrayal and murder. The Pasha's mother was said to have poisoned a rival and to have done the same to the woman's small children in order to make inheritance safe for her own sons after their husband had died.

"We are a hard people, Red Mare, which is why we always triumph. Among our men it is brothers against their cousins, cousins against the world, but it is even harder for women. In the seraglio, a woman has no ally but her own wit. Remember what I tell you, for if you displease the Lady Mother you will be sent to the marketplace, where I'm sure they will receive a good price for your healthy body and red hair—even if you aren't a virgin."

It seemed that as an odalisque, Caterina would be a slave, but she would also be given a slave of her own, who would bathe her, carry her food and see to her wants. She would have to learn the same skills herself in order to care for her mistress, whichever among the kadins chose her. She also learned that many of the women in the seraglio were Circassians or Croats who had been bought as slaves, trained and converted. The household was modeled, as far as this Pasha's wealth allowed, upon that of the Great Turk in Istanbul.

* * *

At the end of the first week Caterina was taken again to the baths. This time, the steaming room was filled with the same women and children she'd daily watched in courtyard. "These are the kadins, their odalisques and the children. They will be seeing you for the first time. Some of them might even touch you, so behave with civility."

This time the bath was a much more amenable experience, especially because the miserable burning paste needed only a brief application. The careful Zehra soaped and scrubbed her until her fair skin was flushed and red.

During the last week she had tried talking to Zehra in German, but the girl had only smiled, patted Caterina's cheeks affectionately and shook her head. Ayhan had explained. "Zehra knows a little Turkish and when you know some too, then you can speak. She is a slave from the east somewhere. Maybe Armenian, but no one here speaks her native tongue, so we don't know. She isn't pretty, but she's a good slave."

All around Caterina, women of many colors were washing each other, bodies and hair. She was surprised to see how free they were in their nakedness, how some of them even put up a leg on the stools and allowed their half naked servants to examine them. Apparently this was a searching for renewed growth of the despised hair, because the paste pot made its appearance after several of these examinations.

Other beauty treatments were in progress as well. One woman appeared to be dying her hair, with the help of several slaves. With the quantities of burning depilatory and black dye that were flowing across the floor today,

223

Caterina understood the purpose of the tall pattens—to keep one's feet above the mess!

All the wives were there, and Cat felt their eyes speculatively upon her. Ayhan had told her that the Pasha had four kadins and had sired children upon them all, as well as upon two concubines and several of the odalisques. The children were everywhere, more subdued than in the garden, perhaps because of the steamy heat. They ranged in color from olive brown to extremely fair. One of the kadins, Ayhan had told her, was an Egyptian.

Today, Caterina saw her up close. She was a beautiful coffee color, very dark, but with fine features and an astounding figure. It was rare, Ayhan said, for this pasha to take a dark skinned woman, but the woman's beauty and some political advantage which Ayhan alluded to had caused him to marry her. Muazzez, as she was called, was the daughter of a pasha, a noblewoman of sorts, if such a thing could be said to exist in this world of absolute male domination.

There were two brown, curly headed boys romping around Muazzez, so she must have been receiving a fair share of her husband's attention. Caterina tried not to stare, but she was so exotic, such a contrast to the well fleshed, ivory figures of the others that it was hard not to. When the bathing and beauty treatments were done, Cat was taken as before to the warm room and wrapped in a large soft sheet. With gestures, Zehra let her know that she was to lie down, to relax. It was easy enough to do, especially after having her muscles so heated by the steam and hot water.

Zehra began to message Cat, hands lubricated with a clean, gingery smelling concoction, beginning at her scalp and then working her way down her straight back, across her firm young buttocks and down her long legs, all the way to the ends of her toes. All around the other women were receiving similar attention from their slaves. Cups of gardenia flavored sherbet, made from the snow of some nearby mountain, were offered.

Caterina had a notion of how dangerous was this luxury. It was easy to understand how a simple peasant girl, sold by her parents, would find this an improvement in her lot. After all, resistance brought pain and death. Acquiescence brought luxuries and physical comfort to a degree that even a noblewoman like herself had never known or even imagined. Still, Caterina was an attentive listener to Ayhan's stories. There was the poisoned sherbet delivered by a rival, the knife in the dark corridor, the silken cord the smiling black eunuch would use as he slowly strangled a woman for some imagined slight given while partnering the Pasha in his bed.

When her own moment of decision came, at the rising of the next full moon, what would she do? She'd been practicing at night, secure in the utter darkness after she extinguished the lamp, with Aunt Teresina's blade, making the killing jab in the direction of her own neck. It was beginning to seem that suicide was the only way out, the only way to retain her self, her honor.

As the days passed, however, she felt her strength, her sense of who she was, draining away. A strange language rang in her ears all day. More and more Ayhan was speaking in it, forcing her to use it. The mocking name "Red Mare" had stuck. That, she was informed, was her name until the Lady Mother thought of a better one.

In the beginning, she'd spent the time when Ayhan wasn't giving instruction, pacing in the little room, her athletic body making her as restless as a caged bear. At these times Cat indulged an imagining of being free, of galloping away on Star, across those familiar flower strewn meadows that graced the rocky shoulders of Heldenberg, Christoph beside her.

How he would catch her, pull her down from Star's back! How they'd wrestle to a fiery conclusion among the bobbing gold and white flowers. She could almost feel his muscular body hard against hers, his mouth caressing, tasting, hear the whispers of his special teasing lovemaking…

Observing her charge's restless pacing, Ayhan had begun a new strategy, one that involved the kitchen. She had seen Caterina's good appetite and decided to use it to tame her.

One day after the noon meal, Caterina found herself not pacing, but lying on the couch, mind drifting. A languorous afternoon passed, wandering in and out of dreams. Stretched out in silken robes, unmoving, she heard with an odd intensity the liquid songs sung by the caged birds in the courtyard below.

It happened the next day too, and the day after that. As she lay there with her eyes half open, curious dreams, ones that seemed to embroider themselves upon reality, appeared. She dreamed that Christoph came through the locked door, that he had come to rescue her, that she was safe at last, enclosed in his great arms. Her face pressed against his broad chest, she felt his hands upon her hair, heard him speak in blessed words of her mother tongue. Sometimes Wili sat beside her, cheerfully chatting. Goran came, leaning on his cane, telling her sternly that she was late for a lesson with the sword...

What tears she shed upon awakening and finding herself still inside a cage!

After such an afternoon, the nights were long and half sleepless, full of sorrow and apprehension. Cat, feeling muddy minded, weary, but incapable of sleep, leaned against the latticed window and listened as nightingales sang in the garden below. Sometimes sad songs rose from the hall of the odalisques, accompanied by the minor key wail of a flute.

On the fourth such afternoon she'd had a dream more disturbing, more real than any of the others. In it, Rossmann, now dressed like a Turkish gentleman, had entered the room in company with a heavily veiled woman. Rossmann stood by her couch, dark eyes shining with admiration, while she, unable to move, lay there her hair loose, wrapped in those splendid robes of blue green silk. Not wanting to meet his eyes, she'd focused upon the tiny embroidered Pegasi, who continued flying off her robes and away through the barred window.

226

Then this creature with Rossmann's face approached, and had gathered up her limp hand and kissed it. Cat was furious, wanting to strike him, but her limbs were too heavy, her throat clogged. She'd felt her eyes widen, her body twitch, but otherwise she'd been unable to either move or speak, while he slipped his hands his hands inside the gown and caressed her breasts.

The anonymous woman's hand was gloved, and now it reached to tug the flowing sleeve of Rossmann's robe.

"Stop!" The hiss was unmistakably Ayhan.

With a grimace of regret, the man retreated. A moment later he was gone. The door latch clicked.

The sound brought Caterina closer to reality—at least that's what she thought it was. The Pegasi continued to fly, to paper the walls of the room with hundreds of tiny, wing beating, galloping figures. She wrapped her arms around the neck of one, and flew away through the window with its bars, straight into a bright blue sky.

* * *

The next morning when Ayhan came to instruct her, she accused her of letting Rossmann in.

"I brought a German called 'Horseman' here?" The woman's black eyes glittered with scorn.

"He's no German, as you well know! And he was here. You were with him! Rossmann is the man who led me into the ambush. He's a traitor Bogomil."

Ayhan clapped her hands and gave a shout of laughter.

"Calm yourself, Red One! I brought a man here? Into Selim Pasha's harem? Do you think I desire close acquaintance with my Lord Pasha's torturer?"

"Stop lying, Ayhan! I know what is a dream and what's not."

"Do you? It's hard to tell sometimes, especially after meals full of the finest white poppy."

"Poppy? Why? That is medicine for pain." Aunt Teresina had told Caterina about the poppy plant and that it should be used sparingly, for great pain only, for the drug

227

"fastens itself upon the user like a leech." All too soon, her Aunt had cautioned, an unending desire for larger and larger doses would overwhelm the life of the strongest willed person.

"Poppy is also for pleasure and for the sake of interesting dreams. You will become most familiar with it in the seraglio."

"Why are you giving me poppy? And why are you lying? Tell me right now why that traitor was here."

"Still giving orders? Perhaps I shall let Sulmah hurt you a little. He's been begging to for weeks. He promises he won't leave any marks."

"I'll stop eating."

Ayhan stared at Cat for a long moment and then heaved an exasperated sigh.

"You won't be able to starve yourself. Life is too strong in you. And why do you object to such a treat anyway? It makes time pass pleasantly."

"It enslaves."

"You are already enslaved. Foolish one! Enjoy the pleasures of your new life. The poppy will help you forget the past, the past you still weep for, that world you will never live in again. Besides, you have too many muscles. They make you too restless to settle down here properly. You need to sleep more, to gain weight. You are far too thin."

"I won't poison myself with poppy." It was, Cat knew, not the cleverest thing to say, but she couldn't stop herself.

"Such stubbornness! Such pride! Too much of the carrot and not enough of the stick, I think," Ayhan grumbled. "But I am ordered not to let the eunuchs amuse themselves with you. Your new Lord says," she added with gleeful menace, "he's looking forward to instructing you in submission himself."

"The Pasha?"

"The Pasha, indeed!" Ayhan sniffed. "No, skinny barbarian, praise Allah, you won't trouble me much longer."

"What?"

228

"A friend of the Pasha wants you and the Lady Mother fears ..."

"What? Someone else is to have me? Who?"

"You shall be given to Ban Nijaz. Now, are you any the wiser?" Ayhan had on a look which meant there was not another word on that subject to be got from her. Pleased that she had frightened Caterina, she turned on her heel and went out, locking the door.

The next afternoon, Ayhan unlocked the door and said, "Prepare yourself, Red Mare. You are to come with me and see what happens to women who do not please their men."

Ayhan's evil smirk did not bode well, and Caterina set about veiling herself, feeling the sharp prick of fear. She put on the yashmak, extinguishing the flame of her red hair beneath it and making certain she had brought the fabric tightly against the bridge of her nose. When Ayhan was giving instruction, she'd taught that if a woman showed her nose, it was the advertisement of a prostitute.

After she was ready Sulmah appeared and he and Ayhan accompanied her along corridors, unlocking doors that led in a direction she'd never traveled before. As they approached the stairs, she found herself walking among a crowd of veiled women of the seraglio. Most kept their eyes down, and Caterina could sense the tension. Beneath the scented bodies, she could also smell perspiration, and knew that the co-wives must have all been summoned to see whatever horror was planned.

As a slave held aside a curtain, and they entered into a latticed gallery overlooking a courtyard and began to settle onto cushions, carefully attentive to rank. Some of the women, despite their elaborate veiling, she thought she recognized from the baths. One pair, she'd often thought, with large, expressive dark eyes and harmonious pale foreheads, might have been sisters. Like bright birds, they all settled and sat unnaturally still, not a whisper to be heard among them. It seemed that they were all equally anxious, even the tall black kadin, who was seated first among them.

Finally, a door opened, a line of men entered the courtyard below. They too settled quietly, ranks of what appeared to Caterina to be gentlemen and house servants. Last of all came the Pasha, a burly middle-aged man with a neatly trimmed beard. She thought that even if he were stripped of all his attendants and all his silks and jewels, he could have yet passed for a prosperous German knight. There was assurance and power in his movements.

"Look upon the Master of this city and tremble." Ayhan leaned close to whisper. "And there are the Pasha's own eunuchs, who are men of great power." These men were white, and stood proudly with swords in their belts. They looked far more muscular and dangerous than the ordinary castrati. Ayhan had said that white eunuchs protected the Pasha and his sons. One of the gentlemen who had entered earlier—older, with a long lean presence, silver hair, sallow skin and a great hook nose—approached the Pasha and swept him a low bow. Caterina noted that he too was followed by eunuchs, and how his hands and turban glittered with jewels.

"Faik Pasha," Ayhan murmured. "A close friend of our Lord."

Next, four more eunuchs emerged from the corridors, black like Sulmah. Between each pair, pale arms tied with silken cords, walked a veiled woman. The odalisque who sat beside Caterina gasped as some formal proceeding conducted rapidly in their language began below. Caterina could catch a stray word here and there but not enough to make any sense of it.

At the end, one of the bound women was brusquely unveiled and pushed to her knees before the Pasha. While Caterina watched in horror, the largest black eunuch, the one who had examined her for imperfections on her first day, stepped forward and placed a silken cord around the woman's neck. Without any further preamble, he strangled her.

It seemed to take forever for the awful struggling, the white hands clawing to disengage the cord, to finally cease.

When all movement stopped, her limp form was allowed to fall onto the colorful mosaics.

From the odalisque nearby a single sob escaped. When Cat turned to look at her, she saw a black teary streak running from one kohl lined eye.

Caterina had never witnessed an execution—not even a hanging in Passau. The whole scene was perfectly horrible, most especially the supreme passivity of the victim, whom she'd recognized as one of the gay beautiful strollers she'd watched daily in the courtyard.

"What—?"

"Later!" Ayhan delivered one of her cautions in the form of a fierce pinch.

The body was carried away by the same servants who had walked her in. The remaining eunuchs hauled the other woman onto her feet and up to the dais. Caterina tensed, fearing she was to witness another execution.

The captive now faced the reclining pashas. For a moment, Caterina wondered if Selim would strangle this one himself.

With a smile, as if nothing unpleasant had just happened, he drew the woman down to kneel before his friend, and unfastened her veil. Cat saw the woman's face, the pale flesh and translucent skin baby-like. She had often seen this handsome concubine walking arm-in-arm with the dead woman.

Faik Pasha put a hand under the woman's chin, turned her face from side to side. The kohl with which she had lined her gray eyes now ran down her cheeks. Pasha Selim turned and spoke to his friend. The words "gift" and "pleasure" were two that Cat recognized. Then two strange blacks, ones that Cat had never seen before, entered and threw a long black federage over the woman's clothes and led her away. Next, the two pashas rose. Arm in arm, they followed them out.

Cat thought this would end the awful ceremony, but then something unexpected happened. The curtain at the end of the gallery parted, revealing that kadins had been seated on the other side. From their midst, a tall woman

231

appeared. On every side concubines and slaves knelt, foreheads to the floor.

"Down!" Ayhan hissed. "It is the Lady Mother!"

Although curious, Cat was too frightened not to obey. The alarm on every side was palpable.

* * *

"Leave us at once!"

This was followed by more words Caterina did not understand, although she thought she heard the words "Ayhan" and the scornful "Red Mare." Ayhan put a restraining hand on her arm while, in a hiss of silks, the others crawled away backwards, slipping behind the far curtain.

From her position face down, Caterina heard the great lady rustle onto a low couch, the one which the black kadin had earlier occupied. To her great surprise she heard the woman speak in heavily accented German.

"You may sit and look at me." The Lady Mother struck Caterina's shoulder with a fan.

When she obeyed, a long fingered hand covered with jewels reached to draw the veil away from Caterina's face. Next, to her even greater surprise, the Lady Mother unveiled, revealing white teeth, a generous painted mouth, alabaster skin and moon-shaped black brows. Her forehead was decorated with a glittering band of gold coins and jewels; her black eyes flashed with an icy intelligence. The sight of that gorgeous skin and black eyes reminded Cat of a French noblewoman she'd once met in Passau.

"You are pretty, but far too tall."

"I, ah—thank-you, Lady Mother."

"You have so many freckles! That is not to the Pasha's taste."

Cat didn't know what to reply to that, so she humbly lowered her head.

"You also have too many muscles." The great lady glanced away to her attendants then laughed, and they obediently laughed with her, although they certainly had no

232

idea what she'd said. "Ayhan says you are clever, but far too stubborn, and that is not a good—trait—in a woman. You saw today what happens to those who dare to put themselves before the will of their Lord and Master. Do you understand what happened here today, to the Odalisque Nukhat?"

"It was an execution, My Lady, a show of force."

"Not tactful, are you? Where you will go, the quality may be tolerated. As for the concubine Nukhat and the concubine Leyla, well—Ayhan will explain why one was mercifully allowed to live while the other paid the price for disobedience. Let it teach you the power of my son, who gives life or death as it pleases him. Now," she added after a pause, "you may kiss my robe and depart like the others."

"Am I not to stay here, Lady Mother?" It had suddenly occurred to Caterina that she might dare a question.

"Do you think, Red Jadi, that I would allow such as you to stay?" Abruptly, the older woman was angry. Her black eyes flashed. "Today two troublemakers have been dealt with, so why should a new one stay? You will be given, as Leyla was, to one who has a taste for the unusual—to a man who desires a red freckled woman as big as a horse. Now, GO!"

She threw her fan at Cat's head. Reflexively, Cat ducked. With Ayhan frantically tugging her, she crawled away as fast as she could, sliding at last beneath the curtain.

They scrambled to their feet and hurried away along the corridor and down the stairs. Ayhan pinched her arm and hissed, "Are you mad? You could be beaten for asking the Lady Mother a question! She asks and you answer! Otherwise, do not speak!"

"Ayhan, when am I to leave here?" It had occurred to her that any transfer would provide some chance for escape.

She had to know! And—what unusual tastes? The implied threat hung over her head like a sword.

"No! I know nothing! Now, be silent until we reach your room!"

* * *

"Is that how Muslims treat their wives?" She couldn't stop herself from speaking as soon as she and Ayhan cleared the door of her room. The image of the dying woman, so lovely, twisting, shuddering, contorted in the grip of those strong black hands filled her mind.

Ayhan stared for a moment and then laughed.

"Do you still understand nothing? Leyla was an odalisque, promoted to the Pasha's bed and the rank of concubine. Nekhut was only a slave, another odalisque, like you. The Lord does what he wants with slaves. He sells them, kills them, whatever is his pleasure. Leyla was infatuated with her slave and it offended our Pasha. Besides, that Nekhut was a troublemaker, creating jealousy with her viper tongue. Wherever there was quarreling among the wives or concubines, she was at the bottom of it. She was so beautiful and attentive; all the kadins wanted her." Ayhan paused, reflecting upon the cautionary tale she was about to deliver.

"Did she not—know her—place?" Cat had a pang of guilt remembering what she'd done to Josefa. Although I sometimes felt like it, I didn't go so far as to strangle her, she thought, but I acted judge and jury and exiled her from her family and her childhood home...

"When Pakize Kadin found she did not satisfy, she gave her, as a slight, to Leyla, who was a mere concubine. At first, Nekhut was content, but it never lasted with her. I even heard, although I could not believe it, that Leyla tried to avoid her turn in the Pasha's bed. Then, last week, Nekhut was caught trying to sell at brooch to one of the bundle women."

"For a brooch—she was strangled before her beloved friend?"

"More than a friend, foolish child. Listen to me! Leyla was fortunate that Faik Pasha liked what he saw when she was unveiled. "

"She is now his slave?"

234

"She was a slave here; she is a slave in Faik Pasha's house. Call yourself kadin, odalisque or concubine, there is no change, except in masters. It is said Faik Pasha indulges tastes for things which the Koran forbids, but it is not for me to express an opinion upon any great man."

"She just stood there—" Cat couldn't get it out of her head.

She would have fought them to her last breath!

"It was a quick death. In the Grand Seraglio, she would have been sewn in a sack and tossed into the Bosphorus for insulting her Lord and Master—her lady love with her! It was Kismet, written on her forehead from the day she was born. Nekhut accepted her death because she knew there was no escape, just—" Ayhan paused for effect, "as you have been delivered captive to the Lord Pasha. Accept your destiny, Red Mare. You can no more change it than you can turn back a wave of the sea."

Having made the point, Ayhan turned back to the door. Caterina, at her usual station, the single window that looked down onto the garden courtyard, felt tears rise. Not wanting her guardian to see, she looked away.

No weakness! Show no weakness!

Ayhan sighed with exasperation and with a final backward glance, knocked. Sulmah, eternally outside, opened. Suddenly, Cat knew she had not answered the most important question.

"Ayhan! What is "Jadi?"

Although she'd veiled herself, Cat knew by the way she turned that Ayhan had on one of her malevolent smiles.

"It means "witch," Red Mare. The Lady Mother believes you are a witch, although I have seen nothing— and believe me, I have watched. Why else do you think you arc kept in a room by yourself like a kadin, instead of being kept in the common room of odalisques, sleeping and eating with the others? Just remember, with us as with you, the punishment for a witch is burning."

With that chilling pronouncement complete, she marched through the door. Sulmah, barring his sharp white teeth, grinned as he closed the door.

Chapter Nineteen

That night, despairing, Cat took the blade out, did the exercise and wondered if she had the strength to kill herself. She'd ended weeping in frustration at what she was beginning to believe was a fatal weakness. She just couldn't do it.

She thought, as she often did, of Goran, but this time not only of his unnecessary death and of her guilt. Now she remembered his training, his will to survive, his will to be a man other men feared—even as he was, with one leg. If she was to be given to this "Ban Nijaz" there would be a transfer, a moment when she would be outside this fortress, a time she would have to—somehow—escape or die trying.

* * *

A scrape of a key in the lock brought her rushing back to consciousness and she sat bolt upright. Her hand flew to the locket. Had the fatal moment arrived?

Was hers to be the life of a slave, to be broken, emptied of will, used?

But the open door revealed a slender erect figure, one that was all too familiar. A rolled rug was under his arm. He whispered, "Keep silent!"

Caterina, hand on the locket, stared, wondering if she was again drugged. She had eaten very little but bread since she'd learned what sauces might contain.

Had she, perhaps, eaten enough to be seeing—this?

With a toss, Rossman unrolled the carpet.

236

"A rug the housekeeper rejected. I'm going to carry you inside of it. I'll put you in a cart and we'll drive away. Put on your slippers, and then let me roll you up."

"What kind of trick is this, traitor? Who let you in?"

"Hush. No trick, Lady. I swear. They had to trust me, or they'd never have given me the freedom I needed to send a message. Three days ride from this place, your husband will meet you."

Caterina's heart soared like a hunted bird. Nevertheless, she hesitated. In the last weeks she'd heard many, many stories of intrigue and betrayal.

"You're their man. You betrayed me. Is it your intention now to get me killed?"

"I have never served those pigs. I saved you, saved you from the soldiers, saved you from the marketplace, by convincing them to bring you here. Now come. I have paid the bribes. It's now or never."

"With what have you paid?" Catherina spoke the words while wondering, "Now what am I being talked into—Herr Rossmann or whoever you are today?"

"I have money here, in the street of the Jews."

"And you have used it for me?"

"Your husband and I are more than master and servant, Lady. We are friends."

It was a chance, a thin one, perhaps, but it was the first she'd seen in a terrifying month.

"In three days you will see your husband. This I promise. Now, put on your slippers and this." A feradge was tossed at her and a peremptory gesture was made towards the chamber pot which peeped out from under the bed. "And pee. I know women."

In the dim light of the night lamp, Cat found her slippers, then squatted and obediently tried to do as he said. After throwing the black cloak of the feradge over what she was wearing, she groped her way to the carpet. It was new, smelling of dye.

"No matter what, don't make a sound. Pray to every god you know. If we're caught, I'll give you a quick death, quicker than the eunuchs will."

237

Calloused hands brushed her as he rolled, then he dragged the rug through the door. She heard the click as he locked it. When he hoisted her over his shoulder, she inadvertently grunted.

"Shhh!"

How had he got in there, got the key?

Cat had seen a cluster of these hanging on the housekeeper's belt.

Where were the ever watchful guards?

A thousand questions raced through her mind.

Was it a trap? Whose trap?

The Lady Mother had called her a witch. Was this an excuse to have her killed? Or was Rossmann actually taking her to that friend of the Pasha's, that Ban Nijaz?

Her stomach hurt against Rossmann's shoulder. Sweat trickled down her back. Their joggling passage went on, through terror after terror. Once Rossmann stopped and bantered in their harsh language—at least, so she guessed, for there was laughter. As each gate was passed, certain words were spoken, a kind of formula. Then, at last, Caterina heard the loud creaking of the same wooden portcullis she'd passed beneath on that awful first day.

A little further on, when she thought blood was going to run out her ears, she was suddenly, unceremoniously unloaded. Her landing was hard, but the pain in her middle was relieved and a welcome gust of air blew inside the rug.

With an audible slap of the reins, the vehicle moved off. After they had bumped along for what seemed an endless time, one in which he'd periodically stopped and spoken again—while her heart threatened to burst through the walls of her chest—at last Rossmann called, "Come out now."

She struggled free of the carpet. Taking a huge breath, her first in freedom, she peeped over the jolting side of the cart and saw the torch lit walls of the town rising behind them. Over her head was night, a windy rushing darkness, and thousands of stars.

* * *

238

In a grove Rossmann stopped, leapt out and began to unhitch the horse. Caterina climbed stiffly out of the back to help him.

"Oh, Rossmann! It's Star! How ever did you find her?"

The mare was pleased to see her too. She whinnied and pressed her nose wetly against Cat's hand.

"Coins in the right hand always work. All as we ride, Mistress." He unbuckled the harness. "The Graf will meet us at a place we both know. I've brought some rations and we'll use a twitch to guide her. Now," he said, pulling something from the cart, "Put this on. In case anyone sees us, they will think I am a Bogomil trader with his wife."

It was a yashmak, which thanks to Ayhan's lessons, she knew how to wrap.

"Here, you get up first, then she'll let me get up, won't you, Star?"

"We can't go fast," said Caterina, laying the saddle bags he was handing over the mare's withers. Her own language felt unexpectedly stiff on her tongue.

Rossmann armed himself with a brace of pistols, then belted on a curving sword. "Yes, she's going to have to carry us a long way."

What exultation Cat felt as she swung upon her mare! Even here, in this terrible danger, to have Star beneath her was as thrilling as any imagined flight upon the winged Pegasi...

"Why does she look so dark, feel so greasy?" Cat asked as they rode along the moon-yellowed track Rossmann indicated.

"I've covered her, head to toe, with soot mixed with oil. As far as anyone saw, a black horse went out tonight with me."

"How did you get her out of the Pasha's stables?"

"She wasn't in the stables tonight, but loose in a paddock with a fine Arab stallion." Caterina started.

"Yes." Rossmann chuckled. "If we are lucky, we will have stolen a fine colt as well as a woman from the Great Pasha Selim."

239

For some time they rode in silence. Finally, Caterina asked, "Why have you done this, Herr Rossmann? You seemed happy to be back among your own people."

"I am, but this is for my sake as well as yours. Trust me. Soon it will all make sense."

Nothing he said was logical. Still, she was outside the walled city of the Turks. Despite the fact she did not trust the man behind her, she blessed the strange fortune that had brought her here, and stroked the dull wooden case of the Protector.

* * *

Morning came. Villages where there might be soldiers they carefully skirted. Rossmann often walked beside her, leading the horse. They avoided other travelers. By a well, as they drank and rested, Rossmann produced a bag of oats for the mare and dried fruit and hard traveling bread for Caterina.

As the day passed and she felt safer, she began to ask questions. Rossmann, the cheerful smiling Rossmann that she had known during the summer past, seemed ready enough to answer.

"There was no chance to get you away after we'd been captured. I talked to the captain, told him you were a noblewoman, a rich man's wife, convinced him not to harm you. Selim Pasha is a generous purchaser, but he has a fear of disease. He won't touch a woman whom the soldiers have had. I knew the safest place for you, for a short time, anyway, would be in his harem."

"They told me no one ever escapes, that no whole man ever enters the seraglio. How did you manage?"

"Lies! Men do get in. Actually removing an odalisque is not that difficult. It's simply a matter of money and, of course, Kismet."

Through all those locks and gates, past the eunuchs and reptiles like Ayhan! Still, Cat thought: Here I am. The sun shone on her face, the breeze blew through her yashmak.

"Did he ever summon you to his couch?" The words were soft, but his interest in the answer was far too strong to be concealed.

"No," Cat replied. "Ayhan said the Lady Mother thought me a hexe. She said I was to be a gift to one of the Pasha's friends, someone called Ban Nijaz."

Over her shoulder, she could almost feel Rossmann's smile.

"Lucky she thought so. Perhaps the eunuchs will pretend that you summoned your red horse by magic and the two of you flew away together." He emitted a short, harsh bark of laughter. "You know, it is widely believed that the Pasha's mother is herself a witch."

By late afternoon they reached a golden grassland, apparently endless. At the bed of a shallow stream, they let Star drink, filled a skin Rossmann had brought along, and then forded the water. This time, they took a sharp turn north.

"Every water we cross will help us hide our tracks."

* * *

Slowly the empty miles passed. Cat kept looking back, but although occasionally she'd see a herd of sheep, or a lone rider, no one seemed to be following them. Sun beat down relentlessly. After her month of shadows and a life inside, it made her feel almost sick.

By twilight, Cat's head was aching, her belly calling for food, her feet were bruised and sore from long periods of walking. After the hours of emptiness, there were suddenly all sorts of unique features popping up on every side, upright boulders and curiously bent trees. In the far distance, bathed in the last long rays of the setting sun, Cat spied a bald outcropping. The bare rock shone like the top of a freshly exhumed skull.

Star, who had been plodding head down, suddenly pricked up her ears. Swiveling them forward eagerly, she began to pick her way down a sloping, narrow dirt path, well marked by cattle.

241

"She's scented the water," said Rossmann. "This is where we'll rest until moonrise. Then we'll move again."

At the bottom of a rock-strewn incline, from a cleft in the ground, sweet water rose, a pool of wonderful refreshment for the weary travelers. Star dropped her head and began to take deep draughts even before Cat slid off her back. In the places where legs had rubbed against her sides, sorrel appeared. Cat's clothing and Rossmann's too, were streaked with greasy black.

There was food in the bags and two blankets. Cat unfastened her veil and began to eat hungrily. Rossmann, squatting nearby, watched her.

"Wrap up," he said, tossing her a blanket. "The nights are bitter now, but I don't dare make a fire."

In the last light they found a grassy patch and got the mare to lie down on it. Then, together, Cat in her blanket and Rossmann in his, they huddled against the horse's back. In the darkness Cat could see Rossmann's white teeth. He was smiling to himself, that same cheerful smile that had begun after their capture. It seemed so out of place, both there and here.

"My family slept like this sometimes, against the horses for warmth," he said. "How safe one feels as a child! All an illusion, of course."

When the old moon began to climb, Rossmann roused Cat from the exhausted sleep into which she'd fallen. They set off on foot, leading Star. Only at dawn did they begin to ride again, setting their course straight for the great rock Caterina had seen the night before.

That day it grew very hot, the land shimmering around them, the scent of the water starved grasses, a dusty perfume that dried their throats and made them cough. All day the distant bald grew larger and larger.

It was tall, due west, the stone white. After noon, Caterina saw that there were caves in it, too, like an oddly matching pair of black eyes.

"It looks like a skull," said Cat, uneasily studying the strange feature before them.

"It is called Witches' Head," Rossmann replied. "And that is where your husband will come."

* * *

It was late afternoon when they reached their destination. A thin stream emerged from a fissure at the shadowy base and created a long, shallow pool. Here, once again, they drank beside the horse and washed their sweaty faces.

Within the fissure, the entrance to a cave was visible. When Cat went to curiously peer inside, she saw narrow shafts of light coming from somewhere above, illuminating a damp, mossy floor.

"Where have all the people gone?" Cat turned to ask. The lands they'd ridden through were fine pasture. Even though water hadn't been much in evidence on the surface, it could apparently be got by digging.

"War has driven the people away. There were herders here, many tribes of them, some Christian and some Muslim."

Cat rolled up the legs of her harem pants and began to wade in the pool, splashing Star, intent upon washing the last of the soot away. The mare tossed her head and whinnied, but seemed to be enjoying it. Rossmann sat on the bank and chewed on a biscuit, taking obvious pleasure in the sight of the long bare legs of his mistress.

"Your husband will be here at dawn."

When Caterina led Star out of the pool, Rossmann slit open a bag and offered the contents to Star, who happily thrust her nose inside.

"What have you there?"

"I cooked a special mash for her and sewed it up in this bag. She's been working far harder than we have and she'll need extra strength to get you home. After your husband comes, we'll ride for the Tisza. It's still a hard three day's journey to anything close to safety."

"Herr Rossmann, you've thought of everything."

243

Rossmann smiled. "Yes, the plan was made carefully. Here," he added, handing her a pouch which proved to contain a mixture of shelled nuts and dried apple. "Here's something to keep your spirits up, too."

Crouched by the water, gratefully eating, Caterina felt a growing uneasiness. She noticed that Star kept lifting her head, scenting the air.

"Someone's coming. Look at Star."

"It may be a herder out there, looking for a lost animal." Rossmann seemed disinterested, but Cat stood and shaded her eyes, surveying, once more, the grassy plain. Ever since the ambush, Rossmann had seemed different. She had imagined so many things about him in the two years she'd known him. He'd seemed, by turns, foreign and dangerous, proud and mysterious, handsome and courtly, but now there was a new quality, something slippery. When Cat thought about it—the escape, all of it—it seemed improbable, like one of those romances Wili used to read and weep over.

"Let me show you a back door entrance, so that you know how to escape. You never know when you might need it. Bandits are the only other people who regularly come here, but I happen to know that the Pasha sent an expedition out just a month ago to clean them out. Still, bandits are like rats. There are always more and they always come back."

Had he sensed the drift of her thoughts? Cat felt a stab of anxiety as she followed him into the darkness, but in the last two days he had offered no gesture or word that was less than proper. Last night they had slept close together for warmth, but he had not taken advantage.

* * *

To enter, they had to stoop, but once under the lip of trickling water, they found themselves in a high vaulted room, lit by slanting rays from above. As they moved deeper into the damp twilight, Rossmann paused to use a pocket tinder box.

"Here, Grafin." After lighting a candle, he held out the other hand.

The back of the cave was slimy and green. From above there came a whispery squeaking. Glancing up, Caterina saw a black moving mass. It was, she realized, an untold number of bats clinging to the ceiling.

"Quickly now, or you'll need to bathe," Rossmann said as he followed her gaze.

His candle moved ahead. After a brief climb through a maze of wet, oddly rounded rocks, his light illuminated another low, narrow tunnel.

"Rossmann, where are you going?" Cat cried. "Come back."

"You'll have to crawl," he replied over his shoulder, "but it is important that you see the back door."

His tone was encouraging and his light was receding, so, having no other choice, Caterina dropped to her knees and followed. After a few twists and turns of scuffling, claustrophobic crawling after his outline, she saw him get to his feet. When she reached the same spot, he extended a hand to help her.

The candle in his hand flickered. Caterina saw that they were in the bottom of a dripping, and—except for the light—utterly black hole. Rossmann was turning, shining the candle on the walls, seeking and finally finding the mouth of yet another opening.

"Inside of this next one is what the old ones painted. It's just as I told you the night Star dropped her foal. You, of all people, Lady—must see."

"What? I thought you were showing me a way out."

"It's through here." On hands and knees, neatly balancing the light, Rossmann disappeared again. His enthusiasm for the tour they were making seemed crazy. Cat swallowed her fear, got down on her knees and again followed.

After a blessedly short crawl, she found Rossmann. He was standing, holding the candle high.

As soon as Cat looked about, she forgot her fear. The walls of this tiny space were covered with paintings,

paintings of animals. The colors were bright and fresh, the execution spirited. She recognized cattle, elk, deer and horses, but besides these more ordinary creatures, there were animals she'd never seen before. One was large, furry, and sported a trunk.

"An—an—elephant?" She'd had to make a brief mental search to find the name. "Here?"

"Yes. So it seems. It must have been much wetter in those times. Elephants are very big, you know, eat much."

"Have you seen elephants, Herr Rossmann?"

"Yes, I have. They are wise, perhaps the wisest of creatures, but they are very dangerous to their keepers."

"Where did you see them?"

His bright eyes turned thoughtfully upon her. "In Africa."

"I thought these lands were your home place."

"They are, but I have traveled."

The mystery of Rossmann seemed never ending. Cat returned to studying the beauty and energy of the drawings, pushed away the persistent unsettled sense of-something-not-right she'd felt from the moment they'd entered this dank place.

Among, and sometimes atop, the gamboling animals were hand prints, spirals and squiggly lines. In spite of the fresh, bright colors, Cat instinctively knew that these creatures had been painted a very long time ago.

"This is the Cave of the Red Horse. It's a place a woman with your gift should see."

He raised his candle and threw light high up, upon a painting Cat hadn't yet noticed. Almost directly overhead, a fat red horse galloped. A long legged foal was in full stretch, close by her mother's side.

"Oh! She's beautiful!"

"Yes. She's the guardian of the cave. Long ago a witch lived here. It was said that if a man took her, he'd be a Lord upon this plain, that he would have many sons, many cattle and horses. If her magic resisted him, though, he must die."

He told her this in a sing song tone, like someone reciting a fairy tale. As he spoke, the exhaustion that hummed in her every limb intensified. Caterina felt unspeakably weary, drained...

"I am dizzy, Herr Rossmann. Let's go out."

"Of course. In fact, here is the exit, just behind this rock."

He walked to a pale stone pillar dripping with water, and abruptly vanished behind it. Following, Cat confronted a deeper darkness than the one they'd just come from, a passage as small as the first.

"Watch your head."

Sucking in a breath, Caterina followed. After a far-too-long spell of weary crawling, bumping her knees and her head painfully in that pitch black shaft, Cat again caught sight of his back-lit, scuffling form.

"It's brushy," he called, "but you should have no trouble getting through."

There was a loud rustling and crackling ahead. Although the sudden light was blinding, she hastened towards it. Anxiety at a fever pitch, she pushed through a mass of vines around the opening. Blinking, scrambling to her feet, Caterina found herself facing the sunset on the gently slumping backside of Witches' Head. The slope was dotted with grotesquely bent trees and boulders like a set of worn teeth. At her back, the bald rose in a pale, smooth dome. Cat turned this way and that, brushing herself off while squinting into the low light. Rossmann was nowhere to be seen. A horse whinnied; a horse that Caterina knew wasn't Star.

Chapter Twenty

One pair of rough hands seized her braid, while a second pair wrenched her arms painfully behind her back. A cruel dark face closed on hers.

"Lady von Hagen," the man said, carefully enunciating German. "I am Pasha Selim." From out of the thicket below, armed men appeared. Rossmann tied her wrists with an all-too-familiar fine, silken cord.

She struggled, but after the tightened knots bit into her wrists, she gave up. Exhaustion and defeat fell upon her like two huge stones.

"Exactly as you desired, Great Lord," Rossmann said, in an obsequious tone. His tough hand caught Caterina by the back of the neck and roughly pushed her to her knees.

"Uninjured, I trust?"

"Yes, Great Lord and Cousin."

"And Graf von Hagen will be here at dawn," the Pasha smiled slightly. His eyes were black, fiercely intelligent, like Rossmann's eyes, but Cat thought his smile joyless as a serpent's.

"Yes, Great Lord."

"And I shall have my revenge. I shall steal his wife, I shall kill his men and then my torturer shall have him. He shall pay for what he did on the field of Isvestia."

The Pasha turned to his soldiers, said something bombastic in his own language. Perhaps it was the same speech, for they cheered and waved their swords.

The sun was dropping like a bloody ball below the plain, dying the bald, the men and their weapons in scarlet. Cat swayed, nearly fell.

Blood. More blood. Tomorrow she'd see another battle, more death—perhaps that of her husband. She would use the Protector and take one of them with her..."

"Rossmann! You devil!"

He had not let go of her hair, and now he jerked her back.

"I am Nijaz, a Ban, as great a Lord as your husband. From now on this is how you will address me. My Cousin Selim promises me many things for bringing your husband into his power—and you are the first of them." The smile that grew across his face became enormous, almost boyish. "You are nothing but an infidel and my slave, but if you give me sons, Caterina, I shall make you my wife."

There may have been more to the speech, but it came to an abrupt end when she spat. Rossmann returned the favor with an open handed slap which rang like a shot and sent her to her knees. Tears rushed into her eyes and she nearly fainted.

"Your husband comes," the Pasha sneered, "like a lovesick fool, right into our trap. Imagine risking one's life for a woman! He drew close and murmured, "Tomorrow he shall be on his knees before me. Before his torture begins, he shall know that you are a slave." Steely fingers on her neck, Rossmann directed Caterina down the slope to the mouth of the cave. Once there, he pushed her to the ground and then gracefully sat cross legged beside her. The yashmak that she'd left behind he fastened upon her again, now with a strangely gentle hand.

Armed men, swords tucked through their bright sashes, came to squat nearby. No fires were lit. Food was brought out of pouches, more dried fruit, dried meat and hard biscuit.

* * *

As the light died, the men ate; their language grated in her ears. The Pasha and Rossmann sat together, the Pasha sharing his food with Rossmann, a thing Ayhan had taught was a high mark of honor. After the men had eaten, Cat was fed, although her hands remained bound.

Rossmann himself put small pieces of fruit and biscuit into her mouth. When she spat out the first piece, the Pasha shouted, "It's the last time he'll be serving you, woman, so enjoy it. After tomorrow, you will serve him or you will die."

Rossmann, however, took her resistance calmly. "You had better eat. You will need strength for what is to come, Caterina."

How she hated him! His betrayal was a knife, but this time she opened her mouth and took the dried apricot he offered. She chewed it thoroughly and then swallowed.

He was right. She must be strong. She must be ready, ready to seize any opening. Tomorrow it was escape or death—there would be no second chances.

"Our ways are strange to you, but you will learn. If you obey me, I shall not pen you inside the harem. We will live in tents upon the plain. We will follow herds, those of my family. You will wear the yashmak, but you will ride, Caterina, ride with me."

Solicitously, he raised a dipper of water to her lips. She drank, but answered not a word.

"Tomorrow I shall take your magic," he said. "I shall lie with you beneath the Red Horse, in the heart of the cave. It is Kismet. From the moment I saw your beautiful mare and your power over horses, I knew you were the woman linked by magic with this place, the woman a Ban of my lineage must possess."

Cat tried to keep her face expressionless, to show no fear, but a shudder shook her, one which seemed to rise straight from some ancient, unremembered past.

"This is your destiny. Every step away from Heldenberg has been one towards me." He leaned close.

Desire, intelligence—madness—shone in his pale, intense face.

She wanted to scream denial. Horrible to think that she'd been fooled into thinking he was a friend—a companion! Shameful to think that she had been weakened so much by need, by a stranger's flattery, that she had allowed herself to risk so many lives.

Rossmann hands traveled slowly, caressing her arms. The comfort he was intent upon sending came, despite her hatred.

Whatever he willed was always strong...

"There are many ways to give even a reluctant woman pleasure." He whispered close to her ear.

"I'd rather die."

"Silence, slave!" said the Pasha. "If you don't please Ban Nijaz, there are soldiers here who would—"

"Ah, Honored Sir, I beg you not to threaten her. It's not my way with either horses or women. She will obey me, just as they do."

"And your horses are always magnificently trained," the Pasha conceded. "Well, have your way. If she were mine, I'd flog her, teach her once and for all who is master."

"If I must, Caterina," Rossmann said, putting a hand beneath the yashmak to touch her chin, "I'll force you. Soon, beneath the red horse, you will give me your magic."

It was a long night, but somehow there was sleep. Exhaustion finally dragged her into blessed non-existence.

She awoke abruptly, jerked into consciousness by the awareness of his face close to hers. Pain made her gasp, every muscle aching from the bound tension in which she'd slept. "Come now," he whispered. Caterina drew her long legs close to her body, shook her head. "We'll go through the cave." He'd bent close and now he whispered against her ear. "Your husband and his men are behind the bald." As he spoke, Rossmann cut the silken bonds that held her hands, her ankles.

Once again he had set her free!

251

Cat was half asleep, limbs tingling numb, but she rose and walked. Rossmann's arm tightened as he guided her into the dark opening of the crawl space.

As before, the air was cold and foul. The distant gleam of a candle illuminated the way ahead.

"Is someone there?"

"No," Rossmann said. "Hurry!"

A knee-bruising traverse later, they reached the first candle. It was wavering on the floor of that apparently topless fissure.

As he moved unerringly towards the next passage, he said, "There are Croats and Hungarians outside. Your husband is with them. We all have scores to settle with Selim Pasha. "Now," he commanded, "crawl through here..."

It was pitch black, but finally, after rounding a corner, Caterina saw another light. She prayed for escape, but instead she felt the same rush of panic she'd had during her first hands and knees journey to this place.

Emerging into the painted cave, she saw not one, but three burning candles. Her arrival caused a draft, and the strange animals appeared to prance wildly upon the walls.

"You will be safe here. When the fighting starts, no one will find you."

"I'm not staying." She moved toward the pillar and the exit she knew lay behind it.

"Not yet. It's not safe."

Cat pushed past him, but he caught her just as she crouched to enter the dark shaft. The struggle happened in silence, for they were both afraid of attracting the attention of the soldiers.

A month in the harem had taken its toll. Although Rossmann lacked her husband's mass, he was extremely strong. It didn't take him long to get her down and wrestle her hands above her head. "We will be safe here while they kill each other. Some of Selim's men are mine. When the real fighting starts, they'll hide. Then, when Selim Pasha's soldiers are defeated by your husband's men, they will kill the infidels. Either way, our escape will be easy. There will be plenty of loose horses."

Cat didn't move, hoping that he would be lulled by her docility and not bring out those terrible silken cords again.

"You'll ride, be my wife, not my slave." His lean, hard body forced itself against hers. "You will give me your magic..."

As if talking to a horse he'd taken down for a medical procedure he began a rhythmic murmur.

"Easy. Easy now, my beautiful Caterina."

From above came muffled alarms, rising shouts. There was the clash of steel and crack of gunfire. Cat was terrified, exhausted, mesmerized by the compulsion in his skillfully caressing hands.

"You know your fate." He brushed her lips with his. "You know your new master." His hands released hers, and moved inside her clothing. She trembled wildly, allowed him to touch, for the moment hadn't come.

"You won't be locked away from the sun. You will ride the wide plains, gallop with me on the finest horses. And I'll give you pleasure—greater than you've ever known."

Every fiber of her mind concentrated. The locket was in one hand, just as Aunt Teresina had taught her. Her fingers touched the clasp.

"Good girl," he whispered, nuzzling against the breast he had, without meeting any resistance, uncovered. She gasped at the silken intensity of his touch, fought off the response which some ancient mindless self was ready to make. Cold air raised goose flesh as his lips moved across her nakedness.

"I won't hurt you, not now, not ever. East and West shall breed up strong sons."

In knotted fingers Cat held it, sharp as pain. Fiercely, she pulled her thoughts away. There must be no sign, not the faintest suggestion ...

Rossmann's gaze declined, prizing the ultimate delicacy his fingers had begun to probe. That was when Caterina, in a fluid motion perfected by years of practice, drove the gleaming steel straight into his jugular.

Caterina's flaming red hair!

With no other thought, Christoph plunged into the thickest part of the melee. No one and nothing must stand in his way; death was an impossibility. Blood, severed limbs, and heaving, spurting bodies marked his battle passage.

He saw her gasping with effort, in a caftan drenched with blood. As he approached, his wife jerked a short Turkish sword from the body of a man she'd just killed. On every side was the clash of steel, gurgling of death.

"Cat!" he shouted, lifting his sword, for she had lunged at him, bloody sword raised, eyes wild as berserker's. There was deafening crash as he parried her thrust. His great strength threw her back, but although she hit the wall and staggered, in the blink of an eye she was on guard again.

"Caterina! Hold!" Her upraised sword hesitated. For one of those split seconds of battlefield eternity, Caterina stared. Suddenly, she cried:

"Rossmann's kin are waiting for you and Selim Pasha to kill each other!"

Plunging forward, he seized her arm and pulled her after him. "Come on!"

In a hurtling moment they were at the edge of the now fouled pool, where their path was blocked by a sloe eyed enemy. Christoph parried the man's first blow; then struck like lightning, splitting his opponent's round head like a pumpkin. His skill smashed a path for them, and tall men roared and rallied to assist their escape.

* * *

On the plain she found Star, bucking in wild, tail high kicks. She was saddled but that was askew, betraying that someone had, without success, attempted to mount her.

Ignoring the danger Cat put her fingers in her mouth, whistled and then ran forward. "Star! Star! Komm!"

The ring of steel on steel, the flash fire of muskets, the shouts, were behind her now. The mare was standing about ten feet away, pawing and tossing her head, but not making any move to run. Apparently, she'd recognized Caterina.

"Caterina! Stop! Are you hurt?" Her husband caught her arm, spun her around. She looked up into his eyes, knew at once what he was really asking, all the layers of it, in and in and in, like an onion.

"It's not my blood." She gazed down at what covered her.

She had been forced to submit to Rossmann's hands. She was humiliated, sullied, as much as if he'd finished what he'd started.

"This is Rossmann's blood." Her knees shook as Christoph's arm came to enclose her. "The Pasha gave me to him, but I killed him. Then," she ended in a tone of wonder, "I killed those others."

The sword dropped from her hand. Raising her eyes, she gazed into her husband's face where she saw a swarm of fears. Cat felt sick to her soul.

"Rossmann said I had magic, said he would get it. Oh, if it hadn't been for Teresina, he would have."

She clung to her man, eyes spilling. She knew she'd never forget Rossmann's face as his life pumped redly away.

Oh, but hadn't his betrayal upon betrayal earned the deadly trick she'd played? His trap, of being her friend, her teacher, had been such calculated bait!

"Take me home." Her words came in a wail.

The next thing she remembered, she was on Star, galloping away, in company with Christoph and a crowd of men, wild Hungarians, fleeing from the nightmare, that bloodied place upon the gold and endless plain.

Afterward

When her eyes opened, they met those of a large, homely woman standing beside Christoph. Cat stared. Waking, since her return, was always strange, a lengthy sorting through a flotsam of memory.

"Time to wake up now, love." He spoke gently. "It's almost ten."

Since returning to Heldenberg, she'd found herself capable of sleeping through whole days. He sat down on the edge of the bed as Caterina righted herself and rubbed her eyes like a fretful child waking from a nap. He patted her back.

"This is Trudchen. I sent a messenger to your father and they have sent us this lady to replace our Elsa. Trudchen tells me she was raised on your Aunt Teresina's farm, that your Aunt taught her everything. She says she remembers you when you were just a child."

Trudchen. Cat searched her memory. Had there been a Trudchen at Auntie T's?

"I am the one who nursed you after you got the spider bite, Grafin. Or perhaps you remember 'Die Barin' better."

"Oh, Trudchen! Of course, I'm sorry." Now Cat did remember, especially the teasing nickname "She Bear." Even as a youngster, Trudchen had been a square block of fat and muscle.

"Now, my love," said Christoph, "here is a good woman to help you."

Herr Stocke, after the dismissal of the Walters, had stepped easily into the bailiff's role, but without a chatelaine in the house, even with Cat's best efforts, the housekeeping had been haphazard.

"Trudchen says that devotion to the Tannuci women is bred in her bones. Lucky your mama knew Trudchen could come to us."

The passage of years had not made Trudchen any more handsome. The plain face now had a moustache, yet high intelligence shone in her brown eyes. Cat remembered that this taciturn female had been among her Aunt's human favorites. Now she wondered if she had also been a recipient of Aunt Teresina's special knowledge...

As Cat's memory worked on the subject of Trudchen, she came across another reason for her mother's choice. She remembered that Trudchen had studied midwifery with her aunt. Although Cat had bled during their journey home, a future use for Trudchen's skills was not an unreasonable supposition.

* * *

Winter had come and gone again and now the spring moon grew round over Heldenberg. Beyond, in the misty paddock, she could see the horses and cattle, some standing, some sleeping. Somewhere among them was Star.

Caterina, waiting for her husband to come for dinner, stood at the triple windows in his room and admired the light that silvered the grounds. It seemed impossible that once she had looked through the bars of the seraglio into an exquisite garden, one that had bloomed equally with flowers and her despair.

She lit a candle, leaned against the window and gazed at the distended moon, tonight rising south and low. In the west the summer triangle was rising, blazing Altair and blue Vega, Dench in Cygnus the Swan, those star names that Rossmann had taught her only a year ago. Suddenly, Cat saw herself galloping upon a golden plain beside an upright, lithe man. She wore black, a yashmak modestly covering all but her eyes, riding astride in those loose pants. Rossmann would have had his other wives—but would she have truly cared? She would have had Star; she would have

257

had the strange beauty of that endless sky. But Rossmann's bones moldered beneath the dancing red horses. He'd played a great game, for his honor—and for Red Caterina—and he'd lost everything.

And what, Cat thought, suddenly ashamed, of her husband, who'd come through such peril to her rescue? A true rake would have shrugged and left her to her fate, counted himself lucky to be relieved of trouble, made cheerful preparation to inherit the von Velsen lands without his bothersome cousin.

Overcome, Cat put her head in her hands and wept.

* * *

When the door opened and Christoph strode through, she went straight into his arms. She wore a beautiful flowing undress gown they'd purchased in Vienna, lavender silk embroidered with flowers, but instead of having her hair piled and intertwined with scarves as a Viennese beauty would, Cat's thick red hair was left flowing, an astonishing wealth which now fell almost to her knees. Two fine braids made of the front tresses held back the red torrent.

She raised her mouth and he kissed her warmly.

"Exactly the sugar I was hoping for."

Cat hugged him tight. There were no doubts anymore about the depth of his devotion. In Vienna, he'd gone straight to the Emperor and asked for permission to leave military service. At first the Emperor had been angry, unwilling to let such a successful commander go, but after he heard the young couple tell their story, he had relented.

"Sitting with just one candle?" Christoph studied her face with an expression of concern. "And what are these?" Long fingers touched her wet cheek.

"Don't worry. I, I was just thinking—and I shouldn't do that, I guess."

He drew her into the moonlit window seat. "You know you can tell me."

At first she was silent, turning to gaze at the silver figures of the pastured horses. Christoph didn't pursue with questions, just held her in that safest place, cradled against his chest. After awhile he suggested, "It was about Rossmann, wasn't it?"

Caterina sighed, turned her face against his waistcoat.

"I miss him too." He held her close, so close she could hear his heart beating. "I often think of him now that we're here. I miss his wit and his good advice. Rossmann had our friendship, but that didn't stop him from plotting our destruction. He was a being of pride and mind, not ruled by his heart like the two of us." Tenderly Christoph kissed the top of her head. "He left you no choice but to play the game exactly as he did."

In bed these days he was incredibly tender, understanding of all her new fears and hesitations.

"There, there, Caterina. There, there, my beautiful love."

"Christoph," she whispered. "Make love to me. Now."

"No dinner first?" He winked and stroked her cheek.

"I need you."

Oh, the look in his eyes! There he was, so mighty in battle, so gentle with her, that curly headed warrior who was all hers...

Close in his arms, Cat felt safe again. This was so right, familiar, but still exciting. In the flickering shadows, she caught sight of the naughty tapestry.

How delightful to know that in a few minutes they would be joining those careless, lusty actors!

* * *

A trail of clothes lay behind them. Her satin gown was tossed over a chair along with his pants. The camisole and petticoat kept company with his shirt, and by the bed, silver buckled shoes lay buried beneath his stock, garters and white silk stockings.

"Light a candle." These days, every sense must tell Caterina who her lover was.

"Since the day I caught you at von Beiler's dike, I've had dreams of this beautiful hair on my pillow."

His handsome face shone as he returned to contemplate her naked glory. And how beautiful he was, a lover like a long ago hero, her Lord of Heldenberg.

Cat put her face against his chest and kissed the hardness, while his hand, restlessly moving, slipped straight to heart of the matter. Sighing pleasure, Caterina parted her knees. Her husband kept up his play in the sweet below.

Between her elegant legs, he arched to give a most intimate caress, a tentative stroking of her most sensitive part with his, a voluptuous slide. Grazing the button of pleasure, then descending to a kiss of near penetration, he directed the action precisely with one strong brown hand.

"Don't tease."

She threw her arms around his hard waist and held on to keep him from withdrawing. He obeyed her summons. The sweet tide was already in and spilling everywhere, so his bold attack carried them at once into a wild ride. He rolled over with her, so that she was on top. She gasped at the interruption, but strong hands on her hips quickly rediscovered the lost rhythm.

Panting, she threw her long hair back, braced her hands upon his big shoulders. She was eager to take the initiative, to put him through some slower paces, but her mount was too spirited, too determined to have his own way. In the end she simply sat him, crying delight, and, with breasts hard and flushed, let pleasure buck.

* * *

Star dropped her foal, this one, in the safety of the barn. To everyone's surprise, it was another filly, another replica of her dam.

"Three red fillies in a row." The head groom shook his head. "Is there a colt in her, I wonder?"

"And this one's just as red as the others." Cat eyed the foal. "I never saw the Pasha's Arab, so I have no idea what he was like. Rossmann picked him out and Star liked him, so he must have been a beauty."

She regretted the words as soon as they were out of her mouth.

There were still so many bitter, bitter memories.

"The villain had excellent taste both in horses and in women," said Christoph softly, slipping an arm around his wife's waist. She was round now, full of baby.

Caterina hugged him back, and tried, with the feel and scent of him, to suppress the past.

"Look at that dishy face, that short back! I can hardly wait until she's old enough to breed. I'd love to cross her with the Andalusian, or, even more, with Brandy. I'll wager she'll make the fastest horses in the whole country. I've never held with the idea that the mare is just a vessel."

Arm in arm, husband and wife took pleasure in the sight of the dainty creature frisking her stubby blonde tail as she slipped her head beneath her mother's belly to nurse. They decided while they stood there to call the foal "Lucky."

* * *

"I shall serve you myself, sir."

She cut into the meat pie lying in state upon their table. She'd made it, in that new place of interest, the kitchen. It was a peasant's pie, made of small game: squirrel, partridge and rabbit, as well as carrots, turnips and celery, all lying in gravy beneath a crust, one that she herself had made.

She lifted a wedge for her husband's plate.

"Cook and I made this out of what the Umbergers brought yesterday. She's most economical and a good teacher."

Her husband smiled, although he ate his first portion rather carefully, in case a small bone had escaped her notice. For a time, the couple attended strictly to their supper. Big black Furst rubbed along their legs, meowing. Caterina and Christoph both indulged him with pieces of meat, which he carried under the table to devour.

At the end of the meal, the Graf took his wife's hand and kissed her long fingers.

"It's what I should have done when you first came—dismissed the lot and started over again. The proof is this excellent repast."

"Well, I understand how you felt. They had served you well for many years."

"Until Walters got greedy."

A moment of silence followed. Then Caterina, wanting to change the subject, said "Ever since Frau Lotz came, I've been discovering that I rather like cookery. And, you know, she and I are both learning. I read her my mother's receipts aloud and she remembers them exactly. Her girls are a help too, though one is better than the other. Liza can be difficult. She forgets and then makes excuses. Still, I must allow she's at a refractory age."

Her husband, wiping the gravy from his plate with a piece of rye, greeted this with a grin.

"And what age is that? Somewhere around fifteen?"

"That's it exactly. She has a sweetheart who has been apprenticed away."

"The course of true love rarely runs straight."

"You mustn't be flippant. The young man cannot yet support a wife."

"Does he have a trade? Could he be put to work here? Perhaps that would solve everyone's problem."

"He's an apprentice wheelwright with several more years of his term to serve."

"Well, he had better stay where he is and learn his business well."

"Just what her mother says, but in the meantime the girl is miserable."

There was a pause in which Christoph leaned back and regarded his wife with a mixture of affection and amusement.

"I've been thinking how much this sounds like my parents at table. I used to find," he said, "domestic problems awfully dull, but not anymore." He pushed back from the table and she went into his lap so that they could share a kiss.

"I think," he murmured, "that you've grown again. Those legs!!"

He smiled, surveying the graceful length in his arms. The two new dresses Elsa had made last year now ended above her ankles.

"Yes," Cat sighed. "I can't believe it."

Christoph kissed her forehead. "I don't think you're in any danger of becoming taller than your husband. As it now stands we're a perfect match, especially," he teased, nibbling at her ear, "for good wrestling in bed."

"Hush!"

"And hasn't Herr Stocke taught us both that the goddesses were taller than mortal men and more beautiful than mortal women—just like my Red Caterina?"

* * *

They lay late in bed. He was teasing and kissing her wetly in all sorts of ticklish, unlikely places. She giggled and pretended to protest.

The grandparents to be on both sides were delirious with expectation, but even now, her husband could never seem to get enough of making love to her.

He held her left arm stretched above her head and was busily kissed his way down from the palm. When he had reached the hollow where arm and body joined, it had tickled terribly. She was wriggling and giggling, begging him to stop when suddenly he said, "Hold still a moment."

"So you can tickle more? Absolutely not."

"I promise I won't tickle." He peered down, a thoughtful expression on his face. "What's this? A birthmark?"

Cat felt a sickening wave deep in the pit of her stomach.

"No," said Christoph after another moment of consideration, "It's not a birthmark." He leaned back on his elbow, considered her gravely.

"I've a kind of blue mark there ever since a spider bit me." Cat muttered the words. Abruptly, she was nauseous. "Remember when Trudchen and I were talking about it? It happened while I was staying with Aunt Teresina."

"It's not a birthmark, Kitty Cat. Your Aunt must have had it done to you."

"A spider bit me." Cat shrank away from him into the featherbed.

She couldn't locate the source of the unreasoning terror that had so suddenly gripped her. Memories from her captivity, as fresh as yesterday, came rushing back. She remembered the look on the eunuch's face as he'd studied that very spot.

Then something else began to flash in, something more distant.

* * *

Oh, such a chilly night, but she was not in her warm bed anymore. She could smell fire, hear it crackling. Through a blur she saw masks.

There was the smell of peasants, a smell of sweat, of dirt and leather as they crowded around. There was a sick feeling in her gut, a bitter taste in her mouth.

Here was the nightmare which came if she neglected practice with the Protector! Now, however, she knew that it was not a dream, but a memory.

She had wondered why killing Rossmann had ended both the compulsion and the nightmares. Now, she understood. She could see it all, the events of that long ago night at Aunt Teresina's'.

They had hurt her twice, first under the arm with a needle and then they'd put her belly down over the knees of a terrifying horned creature, a man with a goat's head. He had lifted her gown, pushed something into her, something slippery, smooth and cold. While she'd cried, the masked faces had comforted, had whispered that after this her husband would only give her joy, that this sacrifice to the god would bring her many healthy children...

"It's a witch mark."

She tried to pull away, but Christoph had anticipated. Already she was firmly clasped in his arms.

"Don't be afraid. Your secret's safe. I'll protect you with my life—I swear by every god I know, Christian— or—Pagan."

There was a long moment in which she helplessly shuddered, her mind whirling with the sudden awful clarity, but at last, with his arms girding her like a fortress, she found the strength to ask him.

"How—how do you—know what it means?"

"Because most of our honest, hard working tenants up on the Heldenberg sport one just exactly like it." Thoughtfully, he stroked her long red hair.

* * *

"By the Blessed Mother!" Caterina struggled to get out of bed after a nap. "How dreadfully uncomfortable this is! It's awful to think there are three more months. I'm exhausted all the time and swollen bigger than the biggest pumpkin I've ever seen. I'm forever peeing, just like some poor old grandma, and my legs ache as soon as I stand up. I wish I could just take this belly off for a few hours. Today when I first lay down, the child kicked like a mule. I don't understand how one baby can have so many arms and legs."

Trudchen studied her charge. "I agree, Mistress. It's early for you to be having all this trouble. Why don't you sit still for a moment, Grafin, and let me feel your belly? You may not have three months to wait."

"What?"

"Hush, now. Let me feel and listen." The big hands were already opening her gown, investigating her belly.

She pokes and prods all the time without a by your leave, just like I'm a cow in calf, Caterina thought. Modesty and pregnancy certainly didn't go together.

There was a long pause. Trudchen's hands explored, then she rested her ear against Caterina's belly and listened.

265

When she raised her head, she said with great seriousness. "I will be very surprised if you aren't carrying two."

"Two?" Caterina blinked. "Twins?"

"It would explain a lot of things, Mistress. Not only your size but all the activity. Such things run in families, you know. I've been wondering why your little belly's got so big so fast, why your ankles are already swollen. But, Grafin, time will tell..."

Caterina closed up her gown, feeling a mixture of excitement and fear.

"I shall tell your husband what I think, Lady. And you, my poor darling, are going to have to endure even more confinement. The more you stay off your feet and rest, the longer they'll stay inside, where they need to be. Twins are always born early and small. We'll need to have several women in milk ready to help you. We don't want to take any chances." As she went bustling away, Caterina subsided into the pillows with a groan.

What a wearying and tedious affair this baby business was! Nature, she thought, gazing at the naughty frolicking bed curtains, had set enticing bait to lure womankind into this trap.

* * *

"And now for the names," Christoph said softly. "I've an idea, but I especially want you to name this little beauty of ours."

"Oh, no. You should be the one to name them both."

She didn't want to hurt him, to have him think that she would use these wonderful new creatures they'd made to hurt him again. Right now, she was exhausted, not only from her recent ordeal, but from the whole pregnancy. She had spent the last two months in grumpy and restless confinement.

Today she had pushed out not one, but two, small lively babies. The first was a girl, bald and pink. The second, born about an hour later, was a boy with ragged dark hair like a tiny troll, the long-awaited male heir.

266

"Darling Cat," her husband whispered, lips against her hair, "you never do anything by halves, do you, sweetheart?" His face shone with pride.

Both babies were small, but both were born loudly squalling, appearing more angry than distressed by the perilous journey they'd just made into the world. The labor hadn't been long, either for a first child or a twinning, only eleven hours from start to finish. Trudchen set all this good luck down to Grafin von Hagen's youth and strength.

"I've thought of names, of course, but, oh, I can't—I don't want to—"

Caterina's voice trailed away. She'd slept some, but she was still hurting. Three kinds of nasty brews had been forced upon her, things to shrink the womb, things to dull her pain, things to make milk. She felt dopey and drowsy, not up to saying that she wanted her daughter to be named 'Wilhelmina.' She was afraid the request would hurt Christoph, hurt him at a time when they should both be so happy.

Her husband, however, was joyfully determined to have the naming done.

"It seems to me that a proper name for a child is one that both husband and wife agree upon." He leaned close and kissed her forehead tenderly.

"If this beauty's mama won't say what she wants, I will offer a suggestion."

They'd tried to send him away during the birth, but he'd stayed. "You stay with your horses," he'd whispered against her cheek, "and I stay with you." He'd held Caterina against his chest while she'd struggled to push the babies out. He'd supported her while Trudchen and the others had busied themselves with afterbirth, with the cutting of cords and swaddling.

"What do you say to 'Wilhelmina'? We can call her 'Mina,' and it might be some restitution for a debt of love I owe."

Cat clung to his hand, so strong, which always touched her with such tenderness. It was hard to reply.

"I wanted that," she whispered at last, "but I didn't want to hurt you."

* * *

Four months later, on an autumn Sunday, in the little church of Heldenruhe, with everyone for miles around crowding to peer in the windows at the gentry, the twins were formally christened. The babies were well and lively, gaining weight in a gratifying fashion. They were suckled almost completely by their determined mother, although there was no shortage of peasant woman offering help. Mothers from every nearby farm had come to the big house to offer their milk, "to help their dear brave mistress raise those two angels the Blessed Mother has sent."

The girl was christened "Wilhelmina" for Caterina's sister and "Brigitte" for that staunch protector of Tanucci women. The boy was to be "Rupert Wilhelm" for his grandfathers. Caterina had insisted that "Goran" should be the boy's third name, in honor of the brave man who had died fighting at her side. Not even her father objected.

Both babies had blue eyes, although Rupert's were a slate gray. A shocking scarlet fuzz had just begun to cover Mina's bald head, while Rupert's funny birth hair had been quickly replaced by a luxurious chestnut thatch. Trudchen had observed that this was typical. Baby boys, she said—for the first year anyway—always had more hair and better eyelashes, too."

After the ceremony, a celebration was held at the mansion. The proud grandparents on both sides had made a long journey in order to see this, the fruition of all their hopes.

* * *

Caterina discreetly tucked Mina inside her gown to nurse. Feeling the tug and the responsive let down, knowing she was nourishing her child, that every day her darling was growing, Cat felt a tremendous pride and pleasure, greater than she could have ever imagined.

She was tired but happy. Nevertheless all things sad—and all things beautiful—brought her to tears. Trudchen and her mama agreed it was nursing that made it so, that in time she would be herself again, but Caterina knew in her heart that she'd softened. The pride she saw in every face made her so happy.

"Brave as a woman is brave." Her Mother had said it, and now Caterina thought she genuinely understood.

"I feel like a dairy cow," Cat had complained. "All I do is sleep and feed babies and then eat and feed babies."

"Well, you could use your nurses more," said Lady von Velsen. "I understand that every woman in milk around has offered to share with you. It's wonderful you're so loved."

"I don't mean to grumble, Mama. It's just queer to be so confined."

"New babies are like nestlings, my love. You feed and feed and feed, and suddenly, before you realize what's happened, they've grown wings and flown away." Lady von Velsen studied her tall daughter and sighed.

"I really don't think nurses should have them more than I do. Taking an animal away from its mother is the surest way I know to kill it, and I don't see why people should be any different." Caterina was resigned. "A nurse may help, but Mina and Rupert shall drink my milk as much as possible."

* * *

The night following the christening, propped up in bed, the downy head of Mina Brigitte warmly resting for the umpteenth time against her mother's full breast, Caterina's eye was caught by a red flicker coming through the north window. Sliding out of bed, she hoped not to wake her husband, whose muscular form stretched, like a sleeping panther, on the far side. Neither of them was getting much rest these days.

As she passed the wide cradle the twins shared, she saw Rupert Wilhelm Goran—a grunting, wriggling lump—who was well on his way to soiling his napkin and thereby waking himself up. From the other side of the door where the wet nurse and her infant were, for the moment, sleeping, there came no sound. Privacy, like a night without many, many interruptions, was a thing of the barely remembered past.

Hugging sweet-smelling Mina close, Cat went to the window. There was a huge fire blazing, high up on the shoulder of Heldenberg. All those secret worshipers, Cat knew with sudden certainty, were celebrating with their lord and lady, celebrating the christening of Graf and Grafin von Hagen's miraculous twins.

The End

If you enjoyed this book - please leave a review. Authors need reviews. Please help readers find this author.

Dear Reader. Reviews mean everything to an author. They determine the placement of the book, and thus how many potential readers will see the book. I will be so grateful if you will take a minute of your time and return to the online store where you purchased your copy, and leave, even just a two-line review. It doesn't matter how long the reviews are, just the star rating and a quick comment will suffice. Thank you so much, Juliet

Novels by Juliet Waldron from BWL Publishing

Alexander Hamilton and Elizabeth Schuyler Hamilton
A Master Passion

The American Revolution Series
Genesee
Angel's Flight

The Mozart Series
The Intimate Mozart
Nightingale, Her Lovers, & Mozart
My Mozart

The Magic Series (historical fantasy/adventure)

Zauberkraft: Black
Zauberkraft: Red
Zauberkraft: Green
(coming in 2019)

Pennsylvania Romance
Hand-me-Down Bride

Fly Away Snow Goose
Nits'it'ah Golika Xah
Canadian Historical Brides
(Northwest Territories & Nunvavut) ~ Book 8

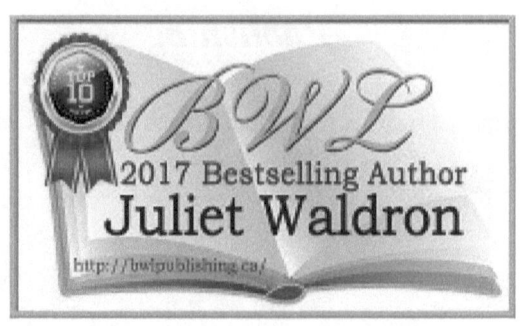

Juliet Waldron has lived in many US states, in the UK and the West Indies. She earned a B. A. in English, but has worked at jobs ranging from artist's model to brokerage. Thirty years ago, after her sons left home, she dropped out of 9-5 and began to write, hoping to create a genuine time travel experience for fellow lovers of the historical genre. She's a grandmother, a cat person, and a dedicated student of history and archeology. She and her husband of fifty years enjoy exploring the by-ways of Pennsylvania on their Hayabusa superbike.